The Black Wall of Silence

A Novel

Paul F. Morrissey, O.S.A.

First published by Dog Ear Publishing
4010 W. 86th Street, Ste H
Indianapolis, IN 46268
www.dogearpublishing.net

dog ear
PUBLISHING

ISBN: 978-1-4575-3250-4

Library of Congress Control Number: has been applied for

This book is printed on acid-free paper

This book is a work of fiction. The characters, incidents, and dialogue are drawn from the author's imagination and are not to be construed as real. Any resemblance to actual events or persons, living or dead, is entirely coincidental. The crisis in the Roman Catholic Church is real. The story that unfolds here is an attempt to show how it may have happened and what is needed to bring hope out of disaster.

Printed in the United States of America

For Thomas Merton, Henri Nouwen, and Pope Francis:

prophets, sinners, saints, lovers, brothers

He whom I enclose with my name is weeping in this dungeon. I am ever busy building this wall all around. As it goes up into the sky day by day, I plaster it with dust and sand lest the least hole should be left. I take pride in this great wall but for all the care I take, I lose sight of my true being in its dark shadow.

—Tagore

CHAPTER ONE

The Bronx, New York 1961—

Clutching the secret I've carried for so long, I move toward the closed door, drawing nearer to the one who always had the power to reward or ruin me with his glance.

I know I can find him there, reading the evening newspaper. Other than the basement, the bathroom is the only place in the house you could get some privacy.

I hesitate a moment before I knock, recalling how he would provide his homemade remedy for too many sweets on the day after Halloween. He would spoon-feed a horrible mixture of sulfur and molasses to my five siblings and me, lined up into the hallway, as though he were giving us Holy Communion.

How can it be that I've come from him and yet we're so different? How did I learn to get by in life by not needing him? Now in this same space, I need Daddy's blessing more than a cure.

"Yeah, who's there?" The old man's stern voice still triggers the child in me, even though I graduated from high school and have been living on my own for almost a year.

"It's me, Zach." My voice sounds muffled, intimate. "Can I talk to you about something?"

Behind the door, the newspaper rustles. Downstairs the silverware clicks as Mama sets the dinner table.

"Sure, come on in." I push against the warped door until it gives. Daddy sits squat-legged on the hopper, the comics section of the newspaper flopped open on his knees. His belly protrudes in a tank top undershirt. He looks older than I remember. His wavy gray hair needs a trim. His gray eyes squint at me over his glasses.

1

"Hi Daddy." I stand still for a moment, imagining how he sees me. The skinny middle son who Mama always tried to fatten up, saving the roast beef juices for me to drink before dinner, making me drink a raw egg with milk in the morning. But it never seemed to help.

Out on my own now, grown up and gone before he really got to know me. Even though he swore he'd do it differently, and not repeat what happened with him and his father. Daddy never finished high school, yet the education he worked so hard to give me only made the two of us grow more distant.

We're like two travelers who reach a fork in the road. By the time we realize we're heading in different directions, it's too late to get to know each other. Giving each other a goodbye glance, we hurry along paths that will lead us forever apart.

Daddy clears his throat. "So what's on your mind?"

I swallow the lump in mine as I slide onto the rim of the bathtub, edging toward him. I need the old man's support in this huge step. He'll be more objective than Mama. I've kept it a secret until now because I needed to be sure the decision was my own.

"I've wanted to tell you something for a while."

He looks at me blankly. We never talk like this, sharing deep things. His head drops a notch.

I can tell him this much at least. "You know those retreats you used to take us on with Uncle Pat and Uncle Brian? Well one of those times I picked up a pamphlet, "Why I Became a Priest."

His moist lips part and sag a little at one corner.

"I hid it in my pocket then because I didn't want anybody to know. But later, when I read it, I couldn't get the idea out of my head."

His head tilts in wonder.

Please believe in me, Daddy.

"What I want to tell you is that I'm going into the seminary."

The comics slide off his knees onto the floor in a heap. He stares at me for a moment as he takes it all in: my mysteriousness and sensitivity, the veil between us all these years. Maybe this distance finally makes sense.

My heart thumps. Breathing fast, a smile of hope creeps onto my face.

His gray eyes get teary as they do when one of the kids breaks a finger or gets hit in the face with a baseball. He doesn't ask me why, or whether I can wait until I get more experience living on my own—or what about Irene?

With a soft voice he searches for the right words, "Well, we always hoped that one of you might become a priest. I never thought it would be you, though."

Never me?

"Does Mama know?"

"I just told her," I blurt out with relief. Wanting to save us both the awkwardness of so many unspoken questions, I quickly explain how I'll be leaving for the Sebastian novitiate at the end of the summer. "Patrick can have my clothes and my car. All I'll need is a black suit." I smile in delicious anticipation of my younger brother's reaction.

"A black suit, huh? Does that mean you'll be one of the bad guys or the good guys?"

"The good guys, I hope." My eyes begin to tear.

"That's swell, Zach." Rather than a kiss on the cheek or hug like the Italians do, Daddy's big hand reaches out to shake mine. The Irish blessing. Soon I am out the door, skipping down the stairs into the future.

When I finally gather my courage to tell Irene, I drive to her home in Yonkers. I want to share my feelings with her more clearly than I ever have. We've dated off and on for five years since we met at a high school dance as freshmen. We often kidded each other about getting married but never seriously discussed it. There was always something that held me back. Now I can tell her why, a vocation to the priesthood.

It's after midnight when we park in front of her house in my secondhand, fifty-seven Plymouth. The dinner of roast chicken, mashed potatoes and gravy, a salad, and half a bottle of wine still rumbles in my stomach. I reach for her hand, but Irene drops it into her lap and leans against the car door with her head cocked to the side.

"So what's up, Sugar-lips? What's on your evil little mind tonight?" she teases me as usual.

I've prayed about this moment for weeks. Now I hope with all my heart that Irene will hear my plans, and maybe sweetly, even if broken-heartedly, accept this awesome sense of calling I have from God.

"I've had something I've wanted to tell you for a while." On the radio, Elvis is panting, "Ah ah ah thought, ah could live without romance, until you came to me . . . "

Dropping her head down slightly, she flirts up at me through a strand of dark hair and licks her moist pink lips. I'm distracted by a small purple stain on her lime-green linen blouse. It's a drop of our dinner wine that rises and falls as she breathes.

"Well, go ahead," she murmurs in a low velvety voice.

My breath comes faster as the aroma of honeysuckles floats through the window. Like a love potion, it urges sweethearts on.

"We've known each other for so many years," I say. "We've done so many incredible things together." I stop talking. I'm losing my way.

Don't stop now.

I feel Irene stroking my hand. She edges a little closer. The street lamp reflects a questioning look in her eyes. I remain still so the shadows hide mine.

"Irene, once in a while we've said some serious things about our future."

"Yeah." She squeezes my hand, and draws it close to her breast.

I can feel her heartbeat. Elvis keeps moaning, "But now ah ha know ho, that ah hah love you so ho . . . "

I'm desperate. There's got to be another way. Maybe I can throw self-protection to the wind, offer my heart on a platter. But it's too late for that.

"I . . . I've not always been as honest as I could have been with you," I stammer. I reach toward her. The gear shift pokes me in the stomach when I try to pull her body to mine. Words tumble out of me like somebody else's. "At the end of summer I'm going into the seminary . . . to be a priest."

At that moment, the sweet and wild girlfriend of my youth, who once called me wholesome in front of a bunch of her friends because we kissed but never had sex, suddenly seems a million miles away.

I'm dying for her to know how much she means to me, how much I'll miss her for my whole life. "If I ever loved anyone, Irene," I plead along with Elvis, "I love you."

I am stunned to hear my pigeon, my little darling, my dove, growl into my shoulder as I hug her, "You never loved anyone but yourself."

CHAPTER TWO

2002—

At Grand Central Station, I catch sight of Penny across the cavernous room. She's gawking like a tourist at the panorama of stars on the ceiling and doesn't see me. My heart skips a beat to see her, my Irish Twin born just a year and a month behind me. An attorney in Boston now, she studied for her political science and law degrees at night after she got married.

I dodge and weave through the teeming crowds, bustling in all directions with Christmas madness. I'm late because the Lexington Line was delayed over a half hour. Now she sees me and waves her funny way. I grin.

The two of us hardly got a chance to catch up at our family Thanksgiving celebration. "You look stressed, Zach. What's going on?" she asked as she slipped up to me at the fireplace.

"Nothing," I told her as we clicked our wine glasses. Usually I hide difficult feelings, even from myself.

Before she disappeared into the crowd of nieces and nephews, she insisted on taking the train down from Boston in a couple of weeks to meet me in New York.

Now she greets me with her sister look as we embrace. I give her a peck on the cheek. Sibling love with just a dash of the old competition we had growing up.

"Hi. It's so good to see you," she smiles. Her hair swirls down on one side with a new look. A thick purple scarf is bundled around her neck.

"Been waiting long?" I check her mood.

"Long enough to feel at home in the New York rat race."

"And Boston's better?" I smirk, knowing she enjoys the pace and hustle of the Big Apple.

Her gaze takes mine in while the train schedules blare over the loudspeaker. Without another word she flips over her Boston Globe. Oh God, another screaming headline about priests sexually abusing kids.

"It never stops, dammit." I groan, meaning the headlines.

Penny drills me with her look. "It's the abuse that never stops, Zach."

I grab her elbow, needing a respite from the cascading insanity of the news reports about the crisis that's been rocking the Church over the past few months. "Let's walk," I say, steering her toward the Madison Avenue Exit. A woman babbles in a foreign language as we pass by. The man beside her gapes up at the train arrival board looking lost.

"It's like when the World Trade Centers crashed." Penny shakes her head. "Only now the Catholic priesthood is the bed of ashes at our feet."

Penny's one of my five siblings who is still a practicing Catholic. The anger and disappointment in her voice hits me like a punch to the chest. I'd like to console her, but don't want to take sides right away. We edge toward the stairway to the street while a heavenly aroma of freshly baked buns coaxes us to stay.

"When I walk down the street in a Roman collar now, it feels like I'm wearing a scarlet letter," I say. I grit my teeth and widen my eyes to show her what it feels like. "It's like being trapped in a nest of hissing snakes."

Penny gives me a look back. She doesn't actually say it, but the way things are she could even be thinking, *Yeah brother, and are you one of the snakes?*

I halt in my tracks. Should I ask her?

"The Church is in such a mess. Why do you stay?" she asks instead.

She doesn't understand. I grab hold of the railing. "Penny," I flash my scorned lover look, "I've devoted my whole life to the Church. The priesthood has always felt like a holy profession to me. Just because it's under attack doesn't make me want to quit." I pull her toward me so a group of college guys can rush by. "Don't you get it? It actually makes me want to stay and fight even more."

But Penny the lawyer is speaking. She flips her hair back and glances around. "Lots of the media are circling this story like sharks. I'm worried for you. You're always so outspoken and honest. You better be careful." She moves up the stairs ahead of me.

When we reach the revolving doors, I ask, "How's the family dealing with this?"

She halts for a moment and blinks. "The ones who've already left the Church aren't surprised. They almost seem to be saying I told you so. Those who are still trying to be Catholic are angry, devastated." She stares at me to let it sink in before pushing through the doors.

When we reach the street, a homeless guy lies curled up asleep in a ratty blanket in a doorway. A skinny dog with mournful eyes lies at his feet. The sky beams crystal blue and brilliant in between the towering buildings. There's a chill in the air. Cabs and shoppers rush by. Horns honk. A siren wails in the background. Manhattan!

"What's so upsetting is that the Vatican seems to be in denial," I tell her, tossing some change in the guy's cup as the dog wags its tail.

"Yes. The Pope and other bishops seem caught up in this too. Apparently, they've been reassigning these pedophile priests."

Pedophile priests! The phrase boils me.

"And then they abuse again," she says. "Now they're trying to cover this up. The whole thing's a disgrace."

My voice starts getting louder. The dog looks alarmed. "The bishops think they're protecting the Church, but they're really destroying it. And they're hell bent on finding some scapegoats." Noticing people passing by us, I lean closer. "Guess who they're trying to pin the blame on?" I search up and down the street for a taxi and whisper, "Gay priests."

"Oh god!" Penny purses her lips with disgust.

"Gay priests aren't the real problem. I can't believe the Vatican doesn't know this. Certain bishops just want to get the spotlight off themselves and their coverup. If they can find some group to blame, it solves the problem quickly, right?" I watch her mind whirl at this Vatican roulette.

"The bishops are a bunch of queens themselves," she spits out suddenly. *Whaaat?* Together we laugh at the image. I wave my hand toward a line of taxis, but they speed by.

I think of certain priests who drool over all the costumes and liturgical rubrics. "Yeah, some of them love the lace as well as the power," I admit. "But we've got to do something. Trust is broken, trust that is at the heart of the priesthood." A taxi screeches to a stop in front of us, blocking the intersection. People yell at the sudden obstruction.

"Ninth Avenue and 46th Street," I shout through the window to a cabbie who looks like Bin Laden. I have a cozy West Side restaurant in mind for us. He nods a stoic face and we jump in. Slamming the door, I tell Penny, "If people don't trust us anymore, it's all over." Part of me feels like it already is.

We ride in silence while the driver dodges buses, other taxis, and pedestrians. Staring out the streaked window, I let the sights and sounds of Manhattan wash over me. Traces of snow on parked cars and shop awnings. People of all races rushing somewhere. A crazy but wonderful mayhem. A bicycle messenger suddenly jumps in front of us, and the cabbie curses in a foreign language. The meter clicks.

"Zach, did you know anything about this abuse?" Penny murmurs in a low voice. She doesn't look at me at first.

Hurt and thrown by her question, I quickly scan back across a Rolodex of thirty years. What could I have known? What might I have heard or seen, even possibly ignored for the sake of solidarity with other priests? I stare at her until she looks into my eyes. "If I did, I would have done something about it, don't you think?"

Her gaze drops to my Roman collar that peeks up above my scarf. "I'm not sure." She pauses to glance back through the window. "The Church is so secretive and controlling, Zach. Celibacy, gay priests forced to be in the closet, shady financial practices. Lots of people are wondering and asking out loud: Why didn't they protect our children?"

Stunned by her doubts about me and her examples, my stomach roils. I search for some explanation as the taxi races through a red light. The cabbie eyes me through the rearview mirror.

"At the same time, Zach, other people are defending the Church and the Pope. It's like the Church is a ship without a rudder. Somebody's got to do something."

The taxi stops in front of the restaurant. Bin Laden still doesn't smile. I give him a tip anyway.

"Oh my god, Penny," I wait until a couple pass by. At the sight of her questioning face, my heart wrenches. I've grown up seeing my own reflection in hers my whole life. "I feel like the Church in which I've served as a priest for over thirty years is a prison now, Penny. Priests wear its black uniform." I yank at my Roman collar like it's a metal cuff. "Even if we chuck these uniforms to be invisible, the sentence will follow us, don't you see?"

I need her more than ever now, need my sister to understand my situation. "We'll be on the lam like any escaped convict. The public will track us down to shame and punish us: You must have known something. Why didn't you stop them? Are you one of them? We're all guilty by association now. Who would want to become a priest today?"

Penny bobs her head slightly. Her hairdo hides one eye. "Let's try to put all this on hold so we can have a good time tonight," she says.

"You're right." Reaching for her arm, I lead her into Swing 46, a jazz and supper club I love.

With a new sense of urgency, I begin to look for a way that I can do something crucial for the Church during this time of crisis. My religious order, the Sebastians, is more committed to peace and justice than the Church as a whole. Of course I can use my pastoral counseling training to help some individuals and families. Yet even this ministry doesn't address the mud down in the Church's basement, the structural issues like its teaching on women and gay people, which keep causing pastoral problems.

About this time, in my priests' support group I hear about a Catholic Chaplain's position that has opened up at the New York City jail on Riker's Island. Intrigued, I search for the info on their website and the following day make a call to Norma D'Amore, the Director of the Archdiocesan Prison Ministry Program. I listen to her answering machine sign off, "Have a peaceful day," and I leave a brief message. Soon Norma phones back and suggests I come in and meet her at her office later that week. My prayer for guidance is moving fast.

On the wicked–cold day of our meeting, I drive down the Deegan Expressway to her office, located on the second floor of St. Dymphna's former grade school, about a mile and a half from the bridge to Riker's Island. Norma, an attractive woman with mahogany hair and buxom figure, eases herself into a soft chair. "They call me The Mother of All Captives," she announces with a whimsical smile.

"Hmmmm, that's quite a name. I'm Zachary, but people call me Zach."

"Zach. I like that." She brushes a lock of hair from her face. "The inmates gave me my name. They give us all names. They'll give you a name too. Here, have a cinnamon bun."

"Oh boy. Can't wait for that." I reach for the treats she's brought.

While hot chocolate steams in our faces, Norma and I exchange small talk. Like me, her brother went to Archbishop Stepinac. Her father and mother, Italian immigrants, had first settled in Little Italy in Lower Manhattan. Later they moved to Mount Vernon where she and her sister were raised. Norma looks about ten years younger than I, in her late-forties I guess. She shows me a picture of her son and daughter in their twenties. "I'm divorced," she mentions casually, searching briefly for my reaction. I imagine Norma's pain in the Church with its rules about remarriage and nod knowingly.

Chewing my nails, I want to be honest but don't want to come across as I sometimes do in my religious community, a kind of rebel in the Church when it comes to authorities. "Norma, I was ordained in 1968 as The Second Vatican Council reforms were being enacted. When I challenged the War in Vietnam and the birth control teachings, standing with my family and students, I got censured for that." I remember her nickname and add, "I seem to have a natural sympathy for the underdog."

"Yes, I do too. But prison is a place where you have to be careful of that instinct. If you're seen as weak by the prisoners or the guards, they'll use you."

"Ohhhhh." Hair stands up on my neck as I imagine various scenarios from films. "My pastoral counseling training will come in handy then."

"Yes, it certainly will." As Norma daintily licks molasses from her fingers, she asks, "So what makes you want to get involved in prison ministry?"

I'm not prepared when a phrase zooms out of my mouth like an escaping bird: "I'm a gay priest." I look into her eyes as she looked into mine earlier. Pausing for a moment so it can sink in, another comment flies out that surprises me even more. "Often it feels like I'm in prison because of this." Memories of hiding this part of myself through the years flash by. The loneliness and self-hatred I had learned as a boy, especially in the Church. The years of struggle to overcome this shame and accept myself. The risks, the danger, the discoveries, the pain and joy and sin all mixed together.

Norma's sunny face goes blank for a moment. Her brown eyes are soft though, inviting. If I'm going to work well with her, she needs to know all of me.

"Go on," she says.

I search for an image that might attract her. Ben Hur comes to mind. "It's sort of like riding two wild horses, one white, the other black," I say. "Think of yourself standing upright with a foot on each saddle, holding the reins to guide them but not too tightly." My voice takes on a dramatic quality and my hands begin to wave as I hunt for words. Norma is nodding, a faint smile on her face.

"Gay and priest, they're like twin energies. The tension between them creates my passion for everything." I point my index finger and thumb forward with a tiny space between them to show her how close these forces feel inside me. "I believe this experience of inner conflict will help me understand the inmates' experience. And maybe they'll help me understand mine."

"Hmmmmmm." Norma rises and silently refills our cups. I gaze out the window with my heart thumping. The only sound is from the radiators banging. Maybe I said too much. Replacing the pot, she turns and asks with a straight face, "Which horse is black?" Her eyes crinkle and her face tilts up.

"I think the black horse is sex and the white horse is spirit," I say while she snickers. "I don't go around advertising that I'm gay, but it's who I am and I think you should know."

"Zach," she reaches for my hand, "we'd be glad to have you join the team. You're just what we need here."

With my heart zinging for joy, I throw my head back and laugh at the prospect of being my real self in my ministry for a change. The Mother of All Captives. Now I understand.

While driving home later, I slip a Leonard Cohen CD into my stereo. The Canadian poet croaks out an anthem I love. Soon I am croaking "If It Be Your Will" along with him.

As my right hand grips the steering wheel, my left palm turns upward. My whole life long it's been a wrestling match. A little kid raised a strict Catholic. Sexual feelings I didn't understand and no one to help me understand them. Becoming a priest possibly to escape them. And then the promise of celibacy.

Glancing into the rearview mirror, I spot a gigantic tractor-trailer bearing down on my little brown Toyota. "Back up, you idiot!" I yell. Boxed in by traffic on both sides, I search for cops while engine-beasts snort smoke all around me. For just a split second, an opening appears and I manage to scoot through it. Then zipping in and out of the traffic like a madman—past the billboard ads for liposuction, casinos, and vodka, past the church steeples in Queens and the Bronx—I finally burst into the open. Yet like some monster from a childhood nightmare, the damn truck is still on my tail.

Flooring the accelerator, the little brown bug chokes for a second before it leaves the truck in its wake. Chuckling, I pat the dashboard and grin like a fool. Floating on for the next couple of miles, my palm opens up again. *Oh God, it's you who created me from my mother's womb. It's you who stand by me each bloody step of the way. So Big Guy, here's your chance. Now you can use all of my prisons: the Catholic Church, the priesthood, and my sexual orientation, to help others break out of theirs.*

CHAPTER THREE

Today is my first formal day as a prison chaplain at Riker's Island. Last night I didn't sleep well, waking and tossing and turning from 2 to 4 a.m. I am out the door by eight-thirty after morning prayers at Our Lady of Angels Parish where I live with the other priests. Before leaving, I wash the ashes off my forehead that the pastor, Father Francis, marked me with earlier. I want to receive them fresh when I celebrate Ash Wednesday service for the inmates at the House of Detention. Norma is accompanying me because she knows the ropes.

In the lobby, one of the officers spots me as I'm signing the entry book. "Got any ashes, Padre?" Tickled that these sacramental signs can help me break across the emotional barrier between strangers, especially two men, I grin at Norma. Reaching into my bag, I peel the Saran Wrap from the cup of ashes and smudge a big thumbprint of ashes on the officer's forehead in the sign of a cross while I say, "Remember man that you are dust, and unto dust you shall return."

"Thanks, Padre."

These interactions amaze me. For the rest of the day, this guy will proudly wear this symbol of his Christianity for everyone to see. Especially on Ash Wednesday, lots of people want this. Something about the fact that it is visible on their bodies, personal and earthy like a tattoo. Catholicism has this way of turning bread, wine, oil, water, fire, and ashes into signs of God's presence. And uniquely with ashes, it helps us witness that we are all sinners and in need of God's grace.

After the guard frisks Norma and me, we head into the cellblocks where we'll distribute the ashes to the inmates. Hardened looking guys begin to line up like children in a schoolyard. You can't be sure who is a Catholic, a Christian, or neither. It doesn't matter. We mark everyone's bodies who steps forward. This includes a couple of people in the medical unit, including one inmate in a wheelchair with a rosary around his neck.

Various prison personnel approach us in the corridor, including social workers, a Filipino psychiatrist, and correction officers both black and white. Many of the African-Americans are not Catholic, but want the ashes anyway. "I need a blessing," they say unashamedly. All the while, inmates keep shuffling past us, coming and going to their cells. For this one day at least, all of us are linked by this sacramental sign, and it feels good.

About two hours into this, we arrive at cellblock "3 Upper" where the protective custody inmates are held. They are dressed in bright orange jumpsuits. "It's to distinguish them," I was told at orientation the day before. I've learned that some inmates in this unit are high pro-file. Their names are in the news. Others are here because they are sex offenders, or cops. Still others because they are gay or transgender. Anyone who might be in danger from another inmate. It makes a volatile mix. I wonder, if I were in jail, would I be locked in here? The plan is to celebrate a Mass in this unit as well as give out the ashes.

When the guard unbolts the gate with a huge key, a young inmate, Billy, leads me into this dingy cellblock that looks like it's from the TV show Oz. Inmates, all male though a few are transsexuals, are hanging around in a long rectangular day room on a lower floor, talking loudly while they watch Jerry Springer's guests throw chairs. Others are locked in their cells on an upper tier. We have to pass them on a narrow passageway to get to the balcony corner in the back for the Mass.

As we pass the cells, some men glance out while others grip the little barred openings. I imagine they might reach out and grab me by my skinny neck as I walk by with my airport traveling bag on rollers filled with the materials to say Mass (missal, chalice, altar cloths, music, hosts, wine, alb and stole, portable CD player, and pamphlets to pass out afterwards). It's like I'm in a trance, hardly believing this is real.

I turn back and hear Norma greeting them, so I begin to smile and offer a hello when I catch their eyes. I can't let them see my fear. Two inmates live in each of these tiny cells, with bunk beds on one side near an open toilet, the room hardly bigger than a large walk-in closet. No privacy here, either in your cell or in the day room. And constant noise that would drive me nuts. Loud talk, a blasting TV, continual commotion. All the while, these guys peek out of their cells at us, a white guy with salt and pepper hair and a black suit and collar to distinguish me, and Norma, the Mother of All Captives in a flowing ankle-length violet dress a few steps behind me. We stroll into their turf as though we are heading for a picnic.

Norma explained to me earlier that the Mass is usually celebrated on the floor. "Yes, on the floor," she nodded with an upturned eyebrow when my eyes rolled. "The inmates sit in a circle," she explained. I try to picture this arrangement as we draw up to a little open space between two sets of cells that face each other with ten feet of dirty concrete between them. Some of these cells look empty, but in one adjacent to where we stop, a young guy peers out through the bars, clasping them with both hands. Olive skin, wavy dark hair, maybe Hispanic, intriguing. I smile and say hello. He just stares back, despondency written on his face and in his dark eyes.

Billy, the young Irish working-class kid, kicks aside some empty milk containers and drops a small bench near one side of the space. "Do you want to say the Mass on the floor or on this, Father?" He drags up to the center of the room what looks like a trash can. Billy asks this as though it is the most normal thing in the world. Imagining myself sitting on the grimy floor and my beautiful linen altar cover being smeared with dirt, the trash barrel with its cover looks like an attractive alternative.

"This'll do," I say, faking casualness. Then Norma and I set up for the Mass with the altar cloth, chalice, missal, hosts and wine. *Lord, be with us here.*

In a few moments, fifteen grown tough guys in their twenties and thirties, whom I'd be afraid to pass on the street, begin to squat cross-legged on the floor around this "altar."

"Hi, I'm the chaplain, Father Zach," I tell them as I pull my white alb over my head. A few of them nod.

"Thanks for coming, Father." Some blank stares.

Oh-boy! I hope we get out of here alive.

Norma passes out some song sheets. "You probably know this one, 'Amazing Grace,'" she says. It turns out that quite a few do. Even the guy locked in his cell squints at the hymn sheet and sings as she practices it with them.

15

Billy sits on the bench next to me. A transsexual slides in on my other side, with small breasts visible under the prison garb. Soon, all of them are listening attentively as I try to offer some words exploring the meaning of the ashes on our foreheads. "It's a sign of solidarity with each other as we enter into . . . what's the name of this season in the Church?"

They gape at each other. Is this a catechism test?

"Spring?" the transsexual guesses with lips pursed.

I shake my head no.

"How 'bout Mardi Gras?" She flashes a sheepish smile.

"Nope."

"Holy Week?" a guy leaning on his elbow on the floor offers.

I shake my head again. They need a hint. "It's got something to do with fasting and penance."

Finally Billy gets it. "Lent?"

"Right!" It's like *Jeopardy*. They eye him with envy, and I don't have a clue what's behind these gazes. *What am I doing here? Where are you, Lord? Stay with me.*

When I ask if someone will read the Epistle for me, a burly Black guy with spiked hair and a goatee quickly raises his hand. He has his own Bible spread on his lap. I begin to show him the passage and point out a few difficult words to pronounce. He turns to me with an annoyed look. "I'm a college graduate, Pastor." Norma chuckles.

"Oh, okay, I just wanted you to feel comfortable. When the time comes for his reading, he proclaims it like Moses on the mountaintop. Others, mostly Evangelicals I learn later, read along silently from their Bibles.

After the Gospel, I give a homily I've prepared. "There are some passages from the Bible that struck me," I begin. At that precise moment, raucous shouts boom up from the guys on the level below us. Everyone turns to look. Two of them are chasing a rat with a broom. My little congregation runs to the railing to cheer them on, "Go! Go! Get 'im! . . . Kill the motherfucker!"

When we finally reassemble, I make a disgusted face and shudder, "A rat!"

"Oh that's nothing," Father," Billy boasts, "that was a small one." Knowing laughter and nods all around.

"You're kidding."

"Nope. But you get used to it after a while. You should see them scampering across the floor at night when they let us out for showers." He holds his hands up to show me their two foot size. More laughter.

I can't imagine getting used to it. "Okay, okay, let's get back to the homily. Hmmm, do you know I can't remember what I was so struck with in the Bible passage?"

They all howl at this admission, relaxing back on the floor as though we are in a cabaret now. It's like they are glad that the priest is able to make a mistake like them. I remember the phrase I had forgotten and tell them, "Why should they say among the peoples, 'Where is their God?'" Some nods of recognition.

After the homily, Norma invites them to stand and come forward to receive the ashes on their foreheads. She and I stand a few feet apart as we do so. As we finish this part of the ceremony, I notice her rubbing the ashes from her thumb with a tissue and some holy water she brought.

"Norma, I need some ashes too."

Easygoing but surprised by my switching of roles, she places some ashes on my forehead with her own version of the prayer, "Remember that you're from the earth, and someday you will return to the earth."

At communion soon after this, her earth-to-earth image returns to me. As the inmates hold out their rough hands for the host, I say, "The Body of Christ." They say, "Amen" as they receive it. I'm filled with wonder: The Body and Blood of Christ entering into the body and blood of prisoners in jail. Jesus Christ entering into the hearts of thieves and sexual abusers, murderers and transsexuals. Yeah, I think, and into me too. A glimpse of what the Mass on the trashcan might really mean stirs in me.

We're almost finished. It's time for the kiss of peace. It is the ritual that Catholics perform to show our belief in mutual forgiveness. Earlier I told them we'd wait 'til the end of mass to do it so we could avoid disruption. As we break into this gesture, I notice they each make sure to shake one another's hands, including the few transsexuals. No one, not even the toughest guys, seems to disdain them.

After I hug Norma, a short, muscled guy with a tattoo on his neck reaches to pull me close and purposely taps my shoulder with his. The

Bump of Peace, I later name it and they like that. Most of them crowd around Norma for a hug. "Hi Miss Norma . . . Missed you the past month . . . Did you bring me a Spanish Bible? . . . Can you call my baby's mom for me?" Their weathered faces beam like children's, yearning for a warm female embrace.

I remember the olive-skinned guy. Turning, I don't notice him at his cell window. I finish zipping up my suitcase and decide to roll it over to stand by his cell. Number 187, I make a mental note as I see the correctional officer in his glass bubble scanning our activity like an Eagle Scout.

Quickly I steal a glance into cell Number 187. The young man, in his late twenties, maybe 5'11", is sitting hunched on the bottom level of a bunk. He's writing in a notebook. He doesn't notice me. No cellmate visible. In a moment I call in to him, "Hello."

Startled at first, he rises and approaches the cell window with a stone face. The eyes are inquisitive though. "How are you?" I ask with a slight smile.

"I'm okay. You're the priest, right?" Behind me, I can hear the rest of the inmates finishing their hugs with Norma.

"Yes. I'm Father Zach. This is my first day as a chaplain." Should I offer him a handshake? I decide not to.

We take each other's measure in silence. To keep the conversation going, I quickly peek over his shoulder, searching for a way to understand his world. Socks and underwear are strung neatly on a makeshift clothesline. A circle of what looks like feathers is draped on the wall. Around his neck hangs a tattered rosary cross. He's got a workout build. Thick brown fingers with bitten nails circle the bars.

He sees me searching and says, "I was writing in my journal." He holds up the small notebook.

"I see." I lean closer. "They didn't let you out for the mass?" I frown.

"No. I got in a fight yesterday." He watches my reaction. "A guy egged me on." No further explanation.

I feel a desire to reach through the bars that separate this guy from the rest of us. At the same time, I wonder what he's incarcerated for. Maybe those hands have harmed someone. What's that scar above his eyebrow from? When I glance back to check on Norma, she catches my gaze and motions for us to go. I only have a minute. Better make a connection now. Slowly I reach my hand up toward him. "Can I give you the handshake of peace?" I smile timidly so he isn't spooked. The dark eyes blink twice and stare. We're only a few inches from each other, and his breath smells like peanut butter.

"Yeah, that'd be cool." Two brown fingers stretch through the bars. He's watching me. Slowly I move my fingers toward his. It's like I'm coaxing a wild animal.

The tips of our fingers touch. "Peace," I say.

Bright teeth flash through purple almost rueful lips for a second. "Peace to you, too."

Our fingers remain touching as I ask, "What's your name?"

"Migo!" A raspy voice, sensuous. "My native name is Three Feathers." He pulls his fingers away.

"Three Feathers! Hmmmm."

"My father is part Cherokee."

Suddenly Norma's voice is behind me. I wonder if we're not supposed to get involved, and a shyness comes over me. "I'd like to hear more about that sometime Migo, but I've got to go now."

"Will you come back again?" A plaintive almost birdlike sound.

My schedule is full, but I will make time for Three Feathers. "Yes. I'll be glad to."

"Wait!" He runs to the wall and returns with a rather large brown feather like you'd see from a hawk or pheasant. "Here, take this eagle feather. It'll guide you."

I hadn't yet learned that we aren't supposed to give or receive anything from the inmates, or show any affection. "Thanks, Migo. Maybe next Wednesday. Okay?"

"I'll be here. I'm not going anywhere." He smiles.

When I turn, Norma is waiting. Without a word, we retrace our steps across the same catwalk next to the cells with the little barred windows. This time she leads. A few of them have rigged little mirrors on the outside of their cell doors. Some of them ogle her swaying hips as we pass. A TV blares on the lower level while guys stand and play cards on a long rickety table. "Hi, Miss Norma," one of them waves.

In front of us, a couple of inmates bustle about serving lunch, banging and sliding trays with small plastic food containers under each cell door. I sneak a look sideways into a few cells. Most of them have two inmates in these little cubicles with a dusty slit of a window on the far wall to the outside world. Some guys are rolled up in their sheets, still sleeping though it is almost noon. At the next-to-last cell, a middle-aged, mixed-race guy with a stubbly gray beard shoots a furtive look my way. Somehow during the course of the service I've lost some of my fear and just scoot by him.

As we pass the officer in the glass bubble control booth, I nod to acknowledge him. He just watches stone faced. To him we could even be smuggling drugs or cigarettes as I've heard some official visitors do. He would be held accountable if we did. As we continue down the long corridor to the outside waiting room, Norma throws me a questioning smile, "So? What do you think? I think you were initiated today."

"Oh man!" I toss my head in disbelief. "That's the first time I ever celebrated mass on a trashcan. Unbelievable!"

"Nothing like it, is there?" She giggles. "How could you explain that to the Archbishop? My guys aren't trash though, are they?"

I remember the guy who prayed for all the prisoners on Riker's Island, and for his own forgiveness. "No. Their prayers actually seem more fervent than many in our churches."

She halts in her tracks. "It's because they know they have sinned and need God's mercy."

"Yeah." I think of my own situation. I haven't been perfect. Maybe I can learn from them. We begin to walk on and my eyes fill up. "What a plight for these men and women. These sons and daughters of God, even if they have done some bad things," I say.

"Many of the 12,000 of them are awaiting trial, Zach. Not even judged guilty yet, they don't have the bail money and can wait sometimes six months to a year or more for trial." Her chiffon dress flows as she walks and talks over her shoulder. "Be careful though," she stops and eyes me sideways. "They can be manipulative."

"How couldn't they be? We can walk out of here, they can't."

We reach the last of five doors. I ring the buzzer to alert the correctional officer at the controls. As I do I watch Norma take a dab of the antibacterial gel from a container on the wall and carefully rub her hands. "Always use this. You never know what you've been touching inside." As I take some of the gel too, she beams. "Happy Ash Wednesday, Zach." She gives me a hug.

At that moment the metal door rumbles open. A couple of female correctional officers see us. "Nice job, Chap!" one of them quips. They all laugh, and continue joking and making wisecracks about their own lives as they push by us with their guns and handcuffs jaunty on their hips.

While I'm chuckling, Norma nudges me through the door. It clangs shut behind us. Not yet sure of all my feelings about the Mass and the inmates, I don't really want to discuss what happened any more at the moment. What I do know is that the experience has opened my eyes to a whole new concept of what prison ministry might mean. Before heading to our cars, I agree to meet Norma the following Wednesday at her office for some supervision and lunch.

As I switch on my ignition, my mind returns to the cellblock. The inmates' faces, beautiful in some way. Especially Migo's. Yet the waste of their young lives gets to my heart. Like it gets to God's too, I'm sure.

While I drive back across the bridge to the mainland, I think of the hiddenness of their broken lives from most of us as we roar by prisons on our expressways, zipping past these barbed-wire cages without thinking of the human beings in them. I search in my briefcase as though for an answer. I find Migo's feather and rub it gently.

Later at home after dinner, before going to bed I strip out of my black clothes and get into my pajamas. I light a candle in front of my icon of Jesus and flop into my EZ-Boy chair that looks out on the Bronx Reservoir. Letting my eyes drift shut, a swirl of images and sounds from the day comes up. I begin to pray.

Lord, were you there in that terrible place today? Was that you in the cell gripping the bars and singing, amazing grace that saved a wretch like me? Was it to save people like me too?

I do believe that you were there in the bread and the wine on that trash-can altar. I do believe that you are calling out to anyone who has ears to hear that you have come down to the darkest and most wretched places on earth to save us no matter what it costs you. And I'm beginning to know why I am called to this ministry. To open my eyes to what you are doing on this earth. To understand who you are before I die and go to heaven and you surprise me in your orange jumpsuit.

CHAPTER FOUR

I hop into my Toyota and head down the Deegan Expressway until The George Washington Bridge looms in my path. The maze of ramps and crisscrossing roads that links New York with New Jersey is an engineering marvel as well as a traffic nightmare, especially during rush hour madness. Like any New Yorker, I push my way into the slowing traffic one aggressive inch at a time: "Go ahead! Dent my fender! I dare you!" Chicken at heart, I only half-hope they can read my lips.

I've got an appointment with my spiritual director today. I first met Sister Sophie at a retreat for gay priests that she conducted a few years before in California. It was sponsored by an organization named Twin Spirits. This network consists of over five hundred subscribers who communicate through a monthly newsletter in which gay Catholic priests, brothers and sisters from all over the world share their faith journeys. Some of these are in far-off places like Australia, Ireland, South Africa, and even Vatican City. Given the Church's homophobia, these retreats and the newsletter are not publicized, but announced through word of mouth. Gay priests come from all over the country for these retreats. After that retreat, I began to see Sister Sophie once a month for spiritual direction.

I think of Sophie, a Sister of St. Joseph of Peace, and turn to scan through the bridge's suspension cables to the downtown skyline. Whether it's a hazy summer day with the Empire State Building wreathed in a cloud of smog, or a crisp wintry day with the skyscrapers strung out like a jeweled necklace, this view of the Big Apple means home to me, even with the empty hole where the Twin Towers used to be.

When I first heard about the history of Sophie's religious community in the New York Archdiocese, I was captivated. Anna Cusack, an Irish nun whose religious name was Mother Francis Clare, arrived in New York City in 1878, hoping to establish her sisterhood there. In Great Britain, her community of nuns worked for the rights of the disenfranchised, especially women. Evidently Bishop Corrigan in New York didn't want this activist group of women in his domain, so he let it be known that they weren't welcome. But the Bishop of Newark beckoned from across the Hudson, so off the sisters went to New Jersey where they've been ever since.

Avoiding the other cars and trucks as best I can, I swing North for Englewood Cliffs at the turnoff for the Palisades Parkway. I'm headed toward the only visible building cluster you can see in the Rockefeller wilderness from the Bronx side, the motherhouse of these sisters, where Sophie lives.

Irish in her roots like me, though a few years older, Sophie has white hair in a poodle cut. She speaks in a gentle voice that masks a will of steel. Wise gray eyes in her faded freckled face and a Mona Lisa smile draw me in to share whatever is in my heart. You'd hardly know Sophie is a nun with her beige slacks, pink blouse, and loafers. She has a tendency to smile and say, "Oh, please!" when she thinks you are just schmoozing, or perhaps when you are getting close to her heart.

She also has a therapy dog, a little pearl gray schnoodle who curls up on a chair and listens along with her. Sometimes when I'm upset or angry, Snooky jumps up and rushes over to me, occasionally barking or whining. Sophie calms him down and he goes back to his chair, watching me with mournful eyes and his ears cocked until my voice changes and gets soft. That's Snooky's signal to run over and jump up on my lap. He rolls over for me to scratch his belly. I imagine he throws himself at anyone this way.

"Come in, Zach, come in. You look like you've got a secret."

"I do. I found a great Chinese Spa where I have an appointment for a haircut this afternoon."

"A Chinese Spa?"

"Yeah." I picture the Golden Phoenix with its mostly Chinese clientele, the pencil-thin girls in tight jeans and high heels giving clients a head massage as they wash their hair while Chinese music floats over-head. "My barber's name is Tricky."

"Tricky?" She crunches her eyebrows.

"They all have funny names. Another one is named Happy, and then there's Lucky. Tricky could be a geisha girl with his beautiful pale face and his hair swept up into the latest punk look, a different color every time I see him. I usually tell him, "Make my hair like yours, Tricky.""

"Hmmmm, I'll have to try that. It sounds interesting."

"Not sure they allow nuns there. It might be too sensual for you," I grin, thinking of the head massage and how some of the girls stick their fingers into your ears while they look at you in the mirror with impassive faces.

"Oh, please." Sophie takes her seat, her voice soothing and personal as usual.

I sink into my chair. "When Tricky finishes cutting my hair, with my silver hair scattered on the floor among all the jet black cuttings of the Chinese, he catches my gaze in the mirror and says, 'Handsome.' Maybe this is why I go there."

"Maybe it is," Sophie sniffs. "Okay, let's get down to business. What's going on with you?"

I watch Snooky, looking like he's asleep on the chair. One eye is open, checking me out through his lashes. I smile at him. An ear twitches. "My work at the prison is really challenging. It's like my faith is being tested."

"How so?"

"My god, Sophie. It's like I'm being thrown into situations I've never been prepared for. Like those scenes in the Gospel where people are running up to Jesus to be healed."

"Tell me about it." Her eyes brighten.

"First of all, the inmates' faith seems stronger than mine."

She waits. I gaze out the window.

"I'm serious. They stop me in the cell blocks, asking for prayers, Bibles, blessings, holy water, rosaries. Even exorcisms, would you believe?"

"Really? It sounds interesting."

"Their need for my faith demands that mine be strong. And it's not just my faith in God, but my faith in them."

She begins to rock in her chair.

"Their confessions alone are awesome, possibly a one-shot moment when they are open to God."

"Mmmmm."

"All of this, while loudspeakers are blaring, and we're being watched by the correctional officers and the other inmates." I think of how I have to be quick, ten minutes at the most, while an inmate confesses all his sins of the past fifteen years, seated on a stool across from me while others mill around us.

Sophie pictures this chaotic scene and nods.

"I have to rush because I have a whole list of them that I am never able to finish that day. And this only happens if I can get through the multiple barriers: of correctional officers' moods, lockdowns, shakedowns, lunchtimes, transfers, and other restrictions, in order to get to the inmates, sometimes two to four weeks after they first wrote down their 'urgent' request to see a chaplain." I roll my eyes toward the ceiling, enjoying how dramatic it sounds.

"What does it do to you? To your faith?"

"If anything, their confessions are mostly straight from the heart, inspiring me to relate to them in the same way. When I said in a homily recently that I experience God's activity more in prison than in the parishes, an Afro-American guy piped up, 'We're more humble here, Father.' I asked what he meant. He explained, 'It's because we need God more desperately in here and we know it.' 'Yeah,' another guy jumped in, 'but when we get out on the streets we forget it.'"

Sophie is glued to my words.

"So you can see that I've got to speak from the heart too. I can't fake anything."

"So what happens to you when you do this?"

I close my eyes and think. Soon I come out with, "In ministering to them, I'm more humble too."

"Hmmph," she snorts.

"Maybe the better word is humbled. I can't do this work without a deeper faith in God. And faith in them. I can't just manufacture this. I actually heard myself shouting in the women's prison yesterday during the homily."

"You were shouting?"

"I actually screamed out loud toward the roof of the gymnasium where I was celebrating the Mass. 'I'm so glad you were born,' I yelled." Hearing my voice rise, Snooky leaps up and scampers to my feet, staring up at me, whining.

"Now, Snooky," Sophie croons, "everything's fine." He looks over at her for a moment and wanders back to his seat.

"I realized I was mimicking what their mothers or fathers said when they held them up as babies. My voice became so powerful, Sophie, like it was God who was shouting to them through me. A couple of birds in the rafters got scared by my voice and flew out through a broken window."

She laughs. "Like God was shouting in you. I hear that power in your voice now, Zach."

I let her words sink in. "Yeah, something is happening to me in this ministry. It's like I'm finding my truest voice. Like I'm shouting out to others what I've discovered about God and myself. At one point I looked at the women and said, 'You know, even if your mother and father didn't shout for joy at your birth, God feels this way about you.'"

"Our voices convey a lot about us. It reminds me of your feeling about your father's voice when you were a boy."

"Yeah."

Her gaze probes mine.

Closing my eyes, I rest my head on the chair and go back to those days.

"Sophie, my brothers and sisters and I used to play in the noisy streets of the Bronx. When dusk fell, a booming voice bounced off the buildings three blocks from our house. Startled for a second, we froze in midstep of our stickball game. Everyone knew it was Daddy Braxton, yelling for his kids to come home for dinner.

"When Daddy came home from work in the afternoon, he lifted us off the floor on his flexed bicep. He was strong, but he cried more easily than Mama. His eyes filled up when we brought one of our latest injuries in for him to see. As he held a broken ankle or wrist, the booming voice dropped to a quiver, 'Holy Christopher, smashed!'"

When I open my eyes briefly, Sophie is listening intently.

"Wrestling on the living room floor with him, he'd let me get him down on his back. When I knelt on his chest he groaned in surrender. Then he'd grab me by the ankle and roll me over. I felt the roughness of his beard when he hugged me up against his cheek. I loved it even though it hurt.

"Whenever he caught us jumping on the large double bed where Steve and I slept together as boys, he'd spank us. We'd cry when he pulled off his belt with a flourish and asked, 'What am I strapping you for?'

"'For jumping on the bed,' we'd whimper in unison.

"'This hurts me more than it hurts you,' he'd murmur with tears in his eyes. Who knows? Maybe it did." I sit up.

"We didn't understand, and we'd whine like puppies until he left, swearing to be good. But as soon as the tingling on our bottoms disappeared we'd forget. It was only a matter of time before this ritual happened all over again.

"I think I was afraid of him as a boy. Maybe it was this fear, or something else that didn't allow fathers to get close to their sons back then. It was like there was a barrier that kept me from getting to know him.

"Once when he was spanking Steve in the garage, I heard Daddy shouting. I thought he might kill Steve. Torn between defending Steve and fears for my own life, I ran upstairs and hid in the wardrobe closet with Daddy's powerful voice chasing me all the way. 'Zach? *Zach!*'"

"And how old were you then?" Sophie asks.

"Oh I don't know. Eight, maybe nine. I can still hear that voice after all these years. Sometimes it's softer now, as though he's calling for something out of the past or future. Maybe he still wants to get to know me. It could just be my own voice, or God's voice, it doesn't matter. It's something wanting to be healed."

"Yes. Now stay with the feelings coming up. What are you learning?" Snooky's ears are up and alert.

"Sophie, after I shouted to the female inmates in prison, I asked them in a softer voice, 'Do you believe it, that you are a beloved daughter of God? That you are totally unique, like no other?' A few of them nodded their heads yes, their eyes widening with a half-hope. 'And with a special purpose that God has brought you into the world to fulfill? If so, will you let God forgive your past so you can start fresh?'"

Sophie beams. "And what did they say?"

"I forget their exact words. But I know they got it, at least some of them."

"Can you get it, Zach?"

I brush a few tears back as my head bobs. "Yes . . . All these voices: our fathers', the Church's, and all the other's. So many voices telling us who we're supposed to be."

"There's no need to hide, or shout, is there?" she asks.

"I don't think so."

"If you listen, you'll hear what you were shouting to the inmates: 'You are my beloved child.'"

"Yes," I murmur. Noticing my softer voice, Snooky stands and stretches. Searching my face, he soon bounds off his chair and jumps into my lap. He rolls over, baring his belly, and licking my fingers as I stroke him. Sophie and I glance at each other with a smile.

"Can you pray about these things this month?" she asks.

Breathing deeply, I nod, realizing that our time is up. Snooky knows. He hops off my lap, waiting at Sophie's feet for a treat with his tongue out.

"Thanks, Snooky, you trollop," I say. By the time he cuddles up to the next client, I'll be winging my way home to the Bronx.

CHAPTER FIVE

1966—

It's New Year's Eve and St. Sebastian College is throwing a party. No one else is invited. It's just for us, the seminarians and the seminary staff of five priests. I'm in my second year of a four-year Theology and Spiritual Formation program leading up to ordination. After night prayers tonight, the seminarians are given special permission to stay up until midnight. A special meal of steak sandwiches and hamburgers, chips and coleslaw, sodas and Budweiser—the beer only permitted on special occasions such as this—is spread out like a picnic in the common room.

This room, like a family's living room, is where we come together to relax. It is rectangular and airy, with tall windows that allow plenty of light in the daytime and look out on ancient trees, some of which have wisteria vines choking them. Chairs with dark green upholstered seats line the walls, with coffee tables placed every six feet or so to allow a cluster of us to gather and play cards or shoot the breeze between classes or after dinner for a recreation hour each night. A television hovers like a window to the world on a high shelf in one corner, with seats arranged in semicircles around it so we can watch the evening news or a ballgame. A green and beige checked linoleum floor, waxed and polished each week by whoever has that as his house job, stretches from one set of double mahogany doors to another at the opposite end.

Father Perkins, Father Burke, and a few of the other priests plan to join us from their own private common room. We won't be watching the Times Square ball on TV. We are being offered another opportunity to experience the community life ideal that is spoken of so much in the Rule of St. Sebastian.

Fifty-six of us, between the ages of twenty-two and twenty-eight, are dressed in our black habits, which are gathered around the waist with a leather cincture, and a hood that hangs over the shoulders called a capuche. This habit sets us apart from the world and draws us closer in fraternity, a sign for others and ourselves that we are being singled out by God.

I experience a mix of feelings about this. There are two sides of me and they have been fighting each other since I got here. There's the old party-loving Zach who loves to hang out with friends and drink beer, and the new and holy Zach who left that world behind in order to become a priest. If I have a couple of beers and relax too much, who knows what I could do? In a moment of weakness I might say something revealing, or show too much joy when I'm around Peter.

All of our feelings have to be held in check here. As far as possible in this regimentation of our lives at the seminary, Peter and I have become friends over the past year. He's from a mid-western German family, with crew cut blond hair. Taller, and with a deeper voice than mine, he's a good athlete who shines during the mandatory afternoon recreation periods. Watching his strong competitive drive on the football field, I sense he could easily overpower me, take all my wild Irish energy and tame it. But I don't dwell on such images.

The two of us aren't sexual partners. We never speak about our orientation. Yet one morning I opened my eyes to find him sitting on my bed. It was almost dawn. He'd been up all night, playing poker with the seniors in the boiler room. When he asked if he could kiss me on the cheek, I wondered if I were dreaming and mumbled yes. On lonely nights, I can still feel that kiss.

Another time I snuck into his bed in my pajamas as a joke to greet him when he returned from the shower. "What the hell are you doin'?" he asked as he quickly closed the door. The devilish grin that broke out told me he was glad though. His beefy shoulders and chest filled out the flimsy gray pajamas he was wearing more than mine. With the covers pulled up to my chin, I snickered back, "I just thought I'd surprise you." I wasn't trying to seduce him. I was too defended against the implications for that. Yet my eyes crinkled with joy and my slim body tingled with happiness. Oh, it was heaven to be so close with my friend.

"You'll get us both thrown out," he whispered as he draped his towel behind the door and took a step back.

"Okay, okay, I'll go." But I could see that my bravado had touched him. Besides, I was certain that my feelings for him were pure friendship and would righteously tell the Master so if he somehow found out. *Oh, give it a break, Perkins! Everything's so serious around here! It was just a joke!*

On the other hand, there are those sexual feelings of mine deep down. Everything I read in Scripture and Church teaching tells me these are wrong. In the Old Testament, there are passages that say you should be put to death for them. In the modern Psychology we are being exposed to, homosexuality is considered the result of a stunted sexual developmental process. It is diagnosed as a mental illness. The life of celibacy I'm choosing might hide this from others, but not from me. And not, I guess, from anyone whom I love either.

Half-consciously, I suppose I was trying to show this to Peter by some of these antics. I needed him to love all of me, not just the polished up surface part that society and the Church considers good. While he peeked out from his doorway to watch me try to make it back to my room undiscovered, I turned back and saw a loving look in his eyes. Barefoot and laughing, I ran silently to my room.

The bell tower in our chapel chimes eleven-thirty as I gulp the last dregs of my beer. In the group I sit with by the door, Bart Lomax is raving on about the New York Giants' lousy football season: "The coach doesn't know his ass from his elbow!" The sleeves of Bart's habit are rolled up like he's ready for a fight. The muscles in his forearms flex as he cracks his knuckles. "I'd fire him," he shouts out as though he is God, draining his second beer and licking the foam from his lips. Except for the sarcastic Tom Dempsey, one of the intellectuals in our class, the others egg him on.

Across the room with its shiny green and white tiles, I watch Peter. Portraits of deceased Sebastians and hero saints gaze down on him from the walls. He's describing something to another group with macho gestures. I am restless, bored out of my mind. As though to provide respite, a stream of memories from New Year's Eves of the past flood in: my cousin Mickey and I torching huge piles of Christmas trees at midnight in the schoolyard; the expectation if you are out on a date that you'll be kissing your girlfriend as the clock strikes midnight; always the sense that as one year ends and a new one begins something should be happening inside, though I was never quite sure what. I usually just felt let down at midnight on New Year's Eve.

Suddenly, in the common room at St. Sebastian's, at a party where everyone else seems to be enjoying community life, a deep sense of loneliness comes over me. The clock edges closer to midnight. The voices in the room get louder. My heart feels emptier by the minute. I've got to get out of here. Quietly, as Lomax describes a botched play from a recent game, I slide off the vinyl chair to leave.

"Hey, Zach! Where ya goin'?" With saliva spewing out of his mouth, the would-be coach breaks off in midsentence. "It's almost the magic hour. You're not gonna leave us alone at midnight, are ya?"

"I'm going to the bathroom."

"No! You're probably going to pray." His lips press into a straight line.

"Yeah," I can't resist the dig, "I'm gonna pray for the Giants!" I ease my way into the corridor as Lomax blushes and the rest of them laugh.

After relieving myself at one of the floor-length marble urinals, I begin to return to the party. At the doorway, I stop in my tracks. Muffled voices . . . Lomax! I can join Peter's group. Reaching for the door handle, something stops me. A kind of magnetic force pulls me back and turns me around. Retracing my steps slowly, I turn the corner by Perkins's office and glide down the darkened corridor to the back door. Empty as I feel, I at least need a breath of fresh air. Even more, I need to be with someone I can talk to, talk to honestly. Lomax is right. The only place I can think of is the chapel.

Crossing the concrete path outside the house, I climb the back stairway to the second-floor chapel. Grasping the bottom of my habit so I won't trip, I let myself be drawn to this place of aloneness. An aloneness I recognize in my own heart.

Except for the red sanctuary light flickering shadows off the marble arches, it is dark. Even the stained glass windows are black. Good. I need privacy. I don't want anyone to see me like this. I couldn't explain what is happening if they asked. Slipping into one of the long horizontal choir stalls that face a similar set on the opposite wall, I let down the kneeler in the cavernous tunnel. I turn my head sideways so I can face the altar. Words tumble out silently to Jesus in the tabernacle:

Lord, are you really here? . . . I feel so alone in this place . . . No one knows me.

There's no one on earth to share my heart with tonight. No one who loves me. Loves me for who I am, who I really am.

It feels like I might cry and I stifle it. A faint odor of incense and candle wax hangs in the air. I wait. Nothing. Across the campus, bells begin to ring, deep and melancholy sounds, striking midnight. Bong! Bong!

Is this how you feel in that tabernacle? . . . Is this why you stay locked up there, so someone's there for people like me?

Bong! Bong!

Lord, I'm sorry for having these miserable feelings on New Years. I want to be happy like everyone else . . . You know I'd do anything to belong to you, but tonight I feel like shit.

Bong! Bong!

Should I pretend to be different, is that it? . . . Even if that gets me accepted, would that be good?

Bong!-bong!

You're up there in that tabernacle as another year ends, supposedly as Bread for the Poor, proclaiming Liberty to the Captives, I wonder if even you love me for who I am? . . . I mean for my whole being. My Real Self.

Bong!-bong!

Upfront near the sacristy entrance, I hear a door close silently. In a moment, a shadowy figure rounds the corner and stands still by the organ. My heart stops. Whoever it is seems to be looking back in my direction. Embarrassed at being caught in prayer like some holy roller at such a moment, I remain perfectly still. Hoping to stay hidden in the shadows, I stop breathing. Bong!

"Zach!" A voice whispers. "Is that you?" Bong!

Peter! He's the last one I want to see me like this. Quickly I brush a tear away. Well, maybe the only one.

"What are you doing up here? It's midnight! Everyone's downstairs celebrating." His voice, low and sultry with its Minnesota twang, echoes along with the bells still ringing in my ears as he slides into the pew with me.

"I don't know." I sink back into a sitting position on the pew. "I guess I need to be alone." Only the outline of his head shows in the darkness, but a hint of his aftershave lotion floats between us.

"I was looking for you." He sinks down next to me in the pew and tugs at my sleeve. "I missed you. Let's get out of here. C'mon! It's not too cold out. We can take a walk outside. It'll do you good."

Maybe that's what I really need. To be found by him. To be alone with him, not lost in a crowd. *Stay where you are*, a voice warns. I hesitate, held in place by a vague sense that I won't be able to backtrack once I move. But my loneliness cracks the spell. I follow him out the back door in silence, at the last minute glancing back toward the tabernacle.

Once outside, we start down the path that leads past the little house where the priests live. Voices on the main driveway signal that others have come out for some fresh air too. Peter steers me toward the ball field off to the right. As we step onto the grass, I whisper, "Look! The Big Dipper!" pointing at a constellation I recognize. Though we aren't supposed to smoke, he produces a pack of cigarettes and lights one up. He offers one to me, but I decline.

We draw closer to the front gate. Streetlights splash onto his face, ruddy and square. The cigarette dangling in the corner of his mouth makes him seem like James Dean. "So what's going on, Zach?"

Now that I'm with him, I want to forget any heavy stuff, but can't. It must be the fact that it's New Years. Right now, everyone back home in the city is gathering in Times Square, whooping it up and celebrating. How often will I be alone with my friend like this? Heart of my heart . . . *it's now or never.*

Though we are a good distance from the driveway, and invisible as long as we stay in the shadow of the trees, Chiccone's voice screeches across the field and alerts us that a group of our guys are walking over there. I sure don't want them to see us. I cringe. Peter just keeps dragging on his cigarette. Occasionally we bump into one another.

I turn to face him. "Peter?"

"Yeah?" He stares straight ahead.

I reflect back over the times in my life when I felt disgusted at myself, and the times when I heard someone snicker at a joke about queers. Even though I hadn't laughed at those moments, I never defended them either. The Bible condemns queers, though Jesus never said a word about it. I think of how the soldiers stripped him and spit in his face when he was arrested. I wish I could've stood between them to protect him. "Peter, I need to tell you something about myself . . . "

Something begins to crack inside. Like bile is coming up out of a dark place inside, a poison that's had me in its grip for as long as I can remember. Maybe I can run or scream to keep it down. But no, it wants to erupt this New Year's Eve and nothing can stop it. " . . . something that might make you want to hate me."

"Whaaaat?" He blows out a stream of smoke from the corner of his mouth and turns to look directly at me.

We both freeze in our tracks. Off in the trees by the river an owl hoots. "Peter, you're my friend," the words I partly rehearsed begin. My heart pounds like a bazooka. I breathe in short spurts. Maybe I'll throw up. "I need you to know me as I really am." He keeps staring at me. "Or else you're loving me for something I'm not, and I just can't bear that."

Though I can't clearly see his face, he slowly takes the cigarette from his mouth. Lifting his hands up in a bewildered, helpless fashion, he blows out another stream of smoke. His eyes are glued to mine.

I can't handle him searching me any longer, so I turn and edge forward. Side by side he joins me until the terrible secret just pops out like a New Year's baby. "I'm a homosexual."

Except for the sound of our habits rustling against our legs, for a few horrible seconds a silent void hangs between us, a chasm we may never cross. From off in the distance, muffled voices of our classmates float on the breeze. Peter looks their way and presses his lips into a fierce grimace, then stares off into space for an instant. Suddenly I am chilled to the bone. What seems like a ghost shivers itself out of me and vanishes into the darkness.

When Peter swivels back, a growl comes from deep down in his guts. It sounds more like the groan of a wild animal that's been gored and is dying or fighting back. *Oh God please, please.*

Peter could punch me at this point and I would barely flinch. But no words come from him. I wouldn't trust words anyway. Instead something else emerges from my friend that to this day I count as my salvation moment. Up around my shivering shoulders comes the quarterback's arm, pulling my self-hatred close, melting it by his acceptance. Showing me at last God's love for my true self, which I've been longing for my whole life.

The moon, silvery and serene, floats up behind the evergreens while two seminarian friends stride back and forth on the ball field for a long time in silence. It is New Year's Eve, and finally I've discovered what it means.

With Peter's arm draped over my shoulder, I am the lost sheep finally found. I don't even remember what we said before parting. It doesn't matter. I am a long way from fully accepting myself, but for the first time in my life I feel loved for all of me. I am twenty-four, and two years from ordination.

Everyone is a moon, and has a dark side which he never shows to anyone.

—Mark Twain

CHAPTER SIX

1968—

Today my five classmates and I swear our lives to God at the Cathedral of Saints Peter and Paul in Philadelphia. At a solemn moment in the ordination ceremony, we prostrate ourselves in the middle aisle while our families and friends chant the Litany of Saints over us.

I imagine that others can hear my heart beating with emotion on the terrazzo floor. I'm trying to keep my focus on God but my mind turns to Peter. I still love him more than I ever loved anyone up to now.

Peter wants to do great things for the Church. A year ago, he left the Sebastians to study for the Diocesan priesthood where he expects to have a better opportunity for this. I argued with him, as much for our continued friendship as to make the case for the religious community way of life with the Sebastians—the vows of poverty, chastity, and obedience.

But once he made up his mind, he wouldn't budge. This black-and-white thinking was his style, and not even I could change him. He'll be ordained in the fall and is already slated to be the secretary to the bishop of St. Paul, Minnesota.

I never really got to tell Peter how much he meant to me before he left. I couldn't speak with anyone about this, so I went to his empty room and took the crucifix off his wall and hung it up in my room. In a drawer I found his leather cincture, the belt that friars wear to symbolize chastity. I switched it for my own. For a month, I slept on the floor next to my bed. I read that African people mourn this way, holding onto the suffering for a while so you don't forget someone you love.

My mind couldn't stay on my studies. In our Old Testament class, we studied the Book of Kings. There's a passage that shows how the future King David mourned the death of his friend. "I grieve for you my brother Jonathan, exceedingly beautiful above the love of women. As a mother loves her only son, so did I love you." That's what I felt for Peter.

When it finally sank in that he was really gone, I realized that despite all the talk about community in the Sebastians, I was going to have to take the step for ordination on my own. There wasn't any Buddy Program. I considered leaving too, but my sense of vocational call was even stronger than my love for him.

There were no public models of two guys living together as lovers then. I went ahead with ordination instead, hoping God would transform my sexual longings into a deep care for his people that I would serve as a priest.

It was only a fledgling feeling, but a glimmer of a more radical thought stirred as well: maybe I can do more for homosexuals inside the official Church than outside. As I lie face down on the floor with the choir singing the Litany of Saints, this hope comes back to me.

During the ordination ceremony, there is a key moment when the Church teaches that the formal sacrament takes place. It occurs when the bishop places his hands on the new priests' heads to show that the Holy Spirit has come upon them. They've prepared us for this "ontological change" that stamps an indelible character on each new priest's soul, and we wonder when we'll feel it inside.

It is my turn. I kneel before Cardinal John Krol, the archconservative leader of the Philadelphia Catholic Church, who presides from an exquisitely carved throne. Slowly he places his surprisingly strong hands on my head. With my eyes cast down, against my perspiring forehead I feel the cold metal of his bishop's ring pressing its imprint onto my forehead. At the very last moment I can't resist peeking up at this father figure in faith. He stares down at me with a withering look that demands a lifetime of obedience.

Little does he know how in that moment of pregnant silence, while my family and the whole congregation crane their necks to see, the

Holy Spirit swoops down, gathers me and my gay history up in a flourish, and sends me on my mission.

When our seminary director, Father Perkins, proclaims the Gospel from St. Luke, I hear this familiar gospel verse in a new way. It is as though the words are being spoken directly to me:

> The Spirit of the Lord is upon me
> because he has anointed me;
> To bring good news to the poor he has sent me;
> to proclaim to the captives release
> and sight to the blind;
> To set at liberty the oppressed,
> to proclaim the acceptable year of the Lord.

To have a priest in the family is a great honor for Catholics, and my Irish family wants to celebrate my ordination in grand style. In my home parish, St. Nicholas, back in the Bronx, my parents invite a couple hundred people to attend my First Mass on the day after the ordination. This will be followed by a sit-down dinner. There is one major glitch though. I want to celebrate Mass facing the people. I can't imagine doing it in the old Pre-Vatican Council way, facing "toward the wall and God."

A month before, I explained this to the pastor, Monsignor Brennan, who was previously the spiritual director at St. Joseph's Seminary, the bastion of orthodoxy for the diocesan priesthood of New York. He listened intently before explaining politely, "If you wish to celebrate Mass facing the people, there is an altar for this in the school hall." By the look on his saintly face, he seemed certain that I would balk at not having the main Church for the event.

Equally sure that he would relent for a new priest and his family, I eagerly countered, "I could bring in a portable altar to the main Church."

But two stubborn churchmen glared at each other across a growing divide. He chortled at the insanity of my idea. "There will be no portable altars in the main Church," his velvety voice responded, rising ever so slightly as he dashed my hopes.

I quickly responded to save face, "Oh! I'll have to talk it over with my parents." But I had already decided. It would be in the school hall with the altar facing the People of God.

To me the Eucharist is a sacred meal. As such, it doesn't take away from its meaning as the sacrifice of the cross, the traditional way of understanding the Mass. It's just like my family's dinner table. We share food even with last minute guests one of us brings home.

I believe with all the fervor of a new convert: God is in our midst at Mass as we share the bread and wine that we believe is Jesus' Body and Blood, not up in the sky like some Judge we are appeasing with Jesus' sacrifice on the cross.

I was determined not to be a priest who fostered this fear of a fierce Father-God. No way was I going to be seduced by the stained glass windows and promises of power, even for the sake of doing good. I couldn't believe it had started so soon. Yet I took secret pleasure in the fact that I was already wrestling with religious authorities just like Jesus did.

Mama was stunned at first. Her clenched jaw showed her anger at the pastor. Probably at me too, but in the end she took my side. Mama, the mother of six who attended daily Mass, who enjoyed Dad and the rest of us sitting in the front pew on Holy Family Sunday as though to say to the pastor, "Can you top this?" Now Monsignor Brennan would have to rustle up a crew to polish the floors in the hall, and try to explain to the parishioners why we weren't celebrating such an event in the main church.

Determined to make it something to remember, I hired a cantor who would lead the congregation in singing new upbeat hymns in English like "God is Love" and "Enter, Rejoice and Come In." Excited about the new access to the ritual this offered them, my three sisters flung themselves into decorating the stage with flowers. Above the altar they draped a big banner that proclaimed a phrase from the Psalms: "This is the day that the Lord has made, let us be glad and rejoice in it."

Oh, we were going to rejoice all right! We were a family of dancers ever since my sisters taught my two brothers and me how to dance when we were in high school. I insisted on hiring a rock and roll band so we could dance after the dinner. On the day itself, that plan was quickly dashed when everyone wanted to receive my blessing, a tradition for a newly ordained priest.

There was no way I could bless the long line of people, including many relatives, old friends I'd grown up with, even non-Catholic employees of Dad's from Braxton's Deli, while the band pounded out "Blue Suede Shoes." It broke my heart when we had to send the band home.

I grabbed a mike and announced, "Everyone is invited back to our house for a party afterwards." My parents gaped at each other. We packed the living room, dining room, and kitchen. People brought food, drinks, and musical instruments and we danced and sang songs for eight straight hours. Exhausted but happy around 2 a.m., I tugged the light switch on the lamp and started up the stairs. I had sworn to them all that I would be the last one to hit the sack.

Half-looped from the excitement, beer, and Holy Spirit, I stood on the landing and looked back on the darkened living room where so many events of my life had taken place. The hurtful ones all dim memories now. The good ones all swept up in the vision of my three sisters, singing and kicking their legs like chorus girls to the anthem of the night still ringing in my ears, "You're just too good to be true, can't take my eyes off of you, at long last love has arrived, and I thank God I'm alive . . . "

CHAPTER SEVEN

2003—

Migo's on my mind, one of my jailbird sons who has become dear to me. Ever since I met him, I have visited him a couple of times a month.

When I finally get through the gauntlet of my signature in the official visitors' register, the locked doors, pat downs, long corridors, and badge checks, I take a seat in the small vestibule of the protective custody unit. Noticing the dirty bench, I am careful to sit on my appointment book.

Normally I visit the inmates in this cramped space that links the main outside corridor with the cell-block proper. It is safer for them and for me. After being called, the inmates come down the stone stairs in their baggy orange jumpsuits. Their glum faces light up with a smile at having someone ask for them. "For me, Father Zach? You came to see me?"

We hang out on one of the small benches that face one another and chat about their families, their hopes in regard to their upcoming trials, and if they are in the mood, their faith. Usually the floor of this vestibule is stained with half-eaten sandwiches or spilled juice.

When he finally appears, Migo is a little rumpled and he's got a sheet of paper in his hand. "Something I wrote for you," he says as he sits next to me on the wooden bench. I glance quickly at it, a poem on the unity of all religions. "It's beautiful, Migo." His olive face lights up.

With the scar over his eyebrow and his longish black hair, he could be a pirate. But his lips that make funny grimaces when he speaks and his endearing manner make me love him like one of God's lost sheep.

43

We get increasingly communicative as we spend the half hour together in view of the female C.O. and the other inmates. At one point he runs back to his cell to get a book about Native American spirituality and offers it to me to read. Later he tells me he feels like giving up at times as he lies on his bunk with nothing to do. I draw him out about the depression he has spoken about before. Words like "empty" and "lonely" come up. I go for them, and ask him about trying to write to his father who is "a tough old guy but I love him."

Migo says his dad is not the kind of guy whom you write your feelings to. "He's a fifty-six-year-old truck driver who left my mom when I was nine years old, the oldest of five. My mom was a crack addict who died of an overdose soon after."

"No wonder you feel an emptiness," I say, inviting his feelings, which he doesn't show. We begin speaking about his fears of not making it, even if he beats his upcoming case, which he doesn't describe yet.

"Maybe I can go to a half-way house," he offers.

"Didn't you do that before?" I ask.

"Yeah," he shoots me a rueful look.

I remind him of how he told me about his running in the drug scene, "how you would hustle while your girlfriend waited." I want him to remember that he told me this street behavior of his before.

"Yeah, and then I made her get into a car while I waited."

"What do you mean?" I probe.

"I knew she belonged to me, even though she had sex with a john to get us drug money," he explains, though his grimacing lips show me he realizes how crazy that is.

"Oh man!" I punch him on the shoulder. This reminds me of something I read in Scripture that morning. I pick up his Recovery Bible. A few paper stubs mark key passages for him. "Hey, let me see if I can find something I read today. It reminds me of you." I begin to tell him of the birth of Ishmael, with him picking up the thread of the story. "He was a wild ass of a man," I say.

"What's that mean?" he asks.

I then find the passage and read it to him, while Migo looks over my shoulder: "You are with child and shall bear a son; you shall call him Ishmael because the Lord has heard of your humiliation. He shall be a wild ass of a man, his hand against everyone, and everyone's hand against him; he shall dwell apart, opposing all his kinsmen."

I let it sink in for both of us as he breathes over my shoulder.

I turn and repeat this, "You are like that, a wild ass of a man, Migo." Not sure he gets this or likes it, but I explain a little. "You're always running wild, running to fill up the emptiness."

"Yeah, and doing drugs to escape it," he adds.

"Mmmmm," I tap him on the shoulder again. "It'd kill me to hear that you died from drugs, you know." He stares at me as our knees bump. He then runs back to his cell to get pictures of his family, never shown to me in the past months.

I look at them, faded color copies on thin paper with curled edges, but a good-enough looking dad and brothers and sisters and little ones. Eagerly he points them out and names them. I ask their ages and he tells me these with pride. His father, he explains, raised a few other kids as well as his own five. "They're the children of his second wife. He's been going with her a while but they just got married.

Migo is holding one snapshot of a cousin of his with a little child at his cheek. The cousin, Luis, is about Migo's age. "It's good to see a man holding a kid so close," I say. "Like a father's love should be for his child." Migo gives me his wide-eyed look.

I remember another Scripture passage and try to paraphrase it for him, "God is describing himself as a father," I say, "holding up Israel—no, it's Ephraim!—to his cheek." I make a similar gesture with my hands against my cheek. Then I make a joke about how I am not as good as the Baptists who can remember the precise citations for these passages, before excitedly grabbing his Bible again and searching. "It's from Hosea, I think," and begin to page through the Minor Prophets. Miraculously, I find the passage in a few minutes.

"Hosea, Chapter 11," Migo says as I begin to read it.

"When Israel was a child I loved him, out of Egypt I called my son. The more I called them, the farther they went from me, sacrificing to the Baals and burning incense to idols. Baals are false idols," I explain to him.

"Yet it was I who taught Ephraim to walk, who took them in my arms; I drew them with human cords, with bands of love; I fostered

45

them like one who raises an infant to his cheeks; yet though I stooped to feed my child, they did not know that I was their healer."

I pause, wanting to make sure this young man from the streets with a mother who was a coke addict and a father and family who barely talk to him gets the connection with him and God. I move my face closer to his and look directly into his eyes. "So even if you have done things you are ashamed of, or feel empty and hopeless, let God go down there to that place and love you and claim you. He wants to, Migo, don't you see?"

He nods his head slightly.

"Even if you are a wild ass of a man like Ishmael, God can't bear to lose you. Do you see?" Then I read further, particularly wanting him to hear God's feelings shown in this Bible passage. "Look! It says God *roars*," I tell him. I clench my fists, showing him what I imagine God's passion to be for us.

Migo's eyes are fixed intently on mine.

"It's not just an angry roar, it's a hurt roar. The roar of someone in love," I explain. "God doesn't want to be like humans and simply destroy what has hurt him, left him, or thrown away his love."

Migo listens closely, the dark eyes wide with interest, the scar accentuating this.

"God says he will roar until we return to him," I pause and widen my eyes to make it vivid, "like trembling sparrows and doves."

Migo leans forward with his hands clasped on his thighs. I close the Bible and wait. Soon he asks if we can pray before I leave. We hold hands in our fashion, him gripping mine intensely with his head bowed. I ask if he wants to say a prayer first.

"Yeah," he says without looking up.

I joke, "You're the only one who does. All the others want me to pray first."

Migo then prays, "Father-God, I pray for my family and for Fr. Zach who has helped me see that they are good people. I pray also for the man I'm accused of killing. You know that's not what it's all about. I pray for myself, too. You know how my temptations overwhelm me sometimes. I need your help."

We sit this way in silence for a few moments more before I say, "Amen." As I stand to leave he asks if I will bring him a copy book to write in the next time I come. I tell him that I'll try.

"I'm gonna get a cup of coffee and go back to my cell and read those passages, Zach." He calls me Zach now, explaining that the Bible says we should call no one on earth father.

"That's good, Migo." We shake hands and part.

Later that night, I remember him and our time together. As I walked away earlier I felt some hopelessness in his regard. His addictive patterns destroy even the best intentions. I pray anyway, "Please Lord, bless Migo. I love him as you do." To protect myself, I hadn't planned to get so involved with the inmates, especially a possible murderer, but Migo is different. I make a gesture as of a father pulling his child up to his cheek, "Don't let him be lost Father, I beg you. We can roar later."

CHAPTER EIGHT

1968—

After ordination I am sent to an urban parish for the summer. They want to break young priests into the realities of pastoral life beyond the classroom. They want us to get our hands dirty, make us confront suffering people in hospitals, meet families with problems that no books can explain.

This is no ordinary summer. All over the country, riots are going on since Martin Luther King was assassinated in the spring. And then, the week before we graduate, Bobby Kennedy is assassinated. The country begins to spiral out of control. The Church joins the chaos. *Humanae Vitae*, the encyclical on birth control, splits the Church into two camps. And to crown the year as the most tragic in memory, the great pacifist monk and writer, Thomas Merton, is accidentally electrocuted in a bathtub at an ecumenical gathering in Asia.

My first assignment is to St. Jerome's Parish in the Bronx. Excited to be out of the hothouse of the seminary at last, I arrive at the parish in late June in Bermuda shorts with my tennis racket slung under my arm. I fantasize having some fun as well as parish work after the long years of seminary studies. Finally, I am free to go where God calls me and to live a more normal life.

It is the custom to have dinner with your friar brothers as your first official act of obedience in your community. The Reverend Patrick "Potsy" Cunningham greets me in the doorway in his rumpled habit. My brother, Steve, hunkers beside me with a few of my suitcases.

Famous around the province for his bombastic manner, Potsy's whiskered jowls roar like a scowling bear at the doorway, "What the hell are you doing showing up here late for dinner?"

I imagine Steve, an ex-marine, being rather impressed by this drill instructor priest barking out orders to his latest plebe. I'm about to explain to Potsy that we're late because we drove across the wrong bridge, and that my brother was ogling some college girls in their convertible, but I just mumble instead, "I'm sorry, we got lost."

"Lost! That's no excuse!" He checks out my shorts and the tennis racket. "And what do you think this is, some kind of health spa? You're here to do work!"

Shocked at first by this gruff greeting from a fellow friar, I notice the cook behind him with her lips twisted into a wry smile. She's a bleach-blonde, middle-aged, Slavic-looking woman with Dolly Parton breasts pushing out of the front of her soiled apron. Her face gives me a clue that she's seen this test before.

My voice stays calm. "Don't worry. I intend to work." I decide to go for the test. "But I want to relax too." Crinkling up my eyes and grinning before he can respond, I lift my racket, "Wanna play?" Steve snorts beside me.

Potsy's lips flap. His face flashes red. Finally like a poison potion, he spits out, "P . . . P . . . PLAY TENNIS! *RELAXXXXX?* Is that what this new theology is teaching you? No wonder the Church is going to hell." All of this happens in the doorway while pedestrians wander by and enjoy the show.

Potsy begins to step aside now. He is grinning, though barely. Maybe he won't have a heart attack. Maybe I've managed to claim my space.

"This is Betty, our cook," he says in a more mellow voice, gesturing to the woman. I can tell by his tone of voice that he's sweet on her. She motions us in for the lasagna dinner she has saved. A delicious aroma welcomes us into the cozy dining room with its mahogany table and chandelier.

Potsy invites Steve to join us but he declines. "I've got to find my way out of here," he says, deadpanning a look at me which says, I've got to get out of this maniac's place. Potsy doesn't push him and Steve and I go to the car to get more of my belongings.

After we stack a few boxes, another large suitcase, and my bongo drums in the hallway, I follow him out to the car to say goodbye. "Don't let that bastard get you down," Steve growls under his breath as he grips my hand like a vise.

"Don't worry," I say. Yet now that I am finally being launched on my own, I am beginning to feel a little shaky.

There is something more I need from Steve, but I'm not sure what. "Say hello to Laura for me, and get the right bridge on the way home, okay?" I tell him as he slides into the driver's seat and rolls down the window.

"Right! And I won't say 'Be brave' like you said when I went into the Corps. Keep your head down, you hear?" He winks as though to tell me he realizes what I'm up against.

It dawns on me what I need from him when he turns on the ignition key. "Hey Steve, say one for me, will ya?" My brother doesn't wear his faith on his sleeve like I do. We rarely talk about spiritual things, but with Potsy prowling in the rectory behind me, I figure I'll need all the help I can get. This is as close as I can get to asking for my brother's blessing.

"Sure. No sweat." Then Steve, who is only two years older than me but whom I never really got to know in all the years we slept in the same room together, guns the engine of his '59 Chevy and drives away.

An emptiness washes over me as I watch his car turn the corner at the end of the street. Quickly I brush the feelings aside. I should be used to these goodbyes by now after so many years in the seminary, ready to give up everything for the sake of Christ.

I push my way through the screen door and walk through the hallway into the dining room, hoping Potsy has some other appointment to keep him busy. But he's chatting with Betty in the kitchen doorway.

The table is set for a few people. Betty glances over Potsy's shoulder at me, looking like she wants to say something. Potsy turns as I sit down. Immediately his hands fly up and he screams, "That's my seat!"

"Whaaat?" I'm genuinely flabbergasted at his behavior and almost jump up to apologize but notice Betty smiling. I remain seated. "Your seat?"

Potsy moves toward me, his worn black habit accentuating the fierce look on his face. "Yes, it is my seat," he says sweetly, with his eyebrows standing up like an owl's.

Maybe I'm beginning to grasp his act. I decide to go for a trump card. "Oh, I'm sorry. We learned in the seminary that friars share all things in common," I stare at his bulging eyes, "But if you really need this seat, you can have it." I start to rise.

"Wait! His hand reaches for my arm. "It is my seat, but you didn't know about that yet, so you can stay there for now. And I don't give a damn about what they taught you in the seminary. Since Vatican II, they've changed all the rules that we were taught. It's my rules that we follow here."

I'm trying to decide whether he's serious or not when Betty arrives with the lasagna and a tossed salad. She slides them between us. She hesitates, then asks, "Do you want some wine?" She points to a decanter of red wine on a side table.

"Yeah, I may as well get a little mellow for my first night." I snicker gently before scooping a forkful of the lasagna into my mouth.

Potsy bobs his head up and down as though he's on to something. Is that a glint in his eye? "I'll have a little too, Betty. We wouldn't want Father Braxton to have to drink alone on his first night, would we?"

She glances at me with what looks like pity. "No, we wouldn't." She smooths her apron. Potsy grins at her as she pours our drinks before returning to the kitchen.

The wine offers us a respite that we both grab, a kind of brotherhood underneath the sparring that gives me hope, even for just a moment. Potsy sips his slowly and looks out the picture window into the schoolyard. I drink mine rather quickly and pour a second as Potsy turns to watch.

By the time I finish eating a half hour later, it feels like the two of us actually have some kind of initial bond of mutual respect. Even so, Steve's words, "Don't let the bastard get you down," seem worth remembering as I clear the dishes and Potsy drives Betty home.

A short time later, I almost bump into Potsy as I juggle my belongings up the carpeted stairway toward my second floor room. With a sheet of paper in his hand, he clears his throat demonstratively "Ah, ah, ah."

I halt in my tracks halfway up and turn toward him. "Oh hi, what's up?"

"What's up?" He bares his yellow teeth like a devil, and then chuckles fiendishly to himself. "You have the seven o'clock Mass tomorrow morning." He watches my reaction before adding, "Get a good night's sleep. You wouldn't want to be late for your first duty now, would you?" An ominous tone hovers in his last sweet words.

"No, I wouldn't." He's such a target that I can't resist it. "By the way, do you have an alarm I can borrow?" In a second I wiggle my nose to show him I'm kidding. He glowers like a madman as I head to my room laughing.

While unpacking, I notice the city lights blinking on. The smog-covered Bronx skyline has transformed into a gauzy purple haze. Before I even finish arranging my black priest's clothes and sport shirts in the small closet, I flop onto the bed and fall asleep.

As priests, we hear confessions every Saturday at the parish. One Saturday evening after hearing confessions, I slump down across the table from Potsy.

"Now what's the matter? You just got here and you look like you're ready to bail out." Is that a caring tone in his voice? He slurps some of his cream of turkey soup like a child.

I feel drained and don't want to get into a discussion with this guy. But this ministry is lonely. There's no one to let my frustration out with. The Seal of Confession requires us to hold everything we hear in confession as strictly confidential. To protect people's privacy, you're not supposed to discuss it with anyone. All of a sudden I blurt out, "Did you ever get sick of hearing people confess things they really don't think are sins?"

Some soup drips off his chin onto his habit. "What's that supposed to mean?" His gray eyes stare deadpan. A bus revs up outside.

I take a swig of water. "If someone confesses to you that they missed Mass because they were sick, what do you say to them?"

He blinks a few more times before answering. "I tell them to try harder the next time and give them three Hail Mary's for a penance." His voice is calmer than usual and he's grinning. I sigh and begin to relax.

"But why wouldn't you tell them that if they are sick it isn't a sin? Why make them feel guilty about something they can't help?" Sure of myself, I stare straight into his beady eyes.

"Betty!" He suddenly bellows toward the kitchen like we're on a ball field. "We're ready" Then back to me in a gentler voice. "Did you ever think people NEED TO FEEL GUILTY?" His renewed outburst almost blows me off my chair.

"Need to? . . . What?" I squint in confusion. The door swivels open. Betty arrives with the main course on a cart: baked ham, mashed sweet potatoes, and cabbage. Departing without a word, she glances at me briefly while licking gravy off her thumb and disappears into the kitchen.

"Look," Potsy leans close as though we are hatching a plot. "When they tell you an excuse for a sin, whatever it is, that's probably not the real reason." He forks a couple of slabs of ham onto his plate and hands the platter to me. "Otherwise—do you want some mustard?—they wouldn't be bringing it up in confession in the first place, right?"

I consider his words as I watch him chomp the meat like a savage.

"Usually there isn't enough time to get into the real issues. You gotta get 'em in and out fast." He slices the air with his hand to show me. "Most of the time they don't want you to delve into anything either." He cackles as though only a dummy wouldn't get it. "So in your kindest voice, just tell them to try a little harder and give them absolution. That's what they want." He stabs a hunk of cabbage and pops it into his bear mouth.

I recall that Cunningham received his theology training at the University of Louvain in Belgium. He must've been one of the brains of his day. Even so, at Sebastian College we learned that it is important to help people develop their personal conscience. This is the Second Vatican Council's theology that is clashing with Potsy's understanding along with his generation. I swallow.

He stares across the table at me while I stare back. Two different theologies. Two different churches really, but they aren't in a full-tilt clash yet.

When a married guy confessed to using condoms a little earlier, I heard the pain and embarrassment in his voice. I want to help people like him, not just treat confession like an assembly line. With all of

Cunningham's street-talking roughness, I can't believe that he doesn't hear this pain from people too. "So what do you say when someone comes in and says, 'Father, we have four kids. We can't afford any more?'" I ask.

"Gimmee the gravy," he says while scratching the few hairs on his balding head. "What's your problem? Don't tell me you want to talk to people about their sex lives!" His lips make a smacking sound while chewing, while below the table my hands squeeze my napkin.

"Look," I plead, "I'm twenty-six years old and unmarried. What do you want me to say to these people? If I absolve them of what they simply can't do responsibly, have more kids if they want to have sex, they'll only show up again in a month distraught over their sin." Cunningham's eyes are on his plate. He begins to chew more methodically.

"You've got to understand," he explains, "priests are here to represent what the Church teaches, not to make up our own rules. Even if they gripe about it, the people want it that way too. That way they've got a clean slate after they confess. They are right in God's eyes, even if it's just for a while. What would happen if everyone did just what they wanted?"

When he pauses for a breath I jump in. "But don't you think we should talk to them about it? And if they seem sincere, encourage them to follow their own conscience in the future and not confess it? Why should priests be caught between some impossible ideal and the reality of people's lives?"

"Conscience?" It's as though I've questioned the Blessed Mother's virginity. He sneers at the craziness of the thought. "Conscience! If people follow their conscience, there will be no such thing as sin anymore, don't you get it? They won't come to confession." Some pots crash in the kitchen.

The guy is so angry that bubbles are coming out of his mouth. I decide to shut up before it gets worse. The rest of the meal we eat in silence, passing the plates of ham and cabbage back and forth while we wonder where the Church is going.

From that evening on, Potsy Cunningham and I begin to treat each other like we are in different camps. Trying to bridge this gap, and to keep me a child I suppose, he takes me for a ride each evening to show me the parish and buy me an ice cream cone.

It isn't just in private conversations that these tensions show themselves. In the immediate aftermath of Vatican II, the Church atmosphere is so charged that it is like you have to take a stand on everything. Birth control is the prime example. The media gives so much attention to it that you can't just hide in the shadows. On top of this, it affects so many people where it really counts, their sexual relations.

The encyclical *Humanae Vitae* forbids the use of artificial contraception. Some priests refuse to get caught in the middle of this difficult law. They publicly disagree with the Pope. The Canadian bishops and the Dutch bishops issue challenging alternative interpretations. In Washington, DC, over fifty priests sign a public statement that says they will leave the matter of birth control to people's individual conscience, since "responsible parenthood" is what the encyclical ostensibly wants to foster.

The whole issue becomes quite political in the climate of the times. It may have started as a moral issue, but it soon becomes a battle over which direction authority comes from in the Church, from the pope and bishops down or from the people in the pews up. Priests are caught in the middle.

Feeling his authority on the line, Cardinal O'Boyle, the crusty old east coast defender of the Pope along with Cardinals Krol, Spellman and Cushing, demands that his Washington, DC, priests retract their statements or be immediately suspended from their ministry. Most don't and he suspends them from priestly duties. Shockingly, many of these priests leave public ministry, the large majority of them vibrant young guys who have been educated with the new theology of the Second Vatican Council. Many are my friends.

I begin to wonder if this will be my future, and I've been ordained for less than a year.

CHAPTER NINE

2003—

I swerve into the Administration Building's parking lot for our monthly chaplains' meeting. It's our group time to sign endless policy papers on every aspect of the system, from inmate armband protocol to preparations for where to stack the bodies in the event of a major outbreak of a life-threatening disease.

There are fourteen chaplains: Beverly, the Afro-American Director; Cindy, the Jewish dietician-nurse; Yosuf, the Muslim Imam; ten Protestant chaplains, mostly Evangelical Christians; and myself. There are hundreds of volunteers as well, representing every kind of church imaginable. I usually only meet them in the lobby of the various prisons where they are assigned to conduct religious services. Riker's Island, like most prisons and jails, is a magnet for people who believe that God is alive and that people can be saved.

During a break in the meeting, I check my phone. It's a message from Norma. Instead of our regular weekly supervision meeting in her office, she wants us to drive over to City Island today. "Leaves will be falling soon. Let's get some crabs and celebrate the end of summer. Cha cha cha." I picture her making her little dance movement. I text her back. "Great. your office 20 min."

Around twelve thirty, Norma and I head out to the tiny island in the middle of the New York metropolis that makes you think you're on Nantucket. We decide to take two cars because I have to leave for another appointment soon after. Norma leads the way in her rust-colored Ford Taurus. I careen after her, my eyes glued on her "Peace is the Answer" bumper sticker.

It's still a warm day for mid-September. Wispy clouds streak across the blazing sun. As we approach the rickety bridge at the entrance to the island, Norma points at the scores of boats huddled in the marina for their weekend adventures. I grin back. Gulls hover above us crying for lunch. I crack my window. A tantalizing mix of salt, fresh air, and fish offers an escape as good as a martini.

Norma reaches back to wave from her window as we stop at a red light. "Hey Zach!" she gestures toward the sidewalk. "The Blue Neptune. This place is cool." She cuts quickly into the only parking spot. I make a U turn and zip into a space across the street.

The little nook of a restaurant with the sea-god statue in its window appears to be crowded as we approach, but we shrug and enter anyway. When the manager approaches, Norma gushes "Ciao." Before I can blink we're being seated at a small table by a picture window. A couple is seated quite near us at the next table. If we want to share anything confidential, it will have to be in a whisper.

Quickly I survey the room. Polished wood plank floors, tiffany droplights over the tables and fish nets draped on the walls. On the front of the small bar is an anchor, sort of a submarine motif, cozy and comfy with a salt water aroma hovering over it all. "Nice," I say, pointing at the lights.

"I come here when I want to forget the city," Norma says, admiring the multiple rings on her hands.

"I needed this. It's good to get out, especially on a work day." Still a little stressed from the tension of the ministry, I start telling her about the women at the female prison I saw in the morning. "The female inmates are so different from the guys. All their feelings are out front."

"That's for sure." She runs her fingers through her hair and sweeps it to one side.

"One of them has eight children, each of them born while in jail."

"Kathleen!" she immediately guesses. "I've helped get some of those children of hers into foster care until she's released." Concern spreads on her face.

"Would you believe the C.O. suggested I tell Kathleen to get her tubes tied?" I raise my eyebrows.

Norma frowns. "Yes, it's a problem."

We know that our role of officially representing the Catholic Church can create a problem for us, especially when an inmate's particular circumstances don't mesh with Church teachings. "So what can you say to someone like Kathleen?"

"Something to drink?" A waitress appears behind Norma, smacking her gum.

"Yes. I'd like a Chardonnay," Norma says.

"Make that two," I notice her nametag. Phoebe. She flashes a smile and glides away to the bar.

"I know, I know," Norma says. But do we just stand by and watch as child after child is brought into the world without parents to care for them?" Her eyes widen as she reaches to touch my hand. "Zach, there are hundreds of such children of inmates in this city alone. Can't you find a way to help her?"

"What can I say to her as a priest?"

"Can't you mention birth control?"

"I could, but what will Bishop Mueller say if I do?"

She starts to choke. "You know him?"

"He and I were good friends in the seminary, before he left for the Diocesan priesthood."

"You were?"

I nod, scanning back over the many years since the night Peter pulled me out of my self-hatred about being gay. He finally got his position of power. Cardinal O'Connor rewarded him for all his deft personnel moves, and made him an auxiliary bishop.

"What was he like then?" She sips her Chardonnay. "I know Peter too."

I gape at her. "You do?"

"You look flustered."

"Oh no, I'm just sort of stunned that you know someone whom I knew so well, that's all. How do you know him?"

"You could say he's my boss." She notices the waitress approaching with our drinks. "Let's order first. Are you ready?"

Your boss!

Norma jumps in. "I'll have a basket of crabs and the arugula salad with the goat cheese. Put the dressing on the side, please."

I scan the menu, remembering how over the years Peter and I got together less and less. We talk on the phone once in a while. I only see him in the newspapers. "Are the mussels good?" I ask Phoebe as she sets the drinks down.

"Fresh this morning," She's an older gal, with her hair pulled back in a ponytail; I imagine her waiting on lots of tables through the years. She deadpans me while tapping her pencil.

I run my finger down the lunch specials, thinking of all the water under the bridge with Peter. I don't really know him. Does anyone? How can someone live like that? And how is it that I could let someone who changed my whole life drift away and become just a memory? "Okay, give me the mussels in the white wine and garlic sauce. And I'll have the beet and walnut salad. Can you bring us some bread too? Norma, want some water?"

"Sparkling or tap?" Phoebe asks.

"Tap is good. They don't pump it from the bay do they?" I return her bored look.

"Sparkling will do," says Norma, unmoved by my humor.

"No, but the bay water could add a little zest I suppose," cracks Phoebe with a smirk.

"Sparkling it is then," I say.

"Gotcha." We watch as she hurries away.

"So, Bishop Mueller?"

"Your boss?"

"As well as being the personnel director, Peter coordinates the Social Ministries in the Archdiocese. As the prison ministry coordinator, I answer to him. He's a good man." She lifts her drink for a toast.

Mmmmmm, so she's fond of him. I lift my glass and we click. As distant as Peter has become with me, he's easy to be fond of with his quarterback style.

"So why don't you communicate if you're friends?"

"It's a long story." I can't hide a trace of sadness and I look away. "I'd like to, but. . ."

"Hmmmmm. . ." We gaze out the picture windows at the choppy bay waters and sip our wine.

"He helped me accept myself a long time ago, Norma."

Our meal arrives, steaming and mouth watering, strung out on both of Phoebe's arms. A guy with a girl diagonally across from us leans over and motions to Phoebe for their check. Norma puts her index finger to her lips, reminding me we can be overheard.

"Be careful, the plates are very hot," Phoebe warns. The food is arranged with an artistic flair on colorful square plates and designer bowls.

"Scrumptious," Norma says.

We touch hands for a silent prayer of thanksgiving, and I lean closer to breathe in the tangy aroma of the mussel broth. Norma begins to crack open her crabs. She pops one into her mouth and smacks her lips in delight. "I'm a little surprised. Peter doesn't seem that open now."

"When you get in one of those high-up positions, you can build a wall around yourself, you know."

The waitress returns with the couple's check. She checks our wine glasses. "Another round?"

With the mussels tangy in my throat, I'd enjoy a second. "Norma?"

"No thanks. I'm good," says Norma.

"We're okay." I take a gulp of the sparkling water.

"Peter lets his hair down with me sometimes, but he doesn't seem that open to gay issues," Norma muses.

"Maybe it's too close to home," I wisecrack, then wish I hadn't.

Glancing out the window, she smiles slyly. "We've gone away on occasion."

A little stab of jealousy hits me. "Really?"

"We get separate lodgings though."

I imagine her and Peter trying to get away for some special time together. Two men can go on vacation and sleep in the same room, but questions are raised if the two of them want to do so. It doesn't even have to be sexual.

The waitress is back. "Would you like some coffee?" She glances at my plate again.

I push the plate of mussel shells toward her. "I'm done. They were great. Coffee Norma?"

She's lost in thought and shakes her "I'll have a regular, and two creamers."

"Give me a decaf."

"Separate lodgings? That's good I suppose," I say when Phoebe leaves. Together we look down in silence. Like me, I imagine Norma thinking of all the sexual issues our Church is so outspoken on: abortion, sterilization, divorce and remarriage, homosexuality, birth control, celibacy and the all-male priesthood. The whole bloody litany linked together like a house of cards.

Taking a small mirror out of her bag, she begins to reapply her lipstick. "What a world of subterfuge we live in," she says, then presses her lips together.

"Yeah, these sexual issues have become the identity of our Church."

Norma runs a pencil around her lips, turning her head from side to side to check out the effect. "The overarching doctrines are too much for me to deal with, Zach." She clicks her compact shut. "The personal is what really matters to me."

"Me too, Norma. You can get away with it, but priests can't. We're not allowed to disagree with these teachings, at least in public. They want us to have a united front."

Our coffees arrive along with some chocolate biscotti.

"Mmmmmm," she ponders them like a child. Picking one up daintily, she dunks it. "You know what it's like? A black wall. The clergy with locked arms, especially against women."

"Really?" I notice the anger under her words.

"It's a wall of silence, and no one can break through it."

"Not even with Peter?"

She sips her coffee, then places the cup down and runs her finger around the rim. "If you'd let us in, a whole new Church could emerge. It will be painful though. Priests will have to let go of some of their privilege, their pomposity. Bishops even more." The restaurant begins to empty out.

"You're right about the personal," I say. "I suppose the big issue is how Peter and you and I will relate to one another. I don't want the past to get in the way."

"It will. You can be sure of that. You can't make the past go away, but you can learn from it." She presses her lips together to fix the lipstick.

I know Norma cares for me from how we share about the inmates. I'm not yet ready to tell her everything about my past though. I want to keep the supervisor relationship I have with her. Maybe it's part of the black wall. Let a woman in, but not too close. Keep her in a role. If you're just interacting with feelings, it can get too messy.

Together we gaze through the picture window. The wind has died down and the water is serene. A sailboat heads out for a jaunt. A lone gull dives and swoops away toward the horizon. An image from my past stirs, a time when Peter and I stood at that wall of secrets.

Peter and I stood shivering by the back door to the seminary in our habits. It was about one o'clock on New Year's morning. Just a half hour before, he had been the arm of God's love for me as he pulled me close. We had walked and walked across the ball field until the other friars had finally gone in. I'm sure Peter sensed the enormous turning point it was for me to have come out to him. But he seemed to need some space now, maybe to deal with his own feelings.

I waited while a breeze ruffled the trees. Soon Peter reached out his hand toward me for a shake. Not wanting the special night to end, I hesitated before grasping and holding it for an extra couple of seconds.

"You okay?" he asked, gradually releasing my hand.

"Yeah, sure."

"Good." He started moving toward the door before his head turned back like an afterthought. "Hey man, do me a favor, will you?"

My eager face gleamed in the door's light. "Sure. What?"

He glanced sideways. "Let's keep tonight to ourselves, okay?"

Just a half hour before it had felt like a miracle happened between us. "Oh . . . okay." Now my jaw dropped along with my heart.

"I'm not saying . . ." he searched for the right words. "What happened between us tonight was special," his deep voice cajoled. He punched me on my chest lightly. "It'll be our secret, Buddy."

Our secret. But Peter, don't you see? I feel like screaming your acceptance of me to the whole world.

He saw the question in my face. "A secret just between you and me, Zach. Okay?"

His voice was soothing, caressing even. I took a deep breath while my habit whipped around my legs and a crater opened up in my gut. "Okay."

I watched my friend disappear through the doorway, watched him bound two steps at a time up the stairs to his room where I once surprised him in his bed. As I backed up into the shadows and the emptiness, my heart fled back to me.

"Ohhhh! I've got to get back to the city," I suddenly announce to Norma. Quickly I put on my public face.

"Okay," she says. She was watching me but doesn't probe. "We can pick this up again sometime soon, all right? She finishes her coffee and takes the check. "And this is my treat. You can get it next time."

Back at the parish later, I call out a quick hello to the other friars as I pass them in the kitchen. My mind is still whirling from my conversation with Norma. After changing into jeans and a sweater, I decide to take a quick stroll around the neighborhood before dinner.

Under the el, the traffic is dense with honking limo-cabs and jaywalkers. I jiggle my foot nervously at the curb as I wait for the light to change.

Storefronts blare out Latin rap music that pulsates to the energy of teenage moms pushing strollers, sometimes with two babies, occasionally accompanied by a teenage daddy in baggy jeans slung halfway down his butt. Their tattoos and body piercings seem to boast, "My body is mine and I'll do what I want with it!" Above us the #4 train screeches to a stop at Kingsbridge Road, the heart of the North Bronx.

Usually I can count on this orgy of sights and sounds to drag me out of any mood I'm stuck in. Yet I can't get my mind off Peter and Norma. They go away together. Get separate rooms. *He's a good man, Zach.*

It makes me wonder about Peter and me. When was the last good interaction we had? Was it the time about ten years ago when he was named a monsignor? The Diocese had called a meeting of all the priests to deal with the sexual abuse crisis. It was the first time the exploding outrage had been brought into our consciousness. Since then it's been a runaway train.

CHAPTER TEN

1993—

After dinner, Francis, Geraldo, and I sprawl in the common room at Our Lady of Angels Parish, watching Seinfeld. Geraldo, a lonesome young jock in a friary community of gardeners and interior decorators asks, "Are any of you going to the meeting the Cardinal called at Dunwoodie Seminary next Tuesday afternoon?" Francis and I keep watching the Pillsbury Doughboy commercial.

"I might be going," Francis says with a yawn, "but I've got a wedding rehearsal that evening and I don't want to be late." As pastor, he's constantly complaining about weddings and how the brides' mothers are like dictators.

I am planning to attend. Peter and I are meeting beforehand so we can catch up; I don't want any company. "No way am I eager for this command performance by O'Connor," I say.

"You know these sexual abuse cases are a shout for us to wake up," says Geraldo. He's from the Dominican Republic, a rare mid-thirties guy among the older friars. I like his energy. He's in the midst of a pastoral immersion year with us before he gets ordained, and he enjoys popping theological questions to us when we least expect it. I decide to egg him on.

"It'll offer a clue to how the Archdiocese plans to respond to the stories accusing priests of sexual abuse," I say.

I can see Geraldo musing on this so I add, "Do you think we'll get to discuss how celibacy relates to this?" Francis smirks and rolls his eyes.

"We better," Geraldo says. "Some of these Church teachings about sex can actually lead to violence." His macho voice resonates and we both glance at him.

"You're right," I agree.

His dark liquid eyes check to see if I am serious. "There are kids who are taught, you know, to hate that they're gay." He shifts his leg until it's draped over the armrest.

Francis' eyebrow arches. Though we live together in community, rarely do the friars speak personally about something as crucial in our lives as our sexuality. It's as though once we make our vows, our sexuality becomes spiritualized and hidden, not just from others but even among ourselves.

"There are kids at home who've hung themselves." The young Latino's voice takes on a pleading quality. "In my country, the Church teachings foster this self-hate."

"Oh god." When an older priest is loosened up with a sip or two of brandy on a feast day, you might hear him refer to this mysterious hidden part of our lives. "The feelings never stop. Not until you're six feet under," he'll wink as he pours another Scotch. "And even then they're not sure."

"If young people could find a place in the Church to talk about their feelings, it could help," Geraldo continues.

When a friar does actually try to open up, someone usually distracts us and the issue goes underground. Except for a few gay guys in support groups, most friars never talk about how we deal with our own sexuality. It's like it's only between us and God, and most times God doesn't seem to care. "We've got to help these kids, Geraldo, and find ways to share about our own sexuality," I tell him.

"I told you, the Fat Lady's singing." Francis flings out his campy smokescreen. He makes this wisecrack often, insinuating that the Church is in trouble because of the sexual abuse crisis and lack of vocations, even that the ballgame is over for us. A pessimist by nature, he'd be happy to be living like a cloistered nun, walled off from the world with its brides and murky moral issues.

I scowl at him. It's not over for the Church as I see it. Rather, I believe there's a new Church being born, yowling and thrashing to burst out of the womb of a creaky old Mother Church who's on her last legs. She needs us to be the midwives, but we'll need to risk getting some blood on our hands. I glance over toward Geraldo, "Friars like you can help us."

His fierce eyes sweep back and forth between us. Rising, he places one hand on his hip and the other on his flat belly. "The Fat Lady, she may be singing, but if you listen closely she's singing with a Latin beat now." He makes a sultry grinding gesture with his pelvis and sneers with his lip up. "And this beat—he thrusts his pelvis forward and grunts 'Mira!'—will make all the difference in the world." We burst out laughing, reminded that he and his beat are our best hope for the future.

"Okay Geraldo, I can drive you to the discussion," says Francis.

I speed onto the Deegan Expressway on Tuesday afternoon, while my mind goes back to the dinner party Peter hosted when he was named monsignor a few years before. He pulled me aside in his confidential way and whispered, "Stick with me, Zach. I'm going to need you more than ever now."

Soon after, when he was named personnel director for the Archdiocese, he decided to leave our priests' support group. "Conflicting agendas," he told me over the phone.

"Yeah, but where will you get the personal space you get in our group?" I pressed him.

"Don't worry. You and I can still meet," he assured me. "You're more important to me than the group anyway."

"You are for me too," I say. But after that we've rarely been able to carve out any time for just the two of us. Peter was always so busy. The same with me. It's like our schedules have become our lovers.

After parking my car, I walk out to the Hudson River. A plaque announces that the Recreation Pier was built in 1901 to offer access to the Hudson River for the people of Yonkers, "the largest metropolis North of Manhattan," it boasts.

I'm ten minutes early for our rendezvous and feel kind of anxious, not having slept well last night. I lean on the railing that juts out into the river, and glance south toward the George Washington Bridge, then North to the Tappan Zee Bridge hovering over the river like a spindly giant.

It's a beautiful early autumn day. A tangy hint of salt tickles my nose. I breathe it in deeply, wanting to be relaxed when Peter shows up. It's like a postcard in slow motion, I think. The mighty river undulating like a living being in the dappled sunlight, the trees lush and colorful on the riverbank far across the water, the only sound from a small private plane buzzing in the powder blue sky above. Oh, if only I could hold this moment forever.

I glance behind me just in time to notice Peter pulling up in his bullet-gray, four-door Acura with tinted windows. He's searching for a parking spot and doesn't see me immediately. I watch him back carefully into a space, enjoying how he maneuvers the wheel like a pro. Soon he sees me and his eyes light up like a schoolboy's at recess. "Zaaaach," he calls through the window.

"Peter!" I trot toward him. Emerging into the sunlight, he looks at me up and down. We're dressed the same in our collars and black suits.

Quickly our hands grasp and we hold one another's gaze. Then Peter spreads out his arms at the magnificent scenery. "Terrific!"

I can't believe it. Peter actually seems relaxed, more than I remember him for quite a while. Chuckling at his exuberance, I smile in agreement.

"So, how've you been, Zach?" We stroll over and sit together on one of the benches that overlook the river.

"Good, I'm good . . . and you look great, Peter. The job must be better than you imagined." I loosen the tab of my collar and lean back.

"The job?" Peter makes a face. "You make it sound like it's a nine-to-five deal. Wouldn't that be nice?" A family strolls by. The young child points at a sailboat across the water.

"No, no. I know it's a crazy ministry you do, and you do for us. I'm just glad we could finally get together."

"Yes, it's been too long. Thanks for calling and nailing me down." He loosens his collar too.

Both of us watch the mesmerizing scene before us. My stomach rumbles. I hear him breathe deeply and sigh. Two seagulls float by above us and we glance up. I use it as my cue. "You know when I called you the other night? I wanted to share something I discovered recently."

He keeps focused on the river.

"My father visited me a few weeks ago. . ."

He turns toward me while his rust-colored hair blows in the breeze. He's really listening.

"Daddy and I were sitting side by side on a park bench across from Lincoln Center. We were watching the fountain leap up and tumble back, each with our own private thoughts, a metal armrest between us." I glance down. There is none between Peter and me.

Peter smiles. He knows this quality I have to look for mystical connections. "Go on."

"Suddenly, a thought came to me: my father's almost eighty and I'll be fifty this year. We never talked much as I grew up because he worked such long hours at the deli. He could get seriously ill or even die one day soon. What would I want to say to him if that happened?"

I watch Peter nod. What was his relationship with his father like? I wonder. Rarely has he spoken of him, even in our support group.

"So, what did you say to him?" His voice is soft.

"'Daddy, sometimes it's difficult being a priest,' I said. My Old Man eyed me, not sure where I was going with this line of thought."

Peter leans closer, the story is pulling him in. It's what I'm hoping for.

"My father already knows I'm gay, Peter. I came out to him and the family fifteen years ago, but somehow we never talk about it. Then I added, 'It's even harder to be a gay priest, Daddy. That's why I need your support.'"

Peter's eyes widen. "You said that to him?" He gazes out at the river, swallowing as though to take it in. I watch him until he looks back.

"You know what my Old Man responded? This gruff working-class hero who never graduated from high school? This guy who brought me into the world but never told me I love you?" I raise my eyebrows to show Peter how my mind was boggled at what happened next. "My father wiped the mayo from his mustache, glanced sideways at me with his lip trembling and said, 'I've heard about how they try to change people like that. But I figure God made you that way so you could help other people like that.'"

Peter grabs my arm, his eyes beginning to mist. "Ohmygod, Zack. What a moment to treasure. Lots of people would kill for a moment like that. I know I would. What did you feel like? What did you say?"

"Peter, it was like God himself embraced me, embraced all of me. Like I had finally embraced myself. Yet somehow I needed my father to show me this love. Without really planning it, I just let my desire come out for a change. By doing so I asked my Old Man for his blessing and he gave it to me."

Peter blinks, removes his glasses, and rubs his eyes. Below us we watch a sailboat tip onto its side as it turns into the wind.

"And this all happened on a park bench in Manhattan," I add, "while the Lincoln Center fountain is leaping up, and with homeless people on the next bench, would you believe?"

The two of us sit with these images in silence for a few moments. A breeze stirs up some waves.

Leaning back on the bench with his voice low, Peter mumbles, "I can't imagine my father saying something like that." He checks his watch.

Go ahead, I think. We've got all the time in the world.

"With my Dad it was always, 'Do better son.' In grade school once I ran home excitedly with a second honors card. It had a silver star on the top. 'Dad, dad!' I burst into the living room with my news, 'look what I got.' It was his day off and a baseball game was on TV. Ma was in the kitchen. He waited for the pitcher to throw another strike before he reached for my card and stared at it. I can still remember the expression on his face as he said, 'Not bad, son. Next time you get the gold, right?' Grinning encouragement, he punched me lightly in the ribs before he turned back to the game."

Feeling pulled in by Peter's experience, I reach to touch his sleeve. A couple strolls by and I freeze for a moment, shy to be seen too cozy with another man.

Peter continues, "It was like my dad's love was always dependent on what I achieved, not just for my doing well enough." He scrunches his lips and glances down. "Zack, I never felt like my Dad loved me just for being me."

I want to say, Even your silver stars are great to me, Peter. I hold back though, not sure if my feelings will push him away.

"When my father died years ago from emphysema, I didn't bring up any of these things at his funeral. Even to my mother and brother and sister. But when I'm alone sometimes, I weep over our relationship. I only wanted my father to be proud of me." He shrugs. "Maybe I still do."

For a moment our different trajectories in the church become clear to me. Suddenly I gush like a schoolboy, "Well I'm proud of you, Peter. A lot of people are, you know?"

Our vulnerability lasts until a couple of seagulls fly by to break the trance. Peter's shimmering eyes return to their familiar strength.

"We better get going," he says, checking his watch. "We'll be late." He stands and inserts his Roman collar.

I remain seated and glance up at him. "Hey, wait a minute! Where can we go with this? Let's help each other with these things, okay?"

But he's already out of the feeling zone, his jaw once again the Rock of Gibraltar. It's as though his past jumped out to surprise him and he's fast forwarding to the present.

"The river's making us nostalgic Zach. C'mon, let's go."

Nostalgic, is that it? We walk to our cars and I try once more. "Why don't you come back to the support group, Peter? It hasn't been the same without you."

He clicks his car alarm off and turns to face me. "I can't be myself with those guys now. There are too many decisions I have to make around personnel issues, things that may involve them." He opens the car door, stoops, and slides into the car.

I lean in. "Like what?"

"Like confidentiality." Surely you understand this, his look says. He switches on the ignition.

Recalling our past vacation trips, I lower my face down to his. "But what about us?"

He responds without a beat, "Even you, Zach,"

Confused, I blurt out, "Even me? What?"

"You're a priest serving in the Archdiocese. I might have to make some decisions about you at some point." He guns the engine.

"Decisions? About what?"

He's staring straight ahead, waiting for an idiot to get it. "What if an accusation came to the Archdiocese about you?"

Stunned at first, soon I blink in shock. "My God, Peter! Is that why I hardly ever see you now?" As though nothing in heaven, hell, or earth could intrude on our relationship, I croak, "But we're friends!"

The wind suddenly gusts through the trees while Peter snorts at the naiveté of such a protestation. Between two men, two priests even. "You'll be all right," he assures me, "And so will I."

Tapping my hand lightly, he shifts into reverse and begins to inch his car back. "And we can still get together," he calls through the window. "But we better go now or we'll be late." As he turns and slowly pulls forward, he throws me a backward wave from his side mirror.

I stand still, trying to absorb it all: our long friendship, our different roles in the Church now, the relationship struggles, the Brotherhood of Priests.

I trudge to my car and get in. When I turn on my own ignition, I glance in the rearview mirror. A single tear rolls down my cheek.

Five hundred clergy are packed into the huge ballroom. Almost all except a few religious friars are dressed in clerical black. Awkwardly we gather around circular tables, coaxed by the promise of fraternity and dialogue. Up front on a shiny stage, we observe the panel of experts in the fields of psychology, law, and canon law. They are smart, savvy people who love the Church and are employed by it. A microphone stands on the lectern. I scan the room and notice none visible on the floor.

A hand grasps my shoulder for a moment. It's Peter, sweeping past us as he joins the table of dignitaries up front. I try to catch his eye but he doesn't look back. I spot Francis, Geraldo, and a few other guys from our Sebastian Community and move toward their table.

"So, you came after all," I tease Francis.

"The bride's mother was sick," he says with pursed lips.

Geraldo chats excitedly with some younger priests at the next table. I'm still reeling from the visit with Peter and I grab a seat. *Lonely. Nostalgic. Accusation. Confidential.*

"Please stand, gentlemen." John Cardinal O'Connor's unmistakable nasal Philly voice intones the opening prayer: "Holy Spirit, grant us wisdom and guidance in this moment of great challenge to Holy

Mother Church. Bless us, your pastors, in our desire to be faithful shepherds to the people we serve in your name. And may Mary, the Virgin Mother of Jesus Christ, Your Son, be our special patron as we gather today. We pray this in the name of Jesus Christ, Our Lord."

Hundreds of male voices respond as one, "Amen."

A number of glowing introductions of the speakers follow. Then incisive speeches on the topic of priestly and pastoral boundaries, especially in sexual matters. All of this takes an hour, followed by questions taken from the floor. Cassocked seminarians hustle these to the stage on small index cards that were handed out beforehand. When read aloud, they all have a certain thrust: "What do we do when . . . ?"

What follows is a rapid series of responses from the experts. Swiveling our heads from side to side at our tables, we are gradually being educated to the new world of the priesthood being prescribed for us from now on. The responses are almost completely focused on boundaries, in other words *what not to do* in the realm of pastoral relationships and otherwise, especially anything that might suggest sexuality.

"Don't ever invite anyone, especially a minor, into your private quarters in the rectory. Don't counsel anyone who is a minor without someone else present. Don't offer to drive any minor home alone, even in an emergency. Be careful of any close emotional involvement with those you serve pastorally. Make sure you have a window on the door of your counseling room, and have one installed if you do not." And on and on and on. It's like we are becoming animals in cages.

An hour and a half later, the assembly concludes with another prayer and we are dismissed. Dazed and disheartened, we all wander toward the exits with this new set of rules we're expected to place like a mask over our souls and minds. Not to mention our hearts, hands, and gonads. I spot Peter. He motions me over and whispers, "I've got to stay around and entertain the speakers, so I'll catch up with you later, okay?"

"Okay." I stare at him, numb from the conference as well as from the way we had parted earlier. I want to ask him what he thinks of the event, but he's already heading back toward the dignitaries.

A velvet curtain has dropped. Our friendship will always play second fiddle to his career, I realize. I turn and walk away.

I spot Francis ahead of me in the parking lot. Geraldo is being chatted up by some older priests. Not wanting to be alone with my feelings, I hurry to catch up to them. "So what did you think?" I ask Francis.

He frowns. As he begins to get into the car, he remarks, "Zach, the Church is under a state of siege. We're handling it the way any institution does: circle the wagons, protect the finances. Are you surprised?"

"No. But the round tables. All of us fellow priests gathered around them like friendly strangers. It's as though we're too nervous to address what actually brought us here. All of the talk is directed back and forth to the speakers. It's as though they don't want us to share our experience with each other.

Francis weighs this while Geraldo comes up behind us. I open the door for him.

"What did you think about all the *don'ts?*" he asks as he sinks into the passenger seat. Various cars begin to rev up around us. I stand at the window beside him.

In a sing-song voice, I mock the lawyer's advice: "Don't set the church up by being careless, even if pastoral need requires it! Don't think simply as a pastor would because everything is changed from now on! Don't say anything that would incriminate you! Don't touch anyone unless it is absolutely necessary! Don't ever make a decision from your own conscience! Don't, don't, don't." I poke my head into the car and roll my eyes like a crazy man at both of them.

Francis flashes his Joan Crawford smile. "Remember what they told us in the novitiate, 'If you keep the Rule, the Rule will keep you.'"

"Yeah amigos," Geraldo's accent is thick with affect, "Go ahead and keep the Rule, but you could lose your own soul in the bargain."

Without another word, Francis starts the engine. "Bye-bye," he waves.

Moments later, I'm speeding on adrenalin down the expressway toward the rectory. Careening past the bland high-rises as twilight falls, I notice lights gradually switching on in the apartments above and mutter to myself, "All they tell us is what *not* to do, Lord! No one talks about what we *can* do! What about compassion? What about love? Who can we touch? It's like we're forced to live behind a clerical wall now. Prisoners of love, is that it? What for?"

I glance sideways at the other drivers, heading home to someone they might possibly be real with. Someone they can touch and love before they die. Suddenly pounding the steering wheel with my palm, I shout to anyone who can hear, "Damn! Damn! Damn!"

CHAPTER ELEVEN

2003—

After morning prayer I drive over to Englewood. It's good that I'm meeting Sophie today. When I gave a homily on Jesus as the Good Shepherd at the women's prison recently, one of the inmates told an intriguing story about a cat that struck a personal chord with me. I'm hoping Sophie can help me figure it out.

I ring the bell and notice a memorial plaque in the garden. "For People Infected and Affected by the AIDS Virus." A small fountain trickles below it into a pool with a few hardy gold fish.

I think of a few of our friars who have died from AIDS and repeat their names under my breath. They were my best friends in the community, and I miss them deeply. It's been ages since we laughed and scrapped together, took vacations, and wrangled about the Church's direction. Closing my eyes, I pull them in, pull back the memory of the plague we lived through.

"Silence=Death," the Act-Up buttons, screamed for us to wake up. It took over ten years of demonstrations and thousands of deaths but they finally woke the country up.

"Still sleeping?" Sophie's holding the door ajar for me. Like many nuns, she's put in half a day's work already: bath, prayer, laundry, breakfast, journal and letter-writing. They retire early and are up before the roosters.

I give her a bleary smile and kiss her on the cheek. "I noticed your memorial garden."

"Oh, some volunteers put that in a while ago. We take them down to the shore for a retreat next month. Want to come?"

"Oh no, I'm booked solid until June."

"I told you to get a social life."

We laugh. People don't understand how difficult it is for nuns and priests to make time for ourselves, and to have someone we can relax with. The constant sense of being on-call can be tough and even lead to alcoholism and acting out. "I'm going to spend a couple of days with my brother and his family next weekend."

"Good." We huff and puff up the stairway to her office. Sophie once told me that this is a good way for her to get exercise. "Come in. Take a load off."

I relax in my usual seat that faces the window, noticing the candle she has lit.

After she clicks the phone off, Sophie joins me. "So where were we?" She reaches for her water bottle. Snooky is curled up in his chair watching, his ears perked up and twitching.

"I have a long list of things I want to talk about, but the first thing I want to mention is how I love my job. As difficult as it can be, I wouldn't want to be doing anything else."

"You're lucky. What do you love about it?"

"As I've told you before, it's as though every skill I have learned in my life is being called on now."

"What's your favorite part?"

I think of the Masses, the homilies, the individual conversations, the camaraderie with the other chaplains. But a single image stands out. "Praying with the inmates, and holding their hands as we do." I realize how this might sound a little too cozy, but it's true. It's as though this image symbolizes all the others.

Sophie waits for me to continue.

"It's like the meaning of the whole Gospel. We're together in Christ going to the Father, no matter what our differences are."

"Differences?"

"Yes. On the surface we couldn't be more different. Tough guys and girls with tattoos on their arms place their calloused hands in my soft ones to pray for forgiveness. Hands that may have beaten someone, stolen, or murdered. Hands with curse words on their knuckles placed in mine that consecrate the Eucharist. At first this intimidated me. They could strangle me while I'm blessing them! But I don't worry anymore. Under all the macho masks, they are children. We may be in different worlds but this vanishes when we pray."

"Is it the sacrament of confession when you do this?"

"Whether it's a formal confession or not, usually when I finish a visit with one of them I ask, 'Do you want to pray?' 'Yes,' they usually say. I open my hands face up on the table between us. As though it is normal for two people to pray together like this, they place their hands in mine."

"'Go ahead,' I say, encouraging them to start. 'Oh no, you do it.' 'No you,' I say. But usually I wind up beginning the prayer. They're not quite ready at first to launch out into this God territory with a virtual stranger, though amazingly they trust me because I am 'Father.'"

"I can see why you love this part of your work. It's like an antidote for all the competitiveness in our society, especially for men."

"I bow my head then, feeling the rough hands of a guy who would ordinarily never be resting his hands in another's in such a vulnerable way. Meanwhile I say something like, 'Oh God, bless Anthony. Help him to get out of here so he can be the Daddy his little girl needs. Help him to know that you forgive him and want him to follow this path he is on now.' Then I wait."

"Hmmmm."

"Yeah. If they look up, I might say, 'Go ahead, you pray. Use your own words. That's what God likes.' Sometimes they do, usually in English and usually simply from the heart in a way that must move God because it touches me. If they pray in another language, I kid them and say that God understands that too."

Sophie laughs. "You're teaching them to pray."

"What's really amazing is it seems like an expression of God's longing to touch us and heal us by being one with us in our failures. I close my eyes for a second and feel their hands in mine. I feel our pulses and what I imagine is God's pulse too, rising up through our palms. The inmates must notice this too, I imagine." I think of Migo. Snooky jumps up, stretches deliciously, and wanders over to look up at me.

"Yes, I am sure."

"With this feeling of God's longing, I can listen to the tragedies, often of their own childhood as well as the crimes they have committed. I feel their despair and humility. I can't imagine God not wanting to

77

give them a glimmer of hope, so that's what I try to do." Snooky jumps into my lap and rolls over.

"And what happens to you?"

"Now and then, an inmate will *not* look up. Rather, just allow his hands to rest in mine. This can go on for a few minutes. At first this was somewhat unnerving, me being Irish and not totally comfortable with touch myself. I'd glance up at the tattooed arms, waiting for him to begin, not knowing whether he's praying silently or finally finding a way to touch in the jail that doesn't allow it. Resting in the touch of the Father's love, I think, even for him a criminal. Then I do the same."

"Both of you resting in the touch of God's love? Say more about this."

I want to describe my feelings about this for her, how I feel healed by this interaction as much as the inmates might, but the words don't come. Instead, the sexual abuse scandal comes to mind. "Think of it Sophie, the inmates are certainly aware of the sexual abuse crisis roaring through the Church. What might they think of me? Priests need to be careful, but I don't want to be paralyzed in fear from offering the greatest thing we can provide people, a touch that means God is present. A touch they can trust. This is the awfulness of abuse, that someone you trust enough to touch has betrayed your trust. And when the abuser represents God, it feels like a betrayal by God." I reach to stroke Snooky's belly.

"Yes. So holding the hands of a criminal is a great sign, especially as a priest. They are trusting that you won't abuse them. And if they have abused others, you're offering them a way to acknowledge and seek forgiveness for this."

The cat story from the female inmate suddenly comes to mind. "At Ocean View I preached to the women recently. A group of ten or twelve of them wandered into the upstairs computer room. The warden lets us use it for a mass at the prison every Wednesday afternoon. Often the majority of them aren't Catholic. They're a mix of young and old, black and white. Most look like they have been on the streets for a while. Their plight gets to me even more than the men. I think of my sisters."

Sophie is smiling. I know she has a warm heart for these women.

"The Gospel was about Jesus as the Good Shepherd. I repeated Jesus' words to them during the homily, 'I know my sheep and they hear my voice.' One black lady in the first row began to speak quite freely about how she was strolling the streets one night at 4 a.m., 'to pick up a trick so I could get my drug,' she explained to us. It was brave for her to be so honest."

Sophie nods.

"The key part of her story involved a cat that was following her. 'A cat?' I asked her, bewildered, then stooped down with my hand close to the floor to show her what I meant. 'You mean a cat?' They all howled, understanding my confusion whether she meant *a guy* who is a 'cat.' She continued to describe this cat following her on the city streets "For miles, Father." The other ladies listened raptly to this adventure.

Sophie listens intently too.

"After she informed us that the cat disappeared when she came back out of a place where she traded sex for drugs, she wondered whether God's voice was trying to speak to her."

Chuckling, Sophie asks, "What did you say?"

I told them that I'm not sure.

"'Maybe,' one of the inmates suggested, 'the cat was her soul!' A gal in the back of the room with Afro braids jumped in, 'Yep, it's her soul following her, trying to get through to her while she's wandering around looking for a fix. But when she gave away her body for drugs, it left her.' We all turned to her to take this in."

"Hmmmm. That's quite an image," Sophie says. "Where did they go with that?"

"Well, I was assuring the women in my homily that as the Gospel said, 'No one can take the Good Shepherd's sheep out of his hand.' But, I had also warned them that we can take ourselves out of his hands by our choices. They may get this on a deeper level than I do. 'The wandering cat shows this.'"

"Yes, it does," Sophie says. "And why do you think this image has stayed with you?"

I gaze through the window at the clouds drifting by. "Probably because I do the same thing some times, take myself out of God's hands." My voice wavers a bit.

Sophie watches me. How can I bare my soul to her?

"It's like I'm always wrestling with authorities, Sophie. Like I don't trust myself to be in their hands. Whether it's the Church or the prison, the ones in charge always seem to be so controlling. Like they don't trust those they are in charge of. Like they don't really want us to be free."

"Is that so?"

"It's so frustrating. If I remain silent about a problem in the prison or the Church, I'm rewarded for being a member of the team. But if I ask a question, I'm seen as a traitor."

"Hmmmmm."

"Because of these feelings, I have a love-hate relationship with authorities. I want their approval, but I find myself—maybe place myself—in situations where I am rebellious."

"Were you always this way? What about when you used to be the perfect seminarian? Like the time when you met your brother, Patrick, on the campus after you came back from the novitiate? Remember what you told him when he was so excited to see you?"

I blush at the memory of myself in those days, and that I told her about this. I was so divided in my mind then between the religious life I had recently chosen and the world in which I now saw my brother.

"I see you back then as someone who completely surrendered his soul, his ego, to God and to your superiors as God's representatives."

"It's true. Back then I felt completely right to tell Patrick, 'I can't speak with you because you're a layperson, and the Sebastian Rule says that we have to keep separate from you while we're in the seminary, even if you're my family.'"

"You were such a good little soldier then. You couldn't stretch that Rule when you bumped into your brother. So how did Patrick react to you?"

I laugh ruefully at the memory. "He yelled at me, 'A layperson? I'm your brother, you idiot!' Then he stormed away." Hearing the rough tone in my voice, Snooky leaps off my lap and scampers back to his chair. "I stood there in my habit and watched Patrick storm away from me in my new olive green suit that I gave him."

"And now you're often the rebel, almost the opposite of this obedient side."

I nod. "It seems like a seesaw."

"You push authorities away, and at the same time want them to bless you."

"I want to be aware of this. I'm trying to find a middle ground between being just a rule-keeper or a rebel."

She rocks in her chair while we mull over the different things that've come up in the session. "Do you think you can understand the meaning of the cat story for yourself now?" she asks. I watch her penny loafer bob up and down as she waits.

"What is the meaning, Sophie?"

"You want me to figure it out for you?"

"No." I grin and look away. Before long a phrase bubbles up, "I want my soul to stay with me, Sophie." Soon I am weeping. "I've never . . . "

She offers me a tissue.

"I've never told anyone about this before. I was only fourteen when my life was changed forever. I'd seen this yellow and brown Pontiac with the big tailfins around the neighborhood before, cruising slowly by with a guy looking out of the window.

"One night I saw this car as I was walking up the Grand Concourse after getting off my job after midnight. My heart started racing as it slowed down near me. I stopped to look in a store window, Tom McCann's Shoes. Behind me I heard the Pontiac creak to a stop. Silence at first, then 'You want a ride home?' At first I ignored him, but something made me turn around. The guy was in the driver's side but through the open window on my side I could see his face half-hidden in the streetlight. He was about forty years old and had horn-rimmed glasses. He wasn't sexy or anything, but my young body turned on so easily.

"'You want a ride home, kid?' he asked again. A gravelly voice. A coaxing gentle voice. Hearing my heart pound, I hesitated. Then it was as though something inside me decided for me. I just moved over to the window on the passenger's side and looked in. The streetlight hummed above us. I sensed it would be more than a ride home. Nothing more was said. He leaned over and opened the door. An old Coke bottle fell off the seat onto the street. A cop walking on the other side of the street heard it and looked over. It was a cop I know from my father's deli. Maybe he saw me, maybe he didn't. Maybe he'd tell Daddy who would kill me. But it was too late. I got in anyway.

"As the car began to move up the hill, the guy reached across to adjust my window from his seat, brushing his hand across my lap as he did. I got aroused and felt him staring at me through his glasses. I kept looking straight ahead through the dirty windshield. My heart beat like a bird's wings against its cage. I still had a chance to get away, but I didn't move or say a word.

"'Ever been sucked off kid?'

"*Get out! It's now or never! Run! But then you'll never know.* I took a deep breath and let it out slowly. 'No.'

"He wanted to take me to his house but I said no. Instead he drove around the back into his alley and parked. Trash cans loomed in the shadows. A light from someone's porch turned off. The guy switched off his engine and stared at me. The sound of my heart beating. I'm already hard. He reached for me. . . *Ohmygod!*

"Afterwards I felt so ashamed. I wanted to get out of there bad. He offered to drive me home. I was scared to death that he'd find out where I lived. I was even afraid he might harm me and considered jumping out of the car at a stop sign. Two blocks from home I asked him to stop. It was the same place one of the family's pet dogs got run over by a car a few years before. Sliding out, I closed the door as quietly as I could without looking at him.

"The yellow and brown Pontiac disappeared into the darkness of University Avenue. Hot tears burned my cheeks, and I quickly brushed them away. I'm no longer innocent, I thought, and there is no way I can ever tell anyone about this."

I feel Sophie's gaze taking all of this in without judgment. My lower lip quivers. A soft whine escapes from Snooky on his chair.

"But you're telling me now, Zach. This brings it out of the darkness, out of the silence and the shame where it can kill you."

"Mmmmmm . . ."

"Perhaps your soul left you that night, just for a while. Like the cat who left the lady when she went for a trick. But only so you both can discover how much you need God. The Good Shepherd won't let you take yourself out of his hands forever, will he?" She is smiling.

Something moves deep down inside me. Her listening without condemning me feels like a fresh spring rain, washing me and cleansing me. Never did I imagine I'd pour out this story to anyone, let alone that whoever heard it wouldn't think I was disgusting. "I guess The Good

Shepherd is pretty tenacious," I say. "I feel him putting me on his shoulders." I return her smile.

We sit for a while without speaking. I want to turn away from her gaze but don't for a change.

"Sophie, I'm beginning to understand why praying with our hands held is a new way to trust, not only for the inmates but for me as well. Trusting that it's God who's touching both of us through each other's wounds in order to heal us."

"And these authorities you feel compelled to rebel against so often?"

"Well, as long as they're not driving a yellow and brown Pontiac . . . " Sophie lips press together.

"And I can see them as broken like the inmates and me, and find that middle ground . . . " I let the thought trail off.

She lets me sit with that until I am breathing calmly again. "Is this a good place to stop for today?"

"Mmmmhmmm." A dark cloud lifts from my soul. I'm on my way to healing. "Thank you, Sophie."

"Now don't forget your social life," she cracks. Snooky's tail wags.

"I won't. As long as the cat is still following me."

"Oh, please."

All the true vows are secret vows, the ones we speak out loud are the ones we break.

—David Whyte

CHAPTER TWELVE

1977—

I've been ordained for nine years. I'm strung out from all the battles going on in the Church and society due to the Vietnam War and the Second Vatican Council. I decide to request a year's leave of absence because I feel conflicted. On the one hand, as a priest I have the rules of the Church to uphold. On the other hand, I have my personal life and my conscience. I want both, but is this possible?

During a leave of absence, priests are permitted to work at a regular job and live a more normal life to see if they really want to recommit to the priesthood for the long haul. Some leave the ministry and get married at this stage. I've heard through the grapevine that a few of those on leave are gay.

I arrange to live at Good Earth, a retreat center in Western Massachusetts sponsored by the Quakers. I heard about this organization of rural communes devoted to living in ways that promote peace and justice. I could go to the Catholic Worker or a similar Catholic Peace group, but I need a little distance from the role of a Catholic priest. I believe that I can work some of my issues out with the Quakers. Little do I know what I've bargained for.

Nervous to be heading out beyond the comforting parameters of living in a rectory and being called Father, I'm also excited. Everything is up for grabs at Good Earth: our diet, sexuality, and the role of women and men. The feminist energy at Good Earth is like nothing I've encountered before. Even back at home with my three sisters, the only action bordering on a Women's Movement I remember is when the three of them would commandeer the bathroom before the boys did and keep it until they were all done. That's if we hadn't done so first.

I've never heard of gender equal language until a slim young blonde woman moves into one of the houses a month after me. Julia has a personal mission. Every time one of the guys at Good Earth says "he" and means both men and women, Julia corrects us. With a blank, almost bored, look on her face, as well as her pale eyelids closed but not fluttering, she interrupts us, "And *she?*"

It's annoying, and I try to avoid her and her big black Great Dane, Lilith. *What do you think, we're some kind of dummies?* To protect myself, I vacillate between trying to understand the deeper issues about women that she and the other women keep raising, and avoiding her and bonding with the men.

I'm immediately intrigued by the name—The Bundling Brothers Collective. This is mainly a group of men from Good Earth who meet weekly for support among themselves. It isn't a gay group, but is composed of about a dozen men of all sorts of sexual variations. "Straight, gay, bisexual, and everything in between," one of them tells me. *Everything in between?* I think while I try to fall asleep.

By joining this group, it is presumed that you are actively intent on breaking down the sex role stereotypes men grow up with in our society.

"These roles leave us wounded emotionally and out of touch with our feelings," Rod Mankowietz, the married and bisexual leader of the group explains at my first meeting. "We hardly realize that we are locked into rigid sexual orientations that make us treat each other as rivals and women as pawns or trophies." Bundled up close to each other underneath the quilts and afghans to keep warm on that winter afternoon, we grin our bearded faces at each other and try to imagine how we might ever break out of this box we have grown up in.

One belief of the Bundling Brothers is that everyone needs at least three full-body hugs a day. If you don't get these, you haven't really lived that day. By full-body hugs, they mean not hugging with the lower half of your body held out at an angle like the letter "A" from the other person. It is as though as men we are all scared to death that the lower half of our bodies might touch and something horrible could happen.

It is in the Bundling Brothers Group that I first get to know Toby. At twenty-six, about ten years younger than I, he lives with his girlfriend,

Judy, in one of the other communes, Treetops, while I am one of seven men and women living at Rainbow. Over the course of the first few months of these meetings, I begin to get closer to Toby and Judy when he invites me back to their place on occasion. I even lounge on their bed one day when Toby asks me over to pick out some music for a social we are planning for one of the weekend retreats. It is as though Toby and Judy's intimacy allows me to risk getting closer to either or both of them. On some level, I feel that their relationship provides a boundary that will keep any expectations of mine manageable. It seems like they feel the same about me with my boundary as a celibate priest.

Toby is Jewish. He and I hit it off almost immediately because we are two of only a very few non-Protestants in the Bundling Brothers Group. It isn't just our similar outsider feelings that make Toby and me click. With his olive skin, prominent nose, and long tousled black hair, he brings to mind all the Indians I've been intrigued with as a boy. Their close-to-the-earth ways, their near-nakedness as they straddle their ponies and whoop into battle, even the example of Tonto being the Lone Ranger's best friend, fueled my young boy's hope that there could be a way for me and my feelings in this world.

With a degree in political science from the University of Pennsylvania, Toby loves to rave on like I do about anything. Passionate and intelligent, his brown eyes—the left one with a slight cast in it—gleam when he offers an opinion on everything from music to politics to religion.

He begins to ask me questions that no one ever asked me before. "Why do Christians see Jesus on the cross as a sign of love and forgiveness and at the same time they're intolerant of other religions?" Another time he tells me, "When I see Jesus on the cross, all I experience is blame and guilt." I didn't know how to cope with all of this at first, but the two of us get closer as we keep on talking about anything and everything.

One summer night after the Bundling Brothers meeting, Toby and I look for a place where we can quaff down a pitcher of beer along with some pizza. We decide on The Broken Pony, a working class bar within walking distance from Good Earth. After six months of these meetings, and our occasional visits in between, we know how to entertain each other with our self-dramatized tales of dealing with intellectual WASPS all day long, even if they happen to be Quakers.

My being a priest, and a gay priest at that, intrigues Toby. Even though he is critical of organized religion, I can tell he is fascinated by all the Roman Catholic symbols. He wants to know why I am celibate, and even how.

"So what does celibacy do for you?" he asks while he chews a fingernail. The darts fly by our heads as the beer-bellied guys in the bar complain about the Red Sox recent losing streak.

"It gives me a freedom, Toby. Imagine if you didn't have to be driven by sex all day." He's told me he hates it when Judy gets out of bed first in the morning and leaves him alone.

"I can't imagine it, Zach. I wouldn't *want* to be free from that." There's a fierceness in his voice that I like.

"No?" I peer over my frosted beer mug at him, challenging his sureness. The two of us thrive on challenging one another.

Considering this, Toby licks the foam from his lips. "No. And ya know something? I think you run away from sex by your vow of celibacy."

It feels like he kicked me in the groin. Teasing yeah, but still a kick. My beer-mellowed brain ponders this as I take another swig. "It has more to do with my relationship with God, Toby." I fall back on the traditional explanation that I know he can't puncture.

"And a relationship with God doesn't permit sex?" The wiry black hair on his chest pokes above his tee shirt.

I won't let him into that God-space yet. "Celibacy doesn't have to be against sex, Toby, just different from it," I counter. I think of the Jewish emphasis on childbearing, and how Jesus didn't have kids. I wonder if that's why he wasn't accepted by his own people.

"Different?"

"Yeah, Toby. Different." I feel myself getting pissed.

Our verbal tussle continues, making us closer. At the same time it provides a protection from closeness that guys seem to need. In the background, the Beer-Bellies yell profanities and more darts fly.

Gradually, what started out as intellectual wrestling develops into a different kind of electricity. Playing around with the questions about celibacy begins to stir up sensual vibes in me. Our knees jostle under the table. Occasionally one of us touches the other's forearm to make a point. For a few milliseconds, we lock eyes in silence. Maybe you can pull me out of my sureness tonight, Toby.

"Yo, Vera!" Toby suddenly hollers for the barmaid. He holds up the pitcher for a refill. I check my watch, remembering that Rainbow has a house meeting in the morning. "Hey, relax, will ya?" Toby says emphatically. He grabs my arm and we get mellower.

Forty-five minutes more of this and Toby says, "You wanna crash at my place tonight? Judy's with her family in Ohio." A dart flies by.

It's not like I haven't fantasized this before. Already buzzed, my heart thumps. "Nah, I better not. I've got to get up early."

"Whatever." Toby's cross-eyed look searches me. We down another mug and play some darts ourselves before heading home.

The two of us wobble up the stony road to the Good Earth compound of houses. The summer air, thick with lightning bugs and the smell of roses, flows back and forth between us as we occasionally bump against each other. As we pass a house on the corner of his road with a thick hedge around it, I suddenly shove Toby into it.

"Hey! Cut it out, you jerk!" he yells, but he's chuckling.

I offer my hand to help him up. Halfway up, he turns quickly and shoves me in.

"Hey!" I lie there protesting. Toby waits, his khaki pants hanging low on his hips.

"Well, arntcha gonna help me?" I fake a drunken drawl. His sweaty hand would feel good in mine.

"You can do it yourself."

"C'mon Tonto, help the Lone Ranger!" For a long moment Toby stands there, thinking. His hand reaches for mine.

Brushing each other off, we head toward his place. "Tonto? Hmm-mmmm . . . " he murmurs.

"'Member him?"

"And the Lone Ranger."

"Kemosabe." We weave the rest of the way in silence.

"See ya tomorrow," Toby announces when we get to Treetops. He's already on the landing, halfway up to the porch with its old rockers.

I stand at the bottom looking up. Rainbow is just a block and a half further. I think of my lonely bed back in my room. "Kemosabe need a goodnight hug," I sing-song into the dark.

The moonlight on Toby's nose casts a shadow on his face from the streetlight. I can't read his expression. He glances up and down the road before his head makes a motion. "C'mere."

Before I know it, I am up the stairs and Tonto is hugging me. The Bundling Brothers hug. When his body curves to meet mine, I do the same. His cheek is warm against mine even through his long hair. "Oh man!"

"You sure you don't want to stay over?" he asks, stepping back.

My mind is racing. I glance upstairs and notice that all the lights are off. "But the others?" I ask, thinking of his housemates.

"I've got a sleeping bag. You can sleep on the living room floor if you want."

Wanting to remain close to him, my heart sinks. I guess it shows.

"I've got two. We can sleep there together."

With my whole future stretching before me, I search Toby's face in the dark. Suddenly the space around us comes alive. Perched on a spruce tree behind him, like crows on its ghostly branches, I imagine all of my seminary masters squawking their pointy beaks in unison: "Remember the Rule! Remember the Rule!" while in my right ear, my Provincial's voice whispers, "Don't Zach, don't." My legs start to wobble.

Higher up in the tall trees, the crickets rub their legs together in a mating dance, drowning out the negative voices with their pulsing waves, while Quaker mantras come to mind like answers for an exam: *Consensus. Follow your Inner Light. Conscience.*

A dam gives way inside me. The tide surges past the sandbags. Sighing from down in my toes, I hear myself say the unthinkable, "Okay, Toby. I'd like that."

"Good." He grabs my bicep. A warm feeling rushes over me as we turn and push our way through the broken screen door into Treetops.

Never before have I consciously reached out for what I desired like this. For what I sense could heal the shame I feel inside for who I am. "Let's take our tee shirts off," I say. "I want to feel your chest. I always wanted to touch my father this way." My heart pounds yet I am strangely calm.

"Me too," Toby says.

Laying my head on his lean muscled body then, manly but open to me wanting him.

The musky smell of his skin, the matted chest hairs tickling my nose, watching his eyes watching me.

Beginning awkwardly to caress him, I lean up on my elbow to just enjoy the wonder of his body stretched out for me in the streetlight pouring in the window, all of this feeling as normal as apple pie.

We strip ourselves naked.

I begin to nuzzle down the whole length of his body, exhilarated at moving for once with only my feelings guiding me.

The sense of joy at such masculine beauty right at my fingertips.

Suddenly feeling the floodgates bursting, as though freed from a lifetime in prison. "Oh, oh . . . ahhhhhhhhhhhhh!"

Reduced suddenly to exhaustion, not being sure how to follow through with him now, kissing him softly on the cheek.

Assuring him as he lay there with his hands behind his head and his eyes closed, "I will not possess you." As though he needs to be reassured, reassuring myself instead.

Later falling asleep under the covers, my back curved against his chest, one of his arms draped around me.

Waking up with the sheet twisted around us when one of his housemates comes down to fix breakfast, eyeing us with a grin.

Not sure exactly what we say as we part, knowing it isn't shame we see on each other's faces, believing that what happened on the living room floor was all right and doesn't need to be forgotten, that we will still be friends.

You've just experienced the most authentic moment of your life! The words rise up in me like an epiphany as I stroll away from Treetops toward Rainbow. It can't have been just a dream, can it? Not the way Toby looked at me. The Blue Danube Waltz plays in my head as I float past the local Catholic Church on a cloud. Beams of morning sunshine bounce off its twin slate spires while kids' shouts from the schoolyard break through my reverie. In their blue and white habits, Blessed Virgin Mary nuns shepherd the kids into lines, two by two.

My first grade teacher, Sister Virginia Marie.

The choir of my classmates' voices singing Happy Birthday to me when I was six.

Innocence.

I can never go back there now, even if I want to. I wait for the cars to pass by on Holyoke Street and another voice inside me mocks, *You're no longer celibate, you know. Now how are you going to fit this together with your life as a priest?*

I feel shaken as well. Not simply apart but shaken together, my body totally at home in my soul. Never before have I known this feeling. Guilty on one level, yet no longer a stranger to myself. For once in my life I've been my truest self with another human being. Even God must want that.

A shout longs to burst out of me to people on their way to work: *Hey everyone! I'm part of the human race with you now! Do you hear? I'll never be the same again! Hallelujah!*

CHAPTER THIRTEEN

2004—

Migo wants to confess. Even though he was baptized Catholic as a child, he wasn't raised Catholic and has probably never gone to the Sacrament of Confession. He pulls me aside at the mass on Sunday and says, "I want to be clean when I stand in front of the judge. Would you hear my confession?" I tell him I'll be glad to and will be in to see him on Wednesday.

Usually, the chaplains don't ask the inmates what their crime is unless they bring it up. Because of his impending court appearance, a C.O. told me that the man Migo is accused of beating to death with a baseball bat was a priest. I am horrified. This allegedly took place during a robbery at the priest's parish. Migo insists he is innocent, the C.O. says. No matter, I'm scared. I've been told that they all say they are innocent.

The day is rainy and cold, making Riker's Island gloomier than ever. Situated out in the East River between the boroughs of Queens and the Bronx, the huge complex of buildings is adjacent to the runways of LaGuardia Airport and has been operated by the New York City Department of Corrections since 1884 when it was bought for only $180,000.

Jets roar over the island day and night. The only access to the island is from Queens, over the small, three-lane Francis Buono Bridge with its sign announcing: "Speed limit 20 mph. Please drive safely." And then a smiley yellow face with the message, "Have a nice tour."

Before the bridge was constructed in 1966, the only way you could reach it was by ferry. With its average inmate population of fourteen thousand as well as seven thousand correctional officers and fifteen hundred civilian employees, it is a small city with an annual budget of $860 million.

The Riker's island complex actually consists of ten jails, which hold local offenders from New York City who are awaiting trial and cannot afford bail, or were not given bail from a judge. It also includes those serving sentences of two years or less, and those placed there pending transfer to another facility. It claims to be the world's largest penal colony.

Migo's building, an old ramshackle structure with little gray slits for windows, looks like something from a century before. The guards joke that it would make a good movie prop. With its large dorms with no air conditioning, prisoners sometimes roam around with their shirts off like caged animals. Yet these same prisoners tell me they gather in a circle to pray at night as well. "We saw the Muslims praying together Father, so we decided to do it too."

I scoot through the usual three or four doors, with the pat down and electronic scanning of my belongings, including the C.O. flipping through the pages of my Bible for contraband. "I've got a hundred dollar bill hidden in there," I tell her with a straight face.

"No you don't Father, I know." She puckers her lips. "But I've got to search you anyway. A psychologist got caught smuggling a cell phone in last week, go figure. I don't want to lose my job."

"No kidding."

Some C.O.s carefully check your waist, back and legs before granting admittance with a huge key. "Do you ever get tired of turning that?" I asked one burly white guy. "Do you ever get tired of preaching, Father?" was the quick comeback. Other C.O.s give a little tap-tap to your body that couldn't discover a gun or pack of heroin, let alone something carried in a body crevice as they say. But most of the contraband comes from the outside. The inmates pay money for cigarettes, drugs, even a knife or cellphone. Some of the C.O.s and other employees supplement their prison salaries by this risky endeavor.

I walk down the long corridor, past the cubicles for inmates' visits with public defenders. I wonder about Migo's lawyer. As Migo explains it, this guy, who was hired by his family, has barely spoken with him over the past year. The lawyer's advice comes down to this: a plea deal.

His contention to Migo and the family is that the circumstances of the terrible crime, which begin to emerge in the media as the trial nears, could possibly result in a life without parole sentence if Migo is found guilty. For this reason, Migo is being discouraged from insisting on a trial even though he professes his innocence. His accomplice actually wielded the bat, Migo claims, yet his accomplice was granted amnesty when he testified for the prosecution. He has since been released and is now living in Florida.

It's all beyond me. I can't fathom the reality that many inmates are actually innocent of the charges against them, yet can be held for years in these places. "I've done some bad things, Father, but not what I am charged with," is a refrain I hear often. Mostly poor and unable to come up with bail money, they are incarcerated at an expense to the city of about $30,000 a year until their trial comes up. They might be assigned a public defender who may or may not show up. Often their trials are postponed two or three times.

If they are judged innocent, they are set free with a Metro card to take a bus back home to resume their lives. Often any equipment they owned for a previous job, including tools, scaffolding, a truck even, has long since been ripped off. Their home might be rented to someone else by a landlord's own need to survive. A spouse and children may be angry and non-communicative, forced into a drug-selling scene to survive, moved in with someone else, or simply vanished from sight. The inmate's own drug tendency and impulsive need to survive make this a combustible and cyclical scenario.

"Father Zach, I was offered free drugs on the street before I got to the bus stop." "How did they know to approach you?" "They could see the sack of my clothes on my back from the jail." "You've got to be kidding!" "I'm not kidding, Father, it's a jungle out there!"

So, many of them wind up coming back and back again in an endless cycle. The recidivism rate is seventy to eighty percent. The poor of this world in more ways than one. Some days I wonder along with them: Does God even care? That's why I continue this work, to show them that God does.

As soon as Migo comes down the stairs, I ask him, "Do you want to meet in the chaplain's office?" Before he can answer I add, "It'll give us more privacy." I want him to feel as free as possible. Actually, it is for both of us. The way they whisk them away upstate to their home prison after they are sentenced, I realize this could be one of our last times together.

Migo sees my face. "Sure, yeah, whatever." The C.O. informs us that he will have to be handcuffed to be taken out of the protective custody area. Migo waves his hand, "No problem," as if it is no big deal. But when they snap the handcuffs on him, I feel terrible. His hands are locked together tightly in front at the waist, with a chain from his wrists going down to another set of chains around his ankles. Migo watches me with amusement, then proceeds to hobble ahead of me as the C.O. leads us to the room. The chains clank in a spooky rhythm on the stone floor.

The chaplain's office is a tiny five-by-six-foot cubicle, which four of us share: Protestant, Catholic and Muslim chaplains and a Jewish Bereavement Nurse. It is crammed with a bookcase filled with King James Bibles and "How to Say the Rosary" pamphlets, a rusting filing cabinet that no one ever uses, and a desk scattered with pink paper messages. This leaves barely enough room for maybe three folding chairs.

A little eight-by-ten-inch plexiglass window on the door allows observance by a guard, "for your protection, Chap," I was told when I asked once. I jostle the chairs together as best I can to make room for the two of us. Migo hunches down uncomfortably with the handcuffs and chains. The C.O. closes the door. A moment later I notice him glance back through the window.

"Wow! I didn't think you were that dangerous," I say to break the ice.

Migo grimaces, looking up at me from his awkward position. "I'm not normally, Zach. But you've got to be tough in here. If someone messes with you . . . " He lets it taper off unfinished.

The scar over his eyebrow reminds me. I can walk in and out of this hellhole, but the inmates are left behind. I recall a young guy whom I read about in the newspaper. Recently arrested for raping a twelve-year-old girl in the Bronx, he's presently in a city hospital from having been beaten up by four guards. Migo told me the guy threw a tray of food at a guard. Then the guard and four others beat him senseless. I shake my head to show him my concern.

"Don't worry. The chains aren't necessary with you, Zach."

Do I really know Migo? Is he really trustworthy? I still can't picture him as a murderer. "So what are they for then?"

"Zach, I fear the C.O.s," he holds my gaze with intense black eyes, "and they fear me." His lower lip protrudes. "That's why the chains." He tightens his fists and stares down at them. "But I know how to take care of myself if it's necessary." His look shows me he means it.

The closeness of the cramped room engulfs me. It's like I'm a foot away from a wild animal. I can hear the two of us breathing together, smell our bodies, see into his bloodshot eyes. He could suddenly strangle me with the chains. Yet I trust that God protects me in this place. That God wants the best for him and sees the best in him. I go to where I can help him. "What about confession?"

"I'm gonna need some help, Zach. It's been a long time since I've done this."

I begin to lead him through the Ten Commandments, mentioning them one at a time, and waiting for him to voice any sins he had committed against them. When I get to the Fifth, I say, "Thou shalt not kill" and wait as I do after the others. No answer at first. In a few moments I add, "Have you ever hurt anyone, Migo?"

Migo's head bobs down. He remains silent. When he finally speaks, his voice is low and muffled. "Yeah, I killed the priest that night . . . with a bat. I didn't mean to . . . I'm so sorry," he suddenly groans. Instinctively I reach my hands out and place them on his, restrained by the cuffs.

A thought stirs. A question I learned to ask the inmates during confession, searching for where they might need to forgive someone rather than the other way around. "Has anyone ever hurt you, Migo?"

No reaction at first. Soon the young man's hands tense, then tremble. Eventually he croaks, "Yeah."

It was that simple question in the shoebox office that set off an avalanche of revelations that changed my life.

It is after midnight now. I kneel and pray in the darkness about these things before the Blessed Sacrament in Our Lady of Angels Church.

"Who hurt you, Migo?"

"He did."

97

"Who?"

"The priest, Father Alan."

"When? How?"

"Long ago. I was fifteen."

"What happened?"

He took us on an overnight trip to his cabin in the country . . . He gave us beer, showed us some porno movies . . . Later that night he came to my room in his underwear, got in bed with me . . . "

"You don't have to say any more, unless it helps to get it all out . . . He hurt you?"

"Father Alan did oral sex on me . . . It happened more than once . . . Finally I told on him."

"Told who? What happened?"

"The pastor told me I should stay away from him, that I was no good for him . . . And not to tell anyone else."

"Did you?"

"No. But I couldn't forget. At night I dream of it sometimes. I think it's why I finally blew up."

"You killed him? Why?"

"He kept doing it again, in the neighborhood, to some kids I know . . . Me and Chooch went to the parish that night. We called him a faggot. He denied it."

"How do you know he's a faggot?"

"He has sex with little kids and teenagers . . . That's when I grabbed the bat. All the rage from the past came rushing out."

"Did you tell your lawyer about this? What triggered your rage?"

"No."

"He ought to know, Migo. It could get your case thrown out, at least reduced . . ."

"I'm ashamed of what happened, Zach. People will think I'm a faggot."

"Migo, this priest preyed on kids like you for years. You are not all faggots . . . To kill him is horrible, but this behavior of his should be brought out in the open."

"I can't say it out loud."

"Even if it would save you from years in prison? . . . Migo, maybe there's something I can do to help you. Testify in some way on your behalf."

"How? What would you say?"

I feel dizzy and crouch back in the pew. Staring at the vigil light by the tabernacle, my mind whirls. Something hidden here . . . some secret . . . something evil . . . *pow!* That's when the revelation hit me like the furies. It's the pattern of reassigning priests like Father Alan, hiding what they've done and endangering other children. It's bigger than Migo and Father Alan. It's the coverup of this, by the pastor, the bishops.

My fists clench toward the tabernacle. Out of my guts comes an insane roar, "PETERRRRR!"

CHAPTER FOURTEEN

At first I suggested the Townhouse, a bar on the Upper East Side that caters to business men. It has a piano room in the back with upholstered wingback chairs where guys sing show tunes late at night. When Peter insists on a more discreet place for fear of being recognized, I agree to meet him at The Regent, a West Side bar near Lincoln Center.

Migo's confession still rings in my ears. Is Peter freaked out by the possibility of being involved in a coverup? My antennae are up to catch any clue of this from him.

"Zach! How's it going for you? How's the family?"

"They're fine. Can we get together sometime soon?"

"It's tough getting away, lots of Confirmations, you know. My secretary may be able to squeeze a lunch in for us in a couple of weeks."

"I've got some news you need to know."

"What kind of news, Zach?" The slightest tremor in his voice.

"It can't wait a couple of weeks. Let's meet over some drinks."

A pause. "Okay. Just don't surprise me like you used to in the seminary." A hearty chuckle. Peter is back in charge as usual.

As I stroll into the quiet place on Amsterdam Avenue a little after 5 p.m., I scan the room for Peter. No sign of him. I pick a stool by a window that overlooks the sidewalk. I'll be able to see him coming and catch a sense of him.

There's so much that's been happening in the Church since Peter and I were in the seminary, especially having to do with different ways of viewing the priesthood. Many newly ordained priests are actually more conservative. It's as though they long for the "good old days" when priests were like little kings with their authority—"Yes Father,

Whatever you say Father." They're in love with the externals: cassocks, lace albs, monsignor titles, special honors, even the Latin Mass, anything that accentuates the separateness of the priesthood from the laity.

And then there's the older guys, priests who've been around for years like Peter and me, our theology forged in the crucible of the Second Vatican Council and the moral battle over the Vietnam War, not to mention the sexual abuse crisis that's setting the Church ablaze now.

Has Peter gotten seduced by his bishop role? He's into power and has always been an enigma about his sexuality. The litmus test you've got to pass in order to be a bishop is that you've got to be a hard-liner on all the Church teachings about sex.

A young couple stroll by holding hands and chatting. I close my eyes and imagine the joy of loving someone in the open like that.

With me, ever since I came out to myself, I've always wanted to be honest about who I am, at least how it energizes my ministry. In the end I'd rather be more real and have less power. Well, maybe have a different kind of power.

It's like Peter and I live in two different worlds—the Church and the prison. Yet there are similar control patterns in both systems.

"Zaaaack!" Peter slides up behind me and whispers my name like the old days. Swinging me around to face him, his big hand with the bishop's ring grips my wiry bicep. "What's up, Buddy?" His pearly grin flashes as he checks out the room.

Quickly I glance at his pressed gray slacks and preppy sweater look. Though he's a bit heavier these days, he's still in good shape. "No purple robes for the occasion?" I tease. I'm used to seeing his picture plastered across the Diocesan newspapers in his bishop's regalia. "Seriously Peter, it's good to see you." We backslap each other while the few patrons eye us through the mirror.

"How long has it been? I miss our regular connection," I lean back on the stool.

"Me too. What are you drinking?"

"Yuengling."

"Just a beer? C'mon man, loosen up." Peter signals the tattooed bartender.

"I've got our support group for ex-inmates tonight in Harlem. Lots of them have addiction issues. I need to be sober."

"Hmmmm. Yeah."

The bar guy arrives. "Sir?"

"Make it a double Dewars on the rocks and a Yuengling."

"That's good work you're doing. This bishop's world is crazy too. Everyone wants a piece of you." He shoots me a look that hints at the crisis we're in.

"Yeah, I bet. It's what you wanted though, to be where the action is, right?"

He gives me a hurt look, and we go to find a table in a dark corner. Soon our drinks arrive.

To warm up, we jabber about the Yankees and other sports stuff. When he shares his thoughts on the new Archbishop, it feels like I'm being taken into his confidence. For a second I notice a troubled look in his eyes.

I can't just throw a bomb.

Leaning closer, in a husky voice he says, "The Church is in a helluva mess. You mentioned some information I need to know." He waits, sips his drink, admires his ring.

"There's an inmate I've gotten close to over the past year. He's up for a homicide charge. It turns out that the one he's accused of murdering is a priest."

His face becomes a mask.

"When Migo spoke to me about this, he said that he might plead guilty because of his fears of a life sentence if it went to trial." Peter must know of this case. I wait for his reaction.

"If he makes a plea deal like you say, he'll be admitting his guilt. The only thing that'll remain is his sentencing. Let it play out." His manicured fingers drum on the table.

There's no other way. Just lay it out. "Migo told me that he and another guy confronted the priest about his abuse of neighborhood kids. When he denied it, they fought and the priest was killed."

He glares at me over his scotch. "And you want to get mixed up in this now?" He slaps the table.

"Don't you see? If the judge hears the circumstances he may be lenient, cut five or ten years off his sentence."

I watch his fist clench. "What? You believe a murderer?" His instant defensiveness tells me I'm on the right track.

"If Migo testifies that he went to confront Father Alan about his continued abuse of young people, a few years after he told his pastor that Father Alan had sexually abused him . . . "

"Whaaat?" He chokes on his drink. "What a bunch of horse shit! Who the hell will believe him? The statute of limitations has passed." His face is red, his eyes narrow.

And this happened while you were personnel director.

His head wags dismissively, and his mouth twists into a leer. "So he wants to appeal to the media's thirst for vengeance with this made-up crap? He'll be laughed out of the courtroom." He flicks a crumb from the table and signals to the waiter for a second round.

So you knew about this history when you reassigned him? Oh how I want to confront him with this, but I need to be careful. I've got to be absolutely sure. I wait until he looks back to me. "I don't think so. They'll take his testimony seriously . . . if I corroborate it."

My old seminary friend looks puzzled at first. "What are you saying?" Soon he pushes his chair back and stands. He looks as though he could punch me.

"Zach," he bends down and whispers loudly with his eyes riveted, "You actually believe this Church-bashing bullshit, don't you?" His voice and actions have built up so that people are looking from the bar in our direction. He pounds the table with his fist. "We have to close ranks or they'll destroy us."

Worried about creating a spectacle, I plead, "Sit down, sit down." He does as the bartender slides our drinks to us quickly and departs. I lock onto his face, "The priesthood has blood on its hands. Are we going to wash it off like Pilate?"

Glancing around the room for distraction, we regain our composure. We nurse our drinks in silence while the Happy Hour crowd starts drifting in.

"Some priests are so demoralized from this scandal that they'd leave the priesthood if they were younger and could get a job," I add. "If I were younger, I'd consider it myself."

Peter continues to brood in silence. While he was the personnel director he had to know the impact on morale this was having on priests. Doesn't he feel like getting a thousand miles away from the questions in people's eyes?

"Zach, the responsibilities of being a bishop of a diocese this size are enormous. You've never had such an executive position, have you? It's real easy for you to look at it from the outside and find fault." His voice is calmer, soothing even. He clicks his ice cubes.

"I haven't had such responsibilities, no. But the bishops are responsible for this coverup mess, and no one is holding them accountable. You want us to just hide? Keep our heads down and hope it all blows over?"

This hits a chord in him. He can always surprise me with another card in his deck. "How long have we been ordained now, thirty-five years? At our age we all need something: positions, perks, a place of our own to get away to on vacations, maybe a relationship." He glances out the window, moistens his lips. "I remember a friendship you told me about. You and—what's his name, Toby?—were quite close once. Do you ever hear from him?"

I can't believe he's mixing my personal life up with the pedophilia issue.

Dumbfounded, I sip my Yuengling, waiting to see where he's taking this.

"Look, Zach. We all need love." Back in his professional mode, his voice is mellow as a counselor's. Stealing a look across to the growing crowd by the bar, he purses his lips knowingly. "See all these young folks? Do you think they're fixated on abusive priests, or even bishops who might have covered these up? No. They're out looking for a partner before they get too old. In the same way, we shouldn't have to be lonely either."

For a moment it's like the old days, his concern touching an empty spot in my heart.

"We all deserve someone to love."

Yeah.

"Someone special to cuddle up with on a cold night." He glances off to the side. "Zach, you can have it all if you want to."

God, it's like we're back at that doorway.

"The priesthood and a lover."

What's he saying? Is this a come on?

"No one needs to know." Downing his Scotch in a single gulp, his tongue makes a clicking sound. "People don't want to know. You just have to keep it discreet."

My head slowly shakes from side to side. An old pain in my heart stirs again at the battle between love and truth always going on in me.

"Peter, if anyone knows, you do, about how I've struggled with the vow of chastity all these years. But I've discovered that I can't really handle having a secret lover on Friday nights, and then stand in front of people as a celibate priest on Sundays to preach to them about fidelity."

"What is fidelity?"

Finishing my beer, I wipe the foam from my lips. Yeah, here come the old ambiguities. I can almost taste them at this Armageddon Moment in the Church: my human desire to touch someone I love, the competing agendas of loyalty and integrity in the Church, the bastardization of the priesthood, and worst of all, the manipulation of our people to save face. My old friend smiles as though he can read my thoughts. I signal the waiter for our check.

Breathing deeply, I lean across the no man's land between us. A cork pops inside as I exhale my passion for integrity into his face. "I'm not going to be bought off with a position, with an appeal to Church loyalty, or even with a lover," Instantly I regret my last dig but it jumps out anyway, " . . . apparently like you have."

He spits back at me. "Like I have?"

"Yeah, like you have. You seem to have sold your soul for a purple cassock. Maybe you want red shoes too. You don't see young kids' lives being as important as the good name of the Church? What happened to you, Peter?" I lift my hands to make my point.

"What happened to you, Zach?" His hand curls as though he's going to clamp my jaw shut. "You only see some romantic idealism as the path we should take. It's as though truth is all there is for you. As though honesty is some kind of God! Don't you see that if you want to accomplish anything meaningful, you have to be willing to play with the truth a little?"

"Play with it?" I think of the scandal rocking the Church, the priesthood collapsing like the World Trade Centers by its linkage with deceit, the victims' cries. "How about making a mockery of it?" The waiter tiptoes up and slides the check between us.

"Zach, do you actually believe a relationship can survive if two people in love are completely honest?" Eyes that once melted mine blaze with his version of the truth now. "That's why you can't hold onto a lover, you know?" Words fly out of his mouth like a dagger.

"Whaaat? You bastard!" *Is that what scared you away long ago, Peter? It'll be a secret, just between the two of us.*

"Your honesty drives people away."

"Maybe it does. But the hypocrisy in our Church has to end. I even think you want priests to have secret sexual relationships, so you can manipulate us."

"So . . . are you finished?" He reaches for the check and scans it.

Feeling dismissed, I go for his jugular. "And it's you who can't really love, Peter. Because you prefer screwing people with your power and calling it loyalty, instead of giving yourself in honest love, even for just a moment."

Horns honk on the street while we glare in furious silence. A cash register jingles. Both of us push back our chairs in disgust. A curtain of lost love crashes between us.

Peter's shoulders slump as he stares at the floor. As he pulls on his tweed jacket, he snorts, "And if you, Father-Holy-Pure-Zachary-The Celibate, if you decide to testify about this in court. I'm going to out you as a gay priest to the Church and to the media." The crowd at the bar erupts in cheers at some sporting event on television. " . . . including your involvement with your inmate friend."

His voice is rising. "That should make your testimony be seen for what it really is, a self-serving way to get into the pants of this poor sucker you want to accuse someone else of fucking."

The bar crowd nearest us turns and gawks with their glasses in mid-air.

I gape in horror as he continues, though he stifles his voice to avoid a scene. "You've always preferred being the victim, Zach. You dream of being St. Sebastian shot through with arrows. Well if you go through with your plan, I'm going to show you how to enjoy being a victim."

I try to speak but my mouth is dry as cotton.

Noticing my disbelief, he's suddenly the bishop in control again. Taking out his wallet, he pulls a folded hundred dollar bill from a corner. Placing it on top of our check, he inches them toward me with a grim smile. "Zach," he says while smoothing his hair, "Let's see how this unfolds, shall we?" Standing, his right hand opens generously, "Keep the change."

Quickly I escape to the men's room, reaching the urinal just before I explode. *So you did know about this priest. Your fury proves it.*

Glancing in the mirror, I'm pale as a ghost. I splash cold water on my face, then stand with my back up against the door to let my heart slow down. Soon someone begins pushing against it so I step aside. A young lawyer type glances sympathetically as he enters. I scoot past him and move swiftly through the happy-hour folks, wishing for a moment I could be one of them.

I cross Amsterdam Avenue for the subway home to the Bronx. A wild bird bangs its wings inside my chest.

CHAPTER FIFTEEN

1978—

After my year's leave of absence at Good Earth, I'm ready to return to ministry. My experience of coming out to Toby and others at the commune makes me want to do the same with my family. Despite the risks of rejection, I need them to know and love me for who I really am. An opportunity comes up when the family is forced to deal with our youngest sister, Megan. After numerous attempts at resolving the problem, she's being expelled from the eighth grade of the local parochial school because of what they call continuous insubordination to the nuns.

As Megan tells it, the nuns continually make reference to the other five Braxton siblings. "Why can't you be like your brothers and sisters? They were wonderful students." And unspoken but screaming underneath, "What went wrong with you?"

So Megan becomes what therapists call the identified patient in the family, the one who everyone conveniently blames for things that go wrong. With my counseling training, I become the facilitator for biweekly family meetings. Mama wants to try to keep Megan from becoming a drug addict or worse.

In the middle of a Megan meeting one late October night, I glance at my watch and see that we have about a half hour left. She is sprawled on the floor with her head in her hands, a petulant scowl on her face. Mama and Daddy sit grim faced in their EZ-Boys. Steve and Patrick are on a fishing trip. Penny and Gwen squat cross-legged on the couch opposite me. All of us are exasperated with the endless cycle of discussing our little sister's marijuana use and other blemishes on the family name.

In the middle of Gwen asking for the third time, "What can we do to help?" I shift off the sofa onto the floor. "I need to talk about something myself tonight," I say. Immediately, Mama and Daddy turn to me. "It's going to make Megan's problems look like nothing," I add. Penny and Gwen sit up, suddenly alert. Megan's scowl relaxes.

My legs start to jiggle. I sigh and jump into what I've prepared. "Did you ever have something about yourself that you were afraid to tell anyone?" *No, it's not cancer.*

Mama's eyebrows arch.

"Even those who love you." *For being a priest?*

Daddy glances at Mama. Does she know something?

"Because you were afraid they might run away from you if they knew?" Wary stares and silence as their imaginations whirl. The clock on the mantle ticks.

"Well I do," I answer my own question. More troubled looks as my heart somersaults.

Penny breaks the ice. "Tell us, Zach. What is it?" She bites her lip. Daddy starts rocking faster. Mama's face goes stoic. Megan sits up on her haunches, her salvation possibly at hand.

Here goes. I can't waste another second. Raising my gaze to the ceiling, I lift my hands plaintively. "So often I've prayed, 'God, you didn't make me weird enough?' . . . I pause for a split second, gritting my teeth. 'You had to make me homosexual too?'" The H word hangs over our little family like a nuclear bomb.

"What? What? What?" they cry out in unison. With her jaw dropped and hands knuckle-white on the armrests, Mama is flustered like I've never seen her before. Daddy searches for a clue from her. It dawns on me that I should have given them a heads up.

"Zach, Zach," Mama pours her heart into the void, "you are our son, and we love you no matter what."

I look at Daddy as she continues, "And as long as you are celibate, what difference does it make?"

As long as you're celibate! Is that it? As long as I'm neuter? Locked in a cage that makes everybody feel safe? My eyes beg, *And you, Daddy?*

"I feel the same as Mama," he says as Penny and Gwen rush up and stoop down on either side of me to show support.

My heart is exploding with relief to have this secret out at last. Megan jumps onto the sofa behind me and flings her arms around my neck, gushing out my new status in the family, "Zach, now you're one of the assholes of the family like me."

Lots of questions follow as Gwen runs to the kitchen and returns with Cokes and potato chips. How long have you known? Do the Sebastians know? Does this mean you'll be leaving the priesthood? What's going to happen next? No one asks if I have a lover or do I want one? Mama comes over, smiles and kisses my cheek. "We love you and are proud of you."

I catch Daddy's gaze over her shoulder. *Oh Daddy, can this make us closer somehow rather than more apart?* He's brushing a tear from his eye. I pray they are tears of acceptance.

Suddenly freed from the spotlight, Megan sprawls like my lifelong pal on the floor next to me. "I told you it'd make your troubles look like nothing," I say with a grin.

"Thanks, big brother," she squeezes my knee.

One by one they gradually drift off to bed with this new knowledge about their priest-brother. They'll have to work at integrating this new piece about me like I have. It'll take time. Suddenly, I call after them as they climb the stairs, "Let me tell Steve and Patrick myself." More than anything I'm going to need my brothers' support.

When I phone my older brother a few days later, he asks "What's up?"

"I need to talk to you and Patrick about something."

"Is everything okay?" I imagine Steve's perplexed face at the other end of the line,

"Yes and no, but I don't want to talk about it on the phone." I don't want to cause him concern. I'm the peacemaker. It's my job to help my family. "I'll let you know where, okay?"

He pauses. Our family rarely probes. It's our Irish way to keep things light and happy. "Okay bro, I'll be there."

Wouldn't it be easier if I wrote them a letter or told them on the phone? No! I need to see their faces: Patrick at twenty-five, home from Vietnam for a few years and about to get married to a girl from Long Island; and Steve, thirty-eight and two years older than me, married with three kids now and still the gung-ho ex-marine. I need to see their faces even if it scares the shit out of me that I might see their rejection instead of brotherly love.

When I pull into the parking lot of a restaurant on the New York Thruway early the following Saturday morning, I spot Steve through my foggy window. Built wiry and strong like me, he's leaning against his Jeep, sipping on a mug of coffee. His head bobs up in a nod when he sees me. I look to see if he's wearing the hunting knife on his belt, the one he wears when he's out fishing or camping. Good, he left it at home today.

Steve loves to posture as the biggest, baddest Republican in New York. I remember a wicked smile spreading over his handsome face once when he warned, "If any asshole ever harms one of my girls, he'll soon be singing soprano." We figure that he is at least half bluffing because, like Daddy, Steve's eyes always tear up at a sad story.

"Hey, what's up?" he yells as he lopes up to the car.

Rolling my window down, I grab his hand. "Hey."

Leaning into the window, he gives me his crooked smile. "Patrick should be along any minute. Did you hear he's got a new motorcycle?"

"No." I picture Patrick, the soldier turned poet with the wind blowing through his sandy locks as he sails through the back roads from his pad in Port Chester. When he came home from 'Nam, rattled and gunspooked and taught not to trust, Penny and I hitchhiked to California with him. Patrick claims he learned to trust again from the fact that complete strangers had picked us up. I have felt close to him and Penny ever since.

Steve waits, sizing me up. My bitten fingernails could tell him a lot, but he bites his too. Just then Patrick coasts into the parking lot like Easy Rider.

"Yo!"

"Hey, you hot shot!"

"Brother!"

The joy of brotherhood tingles in my skinny chest. Even though we don't live at home anymore and bunk together in that third-floor attic room, the guys in our family are close. Every spring, the three of us take canoe trips down the Hudson River with any brothers-in-law and nephews who have the endurance to listen to our endless family stories. While the rest of them fish, hooting and hollering when they snare a shad, I enjoy the scenery and being out on the water with them. Camping out on small islands, we chug booze and tell tales around the campfire under the stars until we fall asleep.

When Patrick shuts down his sputtering metal horse, the three of us pound each other on the back like grinning gorillas and head into the diner.

"Didja see them Giants last night? Yeah, Hammond showed The Niners his fanny a few times, didn't he?" For a second between the small talk, I catch Patrick's gaze: *What's goin' on? Are you in trouble, man?*

As soon as the perky waitress takes our order, I gulp and decide to plunge in. I know if I don't grab the floor, we will wind up shooting the bull with sports' stories and the moment will be gone. "Umm, I need to talk to you guys because some things have happened." I check their faces. Have they heard from the others yet?

Steve keeps it light, "Okay, what protest do you want us to hook up with now?"

I shake my head. It's worse than that I'm afraid. You'll want to protest now.

Patrick jogs the family memory bank, threading our lives together in our ritual of storytelling. "Hey, do you remember when we had Nixon's face on a dartboard on the third floor?"

"Ha-ha-ha!" Steve laughs, "Or the time Patrick laid down in front of the draft board?"

I join the ritual, "Yeah, Mama and Daddy had to go to court to testify he wasn't a derelict. Ha-ha!"

Underneath the table my legs tremble like a racehorse, begging to spring out of the gate. Soon I burst out, "Hey, would you shut up for a minute and listen?" Defiant, I glare across the table.

Their faces swing toward me. Hey, the priest-brother doesn't usually talk like this. Must be something serious.

Fay, our waitress, appears with the coffee pot, one hand on her saucy hip. "Hey, are you guys okay? D'ya want some mud?"

"Yeah," we all say as Steve winks at her. She leans over and pours our cups while I remember my words. *I've been going through some difficult times. I need your help. There's no other way to tell you this.* It's so important that I don't sound like a wimp.

She memorizes our order, checking out each of us as she cracks her gum. Mostly she likes Steve and sees how he enjoys it.

"So what's going on, brother?" Patrick leans closer.

I sip my coffee. My stomach growls when I begin, "Y'know those kids in the schoolyard we used to make fun of?" I fix my gaze down on the place mat. "The ones who played with the girls or lisped?"

"Yeah, like this? 'Thay fella,'" Steve fakes a lisp and flops his wrist. "Ha-ha-ha!"

I clench my teeth. "Look! You're my brothers. I'm going through some incredibly difficult stuff." My legs stop trembling and my voice trails off. "It could even have me leaving the priesthood."

Both of them lean a notch closer and their faces go blank. It's like I am talking about someone else. Like I am taking a whole history of shadowy figures and pulling them around my shoulders with a single phrase. I can barely spit the words out, but finally I do: "I'm gay."

Stunned looks at first. The restaurant hushes like a coffin. You're kidding right? They're trying to absorb it, like when Kennedy died or something. Memories of queer jokes and creeps who may have come on to them. Flashbacks to Steve and me in the bathtub together when we were boys. How normal I seemed then, running cross country, dating and all. Yet somehow different. Now they begin to see. And the priesthood hovering over it all! How does being gay fit into that?

Months of stress and fear rush out of me in an instant. Enormously relieved just to say it, I'm also glad that they haven't run out of the place screaming, *Pervert!* Oh I need to pull them around me now. Show them I haven't betrayed the brotherhood. I don't want to be alone in this. I'm still me! I start telling them how I broke it to the family the week before.

In the middle of this our food arrives. "You boys look like you been out all night. This'll fix ya up." I breathe a sigh of relief for the merciful distraction while Fay hoists the platters in front of us, her black nylon uniform straining at the seams. "You want anything else, gimmee a holler, awright?"

"Okay." We watch her saunter away, her hips swaying invitingly from side to side.

"Hey, I'm famished! Me too!" Like starving beasts, the three of us quickly dive into the savory plates in front of us, relieved to chew our breakfast while trying to hold onto this revelation together.

Together we grab the tall frosty glasses of orange juice as though they are mugs of ale. The juice rolls across my tongue while I listen to Patrick's lips smack. Golden crinkly waffles, smothered in butter and maple syrup, stir our taste buds into action, "Mmmmmmm," we murmur together.

Steve steals a look at me and stabs his fork toward his plate. "Eggs lookin at ya," he cracks, bringing back our younger days working the griddle at Daddy's deli. We watch the golden yolks melt into the hash browns and grab onto a memory that can hold us together.

As though a symbol of how my life feels now, Fay shows up with a side dish of scrapple, the horrid mix of pig's feet, intestines, and other unmentionable animal parts that our cousins in Philly convinced us was the pièce de résistance with their breakfasts.

"All right!" we shout and dive for it, knowing the Pennsylvania Dutch delicacy will zing a spicy kick into the back of our throats. Other than the fact that we hadn't gone to Mass and I had just come out to them, it could be Sunday morning around the dining room table when we were all boys.

"But Zach," Patrick's tremulous voice breaks in, "I know some homosexuals, and you're not like them." Concern riveted on his face, he adds, "Somehow you're more than that to me."

"Like *them!*" I know he means something loving, claiming me beyond a label, but I burst out anyway, "It's not *Them!* That's the problem, don't you see? It's individual people like me."

"How long have you known?" I could see him scanning back over the years. "I never suspected."

Suspected. Like a prisoner being grilled, I try to answer his questions. Steve, mostly silent, keeps poking his eggs and stuffing the hash into his mouth. I flash on a joke he told me years ago when we were at Rockaway Beach. *Hey, did you hear the one about the faggot and the cop?*

"What about you, Steve?" I ask, while a gray, oozing feeling of fear make my arms droop.

More silence. We watch Steve pick a piece of gristle from his mouth, stare at it and place it carefully on the edge of his plate. I hold my breath as we wait for him, the oldest, the one I've been measuring myself against since childhood.

His eyelids remain closed at first, the blue veins in them twitching ever so slightly. Gradually a look of confused disbelief rises on his egg-stained face. The eyes flip open and his jaw moves up and down as he asks, "You-mean-you-like-to-*SUCK*...?" His unfinished sentence hangs between us like a gunshot.

Nervous laughter at first. Even me from the shock of the image he blurts out. Quickly I check around the room to see if we can be over-heard, then slam a volley back at him, "Steve, is that what *your* love life is all about?" I bare my teeth and let that image sink in.

"If someone says they are gay, why is it that people immediately have them in bed with someone?" Oh, I'm on a roll now, the adrenalin pumping from some deep well of pain. "Y'know, being gay is about a lot more than sex. Just like being straight is." Then it occurs to me. Maybe it's his way of asking if I'm sexually active. "Steve, how do you know so much about it?"

More nervous laughter. More checking around the room.

"Hey, keep your voice down," Patrick whispers.

"I'm just kidding," says Steve, as his voice grows softer. I watch his eyes begin to fill up and remember the time in Long Island Sound when he and Daddy rowed us all to shore when the tide was pulling us out. And the time he taught me how to drive when I was sixteen. I can see he is doing mental gyrations as he downs a glass of water.

"So, what's it like?" asks Patrick. "What's going on that we can help you with?" He's trying to smile but his mouth is grim.

Should I get into it? Oh God, why not? "I've had some sexual activity. Not much, but with a friend."

Swiveled heads check out each other's reactions, then glance quickly back at me. It's like I have crossed some impossible line and can never come back.

"But that's not the main thing. It's about what I *do* with these attractions, do you understand? Do I just hide them? Hate them? Find some way to channel this energy for God as I promised? As a priest, I want to be celibate. Yet I know these feelings are part of me now. And no matter what the Church says, I know they are good. I can use them to have deeper friendships and compassion for outsiders in my ministry."

"Whatever you decide to do, you've got my support brother," says Patrick. "But I'm worried what could happen to you in the Church. It's so prejudiced against gay people. Against sex, even." He exhales deeply, scratching his head.

Meanwhile, Steve stares at his placemat. When he turns to look at the people in the booth by the front door, I get ready for another gross comment. Slowly he shifts his seat and locks his eyes on mine.

"I don't get this gay thing," he whispers. "I never could figure out why two guys would want to get it on with each other." Little red splotches appear on his cheekbones.

My heart begins to sink. *If only I could describe it. The whole array of feelings. It's not so different...* "I've been reading this book by a Jesuit, John McNeill," I offer. "He's got a book out called *The Church and the Homosexual.* In it he shows how all the Scriptural statements about homosexuality are really not what we think. Back then they thought everyone was heterosexual, so it was against *their* nature to be involved homosexually. But it would be against a gay person's nature to be involved heterosexually." I can see the brothers chewing on this. But it's too much head talk. I can't really get to the feelings yet. I might fall apart.

"Wait! Let me finish." Steve's hand flies up and his voice grows fiercer though still in a whisper.

"Steve!" Patrick breaks in.

"I may not get it, but you're my brother, right?" Smiling fiendishly like some demon, Steve pats his hip where he usually carries his knife. "And lemme tell you something, if any of these assholes in the Church make any trouble for you," he pauses for affect before ramming home his point, "I'll cut his fuckin' balls off, ya hear?"

"Whaaaah-ha-ha-hahhhh!" We all break up. The other diners turn and stare at us as we double up in our booth, laughing like drunken fools.

Oh Steve! You crazy man! You asshole! I love you! I can barely admit it to him, but for once in my life I am grateful for his macho soldier stuff.

"C'mon! Let's get out of here," he barks, suddenly standing. The patrons by the front door peek over their forks at us as we grab our jackets and head toward the door.

"The service was terrific," Patrick tells Fay as he pays our bill.

"Come anytime, Darlin'," she purrs.

"Thanks, Hon."

A toothpick jiggles on Steve's teeth while the three of us swagger and hee-haw out into the parking lot. We banter a bit about cars and sports and some family stuff before we split. Both of them give me a bear hug as we part. A new joy fills my heart as I head for my car.

CHAPTER SIXTEEN

2004—

Back at Our Lady of Angels' Rectory, my mind is a runaway horse. Migo's court date is coming up and Peter's on a rampage from our fight. I can't just let him bully me. Could he do something drastic? Even immediately? Should I call him? I have to talk to Norma, maybe head him off. Her answering machine: "Have a peaceful day." I leave a message: "Hi. It's Zach. Please call me back whenever you get home. It's urgent."

Have I lost it to spill it all out to Peter? And in a bar! Well, almost. I didn't specifically tell him that I realize he's involved in the coverup. But I need him to know what drove Migo to murder. Oh God, what's going to become of me? Never have I felt so out of control. Lying down, I put my hand on my heart. "Sacred Heart of Jesus, I place my trust in you." Fitful breathing at first, tossing and turning in the sheets, but mercifully I soon fall asleep. When I awake it is dark outside and quiet. The clock says 9:40 p.m. I phone Norma again. "I'm so glad to reach you."

She's munching something, celery or a carrot. "Hi, Darling."

"I really need your advice about something. Is it too late to come over? I don't want to talk about it on the phone."

"I just got in," she says. "Haven't checked my messages yet. Of course, come over now. I'll put a pot of coffee on. Are you okay to drive?"

"Yes. I'll be over in a half hour. Thanks."

Norma lives in Park Slope, a trendy section of Brooklyn where neat brownstones have been grabbed up in recent years by professionals and young families. Near a subway line, they can commute to Manhattan where the rental costs are astronomical. I've been to her house a few times, but never so late at night. I hop in my car and race down the Hutchinson Parkway in a trance.

Before long I've crossed the Triboro Bridge and turn into Park Slope. I pull up to her apartment and she's standing at the doorway in a midnight-blue caftan.

"Come in, come in!" Frank Sinatra is crooning "Fly Me to the Moon" in the background. Her face tells me she's concerned yet glad that she's my confidant in an emergency. We embrace and hold on. It is comforting to feel held for a change, to believe that everything will be alright and that I don't have to be the one to make it so.

She leads me over to a couch in the living room. "What'll you have? I've got coffee, tea, wine. I'm making a salad."

I fall into the cushions and throw my feet up. "Tea will be fine. I'm exhausted. If I start drinking wine I'll never make it home."

She pours my tea and her coffee and joins me on the couch, but remains silent while we sip our drinks. In a while a little wry grin curls on her lips. "So?"

"Your two men had it out today. Peter and I fought at a bar in Manhattan. We said horrible things to each other." My stomach clutches at the memory.

"I know." She shakes her head and waves her hand as though to make the reality go away.

"He told you!" Of course, Peter would have called to alert her. She probably imagines us punching each other.

She nods. I wonder how much he said. "So tell me if you want to. It must have been terrible for both of you."

I don't know where to begin. "Norma, it's as though old hurts from both of our pasts stirred up and we struck back. What we could have said and didn't back then. What we wanted to hear and didn't. Blaming each other for what we are and aren't today. It was terrible."

Her eyes soften.

Sobs rumble up from my belly and I brush a tear away. "How is it that someone I love wants to hurt me so much, and I want to destroy him as well?"

She moves a little closer, pulls me toward her and places my head against her shoulder. Soon her blue gown gets damp from my tears while I tumble out questions with my eyes closed. I feel like a fool. Norma doesn't say much. Mostly I hear her humming. Soon my breathing is more regular.

Frank Sinatra has long since stopped singing. Gradually I pull myself up and take a deep breath. She leans back, smoothing her hair. "So what are you going to do?"

My mind is a blur. "What is Peter already doing? He left the bar with the fire of defending the Church on his face. I wouldn't be surprised if he's already made a report to the Cardinal about me."

"He promised me he would take a few days to calm down before he does anything if you would do the same."

"So he presumed I'd contact you?" I feel some relief. "I'll have that glass of wine now."

She pours us both a glass of Pinot Noir. "Or that I would contact you," she adds. "If you testify in this trial, it would have huge ramifications for prison ministry, Zach." She strolls into the kitchen and returns with some cheese and crackers, and a bowl of vegetables on a cutting board.

"Not just for prison ministry, but for the whole Archdiocese," I say, pausing until she looks at me. "Norma. I believe that when Peter was personnel director, he reassigned this priest whom Migo is accused of murdering. Did he tell you this?"

Stunned, her mouth drops. "What?"

"Even though he must have known of Migo's earlier abuse by him."

She begins to tear the lettuce apart.

"And the priest, Fr. Alan, subsequently abused more kids. It's coming out in the news."

"Migo isn't mentioned in these stories. What are you saying? That Peter deliberately . . . Zach, what I don't hear from you is giving any benefit of the doubt to him. Or even if he did reassign this priest in the past, that as a fellow priest you might understand. Can't you find it in your heart to protect him? We all make mistakes."

"Mistakes! Norma, your love for Peter is blinding you. You're ignoring the young people harmed by this abuse. All the Church is concerned about is its image, so it wants to hide these terrible crimes."

She scrapes the carrots in swift strokes, occasionally glancing over at me. Glad to be getting this out to someone, I reach for my wine.

"Migo's going to be sentenced for the murder of this priest who molested him and others." I picture him clasping the bars. "And you want me to forgive Peter? Do you think he'll say he's sorry?"

"Oh Zach, I love Peter, and you as well. But don't you see? The lawyers are like a bunch of sharks, circling around the bishops, sniffing blood. If the bishops apologize in any way, out loud at least, it's an admission of guilt. Then everyone who has any hurtful memory against the Church will sue it for all it's worth. Do you really think these lawyers are interested in the victims? For God's sake, they have billboards on the expressway advertising for them, for money, for themselves."

"The Church won't investigate itself." I think of the system of closing ranks against the world. "That's why the lawyers must do it, no matter what their intention is."

"You'll see," she says with her chin tilted up. "If we give into them, we won't have jobs anymore because the Church will be bankrupt."

"It is scary. Lots of people would love to see the Church knocked off its pedestal." I refill our glasses.

"You bleed for Migo, Zach. But if these attacks are given full rein, there will be no prison ministry anymore." With her hands damp from the vegetables, she shrugs and gawks at me as though only an idiot wouldn't understand.

"So it's the institution. Individual people must be sacrificed for the institution. Does it always have to be this choice, Norma, loyalty to the Church or to individuals? I can't believe you are siding with Peter. What about Migo? He may acknowledge his guilt in a plea bargain to get a deal. But if I help him by bringing up the fact that Fr. Alan abused him, it could allow the judge to be lenient."

I can see Norma putting it together: Migo's abuse coming out means Peter's involvement in a coverup. She presses her lips together and goes over to the boom box. Soon Nora Jones' caressing voice fills the room, "Why can't I free your doubtful mind, and melt your cold, cold heart?" Gliding back across the room to the music, Norma curls up on the couch and asks, "Can't Migo state his case by himself? Why do you have to thrust yourself into it?"

My mind is becoming jelly. Is it really for Migo that I am so concerned? Or for some reason do I want to get back at Peter? And the Church? Does my own memory of abuse fuel my rage at perpetrators and their protectors? Do these kind of doubts hinder any of us from making a stand? "I don't know, I don't know. Migo has no one to help him. He could get sentenced to life without parole. Imagine, almost thirty years old and never getting out of prison!"

"You really love this kid, don't you, Zach? It's fine with me if you do. Just know why you are as deeply involved so you can make the wisest choice."

"Is that what Peter told you, that I love Migo? I certainly feel warm energy when I am with him, but I love him like a son, Norma."

Her eyes search mine deeply. Suddenly she stands. "Will you help me? I need to finish the salad in the kitchen. Bring the salad bowl and veggies. I'll bring the wine."

Befuddled by our jerky interaction, I watch her move into the kitchen. Soon I follow, juggling the bowl, salad fixings and my wine glass into the cramped space. Placing everything on the table, I find a seat. Norma's at the sink with her back to me.

"What else has Peter told you about me?" I ask, draping my feet up on a chair.

She turns, reaches brusquely for the knife, and begins to chop the vegetables fiercely before looking up. "That you've been involved in some intimate relationships in the past." Her voice is low and controlled.

Damn! That bastard Peter told her about things we had shared in our support group.

"Like I have, and maybe Peter has too," she adds with a quick glance.

Maybe? Where is she going with this? Remaining silent, I stare across the table and swallow my wine.

"That's what gives us compassion you know, even if at times we may have broken vows." Her voice catches.

"Norma?"

"As a divorced woman, the Church says I can't remarry. . ." She peeks over at me with a cut tomato in her hand, her eyes moist. ". . . that my vows are forever even if my marriage has been dead for years . . . and

122

if I find someone to love, I can't receive communion, even if our love is more real than the first marriage."

I get an urge to hold her, tell her I feel deeply for her plight, but something holds me back.

"I do my best, but there are times when I simply make the best choices I can." She waves the knife in a circle. "Don't you?"

"Norma, Norma! What are you getting at? Of course I make the best choices I can at any given moment. That's all we can do."

"Even if some of these choices are technically sins, I believe that some mysterious connection to love makes them a grace too." She drops the tomato into the bowl and begins to flip it around. "I believe God understands this even if the Church doesn't. We all have things we need forgiveness for, Zach."

I watch her toss the salad before glancing out the window. "Okay, I've had a couple of relationships that Peter may have told you about. That was when I was younger and searching, but if he told you about these, he broke confidence." I shake my head to show my disappointment in him. "These are between me and God and I have asked forgiveness." I look intently at her to make a key distinction. "But my relationships haven't been with minors. Is that what you want to know?"

"Zach," she wipes her hands on a towel and moves closer. "I don't know anything in particular about you more than you've told me. It's just that none of us have totally pure hands, do we? Our fear that our own broken vows might be discovered makes people hide the sexual abuse. The real question is: can we forgive others as we have been forgiven?"

"Ask Peter about forgiveness, Norma. Would he risk being censured, or even going to jail, if it would help Migo get a reduced sentence for his crime? In a fit of rage, Migo killed the man who abused him as a minor, and who was still abusing young kids. It's this abuse of minors that we've got to stop." I munch on a cheese and cracker while Norma turns back to the vegetables.

"Oh Zach, what do you want? Revenge for the past?" Her eyes narrow as she hunches her shoulders. "Peter is the one who helped me deal with my divorce when I had no one else. Underneath all that bishop's regalia is a good man, a tenderhearted man, one who might actually be willing to go to jail if it would save the Church." An irony grips her voice as she holds a large peeled cucumber. "The Church is his beloved, don't you see?" She stands the cucumber on its end and I watch with horror as she slices it from top to bottom in a single swipe.

"His Beloved?" I choke on my wine while staring at the poor cucumber. "Really? And *what* Church is his Beloved?" My voice becomes more animated as I speak. "Maybe I'm not ready to forgive. Maybe it's because I'm gay and the Church I serve as a priest is ashamed of me. Maybe I want to sue the Church for the pain of this coverup." I stand as my voice reaches a crescendo. "Maybe some bishops in the Church need to go to jail for *this* crime—teaching gay people that they are objectively disordered. Would Peter?"

Norma stands still with her mouth open and her hands up, one hand clenching the knife.

I step back, trying to speak more softly. "Some young people have jumped off bridges, or hung themselves over this rejection by the Church, Norma." I picture their faces from the Internet, trying to stoke her feelings. "So yes, we need to forgive the Church, but I've never heard the Church say it's sorry about this." I raise my eyes to an invisible jury.

"Look at me, Zach!" She moves a step closer. Her eyes suddenly gleam like a witch's over a cauldron. "As a woman in the Church, don't you think I have similar feelings?" She jiggles her jaw with her lips open. "Women don't have a voice in our Church. Why are you afraid of our experience?"

I notice the carving knife now aimed at my crotch. I nod my head, showing her I care.

"We're waiting for some recognition, but the Church is all we've got: the Gospel of Jesus; our prayers and sacraments, the saints; even the priesthood, as screwed up as it is now . . ." Glancing down, she realizes that she's waving the knife dangerously and places it on the table. "When are you men in the Church going to stop competing for power and consider the rest of us?"

Stunned by her raw feelings, and challenged as a man and a priest, I want to respond. Anything I can think to say or do feels stupid. All I manage to blurt out is, "I'm sorry." I reach to give her a half hug.

She pushes me away slightly. "Try to reconcile with each other, will you? Why can't the whole damn hierarchy get down on its knees in sackcloth and ashes and ask God's and the people's pardon for all of this power stuff. Now that would be a revolution."

In the background, Nora Jones is crooning, "The heart is drenched in wine." We look at each other and Norma's volcano eyes melt a fraction. "For god's sake, don't destroy the Church while you're doing this," she pleads.

Egged on by the hour and the wine and our personal histories, the two of us continue to pour out our feelings. As we retake our seats, Norma leans back and places the knife in the sink.

I feel myself vacillating between anger and a desire to forgive. But forgive what? And whom? "Maybe I should reconsider testifying for Migo. If I could speak to the judge privately, he might be lenient at Migo's sentencing. It could also calm down this war with Peter, help us start over again," I say.

I watch her peel an avocado with a table knife. Suddenly she stops and looks up. "Zach, I just remembered. A prison chaplain isn't permitted to get involved in legal proceedings for an inmate."

"What? I never heard of this before." Could this be my way out?

"Yes, yes. It's because you have a prior relationship with the inmates. Your testimony would be compromised." She sounds relieved.

"Or is it because the prison system wants to keep the public in the dark? Keep its control, hamstring those who might help to change it in any way? Sort of like the Church."

"Probably so." She shakes the salad bowl and her breasts bounce. We chuckle at the chance for some levity at last. "How about some salad?"

"It looks scrumptious, but let's save it if you don't mind." I glance at my watch.

"After all this work?" she pouts with her lower lip curled. But I can tell we've reached some level of peace.

"Honestly, if I don't go home now, you'll be stuck with an overnight guest." I smooth my hair back.

"That wouldn't be so bad, would it? I have a futon." She nods through an alcove to a small TV room.

"Thanks, but no." Gradually, a wave of relief passes through me.

"Y'know, if I can find a quieter way to support Migo, it'll save me from public humiliation too. Peter threatened to out me to the media in retaliation if I testify." I think back to our original pact when she hired me: I don't go around advertising that I'm gay.

She shoots me a pathetic look. "Oh god, that's just what the Church needs now, two clergymen fighting in the media about their sexuality."

Laughing at the absurdity of it, I stand to leave. Yet it's a scary thought that our argument could spill into the public domain. An ambulance siren wails in the background. Norma's challenge about all of us needing to forgive each other for our imperfect relationships hangs in the air. A consoling thought drifts into my mind: You can trust this path now. Even with all your questions, you can do more for the Church in this hidden way. The siren wails on . . . *Don't forget the children.*

A time comes when silence is betrayal.
—James Baldwin

CHAPTER SEVENTEEN

I spoke briefly with Dina, Migo's twenty-three-year-old lesbian sister, on the phone a month ago. It isn't my usual practice to get involved with the inmates' families. It can require a lot of time and there are inevitable complications. Chaotic family systems are the norm for the majority of the inmates and I fear getting overwhelmed by them. Dina is one of only a few of Migo's family speaking to him at this point.

She is a budding graphic artist who sent me a picture of praying hands a few months ago, including one in handcuffs, for our monthly newsletter about the inmates. When we finally meet, Dina ambles into my office at the parish with her close-cropped dark hair spiked up in the center.

"So, you and my brother have hit it off." I steal a look at her cargo pants, flannel shirt, and work boots while she tosses her beat-up leather jacket onto a chair.

"Yeah, Migo's a good guy." As she takes a seat I notice her scoping out my off-duty look of jeans, sweater, and Rockport walking shoes.

"Well, we tussled a few times growing up." She flashes a coy smile. "But he's my big brother and I love him no matter what." Leaning back with her hands behind her head, she surveys my office. "Nice digs, Padre."

"You want a soda or tea?"

"Mmmmmm. Got any Diet Coke?"

"Yep." I get one from the fridge for her and she pops it open. "He's lucky to have you, Dina. Some inmates don't have anyone." Her nose ring glints in the sunlight while she scans the room.

"In case you're wondering, I've got a girlfriend, Gloria. I don't know what Meeg told you." She looks for my reaction.

"Um, he didn't talk much about the personal matters of the family, just showed me some pictures." She notices my leather bracelet.

"As long as we can be real, that's all that matters, right?" Her leg flips up and crosses like a guy's.

Wanting to appear at least as butch as she is, I match her pose. "Yeah, that's what's important. So what does your family expect to happen at court?" I try to imagine one of my family members being tried for murder.

"Padre, if my brother actually killed this guy, well we just can't let people go around popping people off when they have an argument, can we?" Her hazel eyes take on a fierce glow. "But that priest abused Meeg. That's got to change the case."

So she knows. "I agree. Is Migo willing to make this public?" I think back to his fears of being labeled a faggot if he brings the abuse into the open.

"The family's hoping you'll help him in court somehow. He told us you know about the abuse. You're his chaplain. It'll carry a lot of weight if you speak for him."

"Yes, but it'll still expose him, make him look like a victim, which he hates."

"That's tough, yeah. But if my brother wants to spend the rest of his life in jail, then he'll really be a victim."

"Dina, prison chaplains aren't allowed to be involved in a court case of an inmate in their care."

She stares through me.

"I checked this out recently in the prison regulations. Chaplains are actually considered Deputy Wardens here. We're part of the institution. If I didn't have this conflict of interest, I'd do anything for him."

"What! So he's screwed? And in more than one way? What a fucking system! You mean he's gonna get sent up the river for who knows how long, for life maybe, and no one can come to his defense?"

I recall Norma's advice. "He needs to be willing to defend himself, Dina."

"Easy for you to say, Padre. Why isn't the Church willing to defend him? At least try to make up for the harm it's done when it didn't bust this priest's ass long ago?"

"I hate to admit it, but many Church leaders were mainly concerned about protecting the Church's reputation. And they still are, like all institutions."

Dina blinks a few times. There is a teardrop tattoo under one of her eyes. "At the expense of children?" She wags her head in disbelief.

"Yes, but Migo was a teenager." It galls me to be expected to defend the Church in these matters.

"So? He was still vulnerable, and he still is! That's what makes me so fuckin' angry. Sorry Padre." Her leg comes down. She leans forward. "Do you mind me asking, why do you stay in such a Church?" Her voice is sweet, cajoling, but her gaze is intense.

"I love the Church, Dina. I've given my life for it." The pain of her question cuts deeply. I frown.

Suddenly Dina says, "Padre! You can leave the Church, you know? You can still care for people even if you're not a priest."

I've thought of this path before. In the past to have a lover, or more recently to escape the scandal and stigma.

"You could get married or whatever, live a normal life for a change." She searches my face.

Normal? "I don't think I'd be happy, Dina. I wouldn't have access to people like your brother if I weren't a chaplain."

"Access?" Aghast at the implications, her mouth hangs open.

"No, no! That's not what I mean. What I'm talking about is that being a priest helps people trust you, street people like Migo who would never approach a priest otherwise."

"You think so, Padre? Not anymore. Let me clue you in. People see priests now as potential perps. It's all over for you guys unless you do something drastic."

She sees me searching for some common ground, my teeth grinding. I think of how marginalized young people are potential targets for perpetrators of all kinds, not just the clergy.

"Yeah, it's that bad! Meeg trusts you because he knows you."

I think of Migo's endearing way of calling me his "friend-brother-son." "You're right, Dina. That long history of trust has been broken down by the behavior of a few. And I don't know how we will ever get it back, but we've got to try."

"A few?" Her gaze meets mine.

"Yes, a few, compared with society as a whole and other professions. There is actually more danger of being abused by a family member or friend of the family than by a priest. This problem of sexual abuse is epidemic. The Church is easy to attack because we actually keep records. Check out the boy scouts and sport's teams if you want to get the whole picture."

Dina's angelic smile returns. She leans back in her chair, her leg up again. "Father Zach, priests are supposed to be different. We were taught as kids that you're like God, God's representatives. If one of you abuses me, it's like God has raped my soul as well as my body." Her fist crunches the soda can as she finishes this comment. She tries to hook it into the trashcan but misses.

"It's horrible. But if all priests leave, what good will that do? Who will be there for people like your brother? And who will lead the Church, the bishops who are hiding the abuse now?"

"Who will be there for my brother?" She lets it hang in the afternoon stillness. "Are *you* willing to be *now*?" She leans forward with her hands on her knees, the same way Migo does.

"I told you, as a chaplain I'm not allowed to testify."

Her eyelids droop and flutter. She takes a few breaths before looking back at me with her almond eyes. "Padre, the Church is full of beautiful words about love. If you really want to help my brother out in more than words, you'll find a way. You'll be able to heal some of that abuse by the Church, even if it means you get fired as a chaplain to do so. God will find a way to use you. I know you can do it."

Her words are like a stab and a coaxing beam of light at the same time. She doesn't understand that I'm in a religious community, that the prison chaplaincy is a calling I feel from God as well as how I support myself. What will I do if I lose this path I love? "You think it's easy to make such a choice?"

"Well you ought to. Both of these damn systems you work for, the prison and the Church, they each want to swallow your soul, don't you see? What if you left them both and were really free to do what you felt in your heart was best?"

Free? . . . me? "Dina, it's too easy to just up and quit after all these years. I believe God wants me to stay and fight for truth in the Church as best I can, and from the unique vantage point I have as a prison chaplain. Jesus didn't leave, did he?"

"No, and look what happened to him. If you want to stay and fight for honesty in the Church, you know damn well what you're getting into. The Pope or whatever will go down to the mat fighting you on this one. They've bet their fuckin' cassocks on all their sexual rules holding firm because that's all they've got."

I grunt at her imagery.

"People like me and Gloria know." She glares at me, "And you know, don't you? The real Church people like us will be sacrificed for some bloody sexual ideal that even the bishops can't keep. It's as simple as that. They use the rules to hide their own behavior."

My phone is vibrating in my pocket. I pull it out and glance down at the sender. Norma.

"Padre, I still think your best solution is to leave the priesthood and say why, that you want to protest the Church's coverup of sexual abuse by these pedophile priests. In the meantime, you'll be free to testify for my brother."

All of this Dina communicates strongly, yet not simply in anger. Her genuine concern for Migo and for me underneath the harsh words make it even more compelling. But it isn't that simple. What can I say to this young woman calling me to a path of ecclesiastical suicide? I listen a little longer to her pleas to help her brother before saying, "Dina, I promise to think carefully about what you're telling me, but I've got to go now. At Migo's sentencing, I'll be with your family in court no matter what. Even if it's just in silent support."

Dina listens. She surveys the office layout once more: the plants, the pictures, the stack of unanswered letters on my desk, the painting of Christ in handcuffs before Pilate. She nods. "Silent support isn't enough, Padre. Gloria and I will be praying for you." With the trace of a smile she reaches for her jacket. "We'll save you a place next to us."

When she leaves, I tap on the text message from Norma. "Migo wants to see you. It's urgent."

CHAPTER EIGHTEEN

I pedal my bicycle past the caramel popcorn vendors on Fordham Road in the Bronx. The intoxicating sweetness fills my lungs along with the exhaust from the taxis, double buses, and SUVs that I dodge on my way to Ivana's Tea Garden. I grip the handlebars. I'm on automatic pilot. The stress from the upcoming court showdown is turning my legs to jelly. All I hear is my heart pounding to the beat of the reggae music that booms out of the storefronts.

Every spring the priesthood feels like a prison. I wanted this life so I could lay down my life for others, but I'm going crazy. The rush in my veins, stomach, heart, brain, groin—doesn't everyone feel this?

I lock my bike to a spindly tree and flop into a seat at a plastic table by a window that looks out on The Grand Concourse. This six-lane esplanade was built in the early nineteen hundreds to rival the Champs Elysees, but now it's a life-threatening mayhem of traffic.

Another fork in the road. Why these choices all the time? Priests are supposed to help people. I want to defend Migo in court. But if I speak out, I could be thrown out, thrown out of a church I love.

Maybe you want to be thrown out.

"I'll have a cup of Red Zinger," I tell the Hispanic waitress. Blank-faced, she waits until I add, "Tea." I make a silly gesture to explain. I could really use a vodka and tonic.

The Church will try to shut me up if I bring out the truth. One thing I do know, this coverup has to stop. Soon the waitress arrives with the tea in an old-fashioned cup. Except for an occasional curious Fordham University student or homeless person, this part of town doesn't encounter many Anglos. Privacy is what I need now. I stare into the cup, inhale the steam.

Should I testify for Migo or not? Oh God, show me what to do. While sipping rose-colored tea, I glance through the dirty window. On an island between the traffic lanes, a tattered American flag waves in the breeze. Below it is the black flag of the POW/MIA Movement—Prisoners of War and Missing in Action.

Vietnam ... ohmygod, remember? Ten years of protesting in the streets. You had to take a stand then. When I did, it cost me my teaching job and my good standing in the church. Am I going to have to go down this road again?

I can still feel myself crammed into a booth in the student lounge to witness the draft lottery. In 1969, the United States passed a law that initiated a military draft of young men to reinforce the number of combat troops for the War in Vietnam. This would be done by a televised lottery of birth dates. All across the country, young people gathered and prayed in front of the TV, including my students at Sebastian College in Upstate New York where I was teaching Theology. The ones whose birth dates were drawn had to report to the local Selective Service Center to be inducted into the U.S Army. A few students screamed when their birthdays were picked.

I have to do something. But what?

While walking to the monastery from my dorm room for breakfast the next morning, the name Jessie Adams pops into my mind. One of the few upper-class students I've gotten to know at Sebastian, at twenty she's not a lot younger than I am. A few months earlier, she had sidled over to my table when I dropped into the coffee house that she and some of the members of Belle Masque Drama Society had set up in the basement of Dunbar Hall. "Make yourself at home, Father. It's great to have a man of the cloth hanging out with us."

Man of the cloth? Hanging out? I wondered if there was a trace of mockery in her voice? Whatever, her willingness to do something creatively at our conservative school, along with her wide-eyed welcome, intrigued me. Jessie impressed me as someone I could count on if I needed a student's help around campus. A few weeks after that first encounter she was calling me Zach.

The most striking thing about Jessie is her voice. A slender young woman with dirty-blonde hair that falls to her shoulders, Jessie has a voice that easily booms her Boston accent to the back of an auditorium. It is as though she was brought up to be an auctioneer. In addition, Jessie has strong convictions that go along with this incredible voice. She and her drummer friend Ziggie, who is in my eight-thirty a.m.

Theology class and has hair that is longer than Jessie's, are part of an emerging peace crowd on campus.

Jessie can help me—she's got imagination, I think as I walk back to the dorm. That evening I catch up with her in the lobby of the St. Bridget Centre where she lives.

"So Zach, what's going on?" Barefoot, Jessie sports a pair of tattered bell-bottoms and an oversized man's white dress shirt. "Ziggie said you sounded concerned."

"Jessie …" I glance at the security officer and back to her. "Can we talk outside?"

"You bet." She squeezes my arm like a coconspirator. "Wait 'til I throw some shoes on." She vanishes down a corridor and appears moments later in a pair of flip-flops.

It is an early fall evening. Balmy damp air hangs over the driveway. Across the lawn, orange lights twinkle on the front of the townhouses where the senior students live. Jessie slides her small hand through my arm and we wander down the road toward the men's dorm. It feels good to have a strong creative woman by my side. It reminds me of my bond with my sister Penny.

"So Zach, what's up? You seem so on edge." She searches my face in the lamplight.

"Jessie, I want to do something to protest the war." I turn to look at her. "But I feel confused." Her slim arm grips mine tighter. "Kids are being drafted out of my classroom while I'm teaching them about God's reverence for all life."

"I know, Zach. The campus is flipping upside down over this. What can we do?

"I don't know, but next Tuesday morning at six a.m., Ted Rumson, Liam O'Brien and some other Sebastian students will be loaded onto a bus at the Selective Service Office in Auburn. They'll be driven to Syracuse, given a physical, and before they blink twice they'll be in Vietnam crawling in the jungle."

"Yes. They have no choice. If they refuse, they can go to jail."

"They may not have a choice, but I do." Despite my ambivalence, my voice takes on a fierce quality I barely recognize. "That's where I need your help."

"Mmmmm … go on, I'm listening." As though to hold the turbulent feelings in check, her voice remains calm, with her perfect diction. Suddenly I stop dead in my tracks to face her. "Jessie, you know what it feels like to me?"

She stares at me, deadpan.

"It feels like Death is presiding over all of this killing, and we are helpless." My hands wave in circles. "I've been reading about Gandhi. He would do something nonviolent to challenge this."

She studies me for a moment. "Well y'know, the Drama Club has been experimenting with some skits about this. We're planning on making some big puppets, maybe break into a faculty meeting with them to demand some action." Her eyes narrow. "Maybe we can do something together."

We turn and begin walking again. While the sand crunches under my heels, and Jessie's flip-flops make slapping sounds against her feet, our imaginations soar. Her willingness to do something with me is really beautiful, but I don't want to drag students into this. Right now I need to do something by myself. Remembering the scene that came to me the night before as I lay awake in bed, the helpless feeling begins to lift.

"Jessie, you know my religious habit? The long black tunic with the leather belt? The shoulder cape with the hood? Well, I'm thinking about wearing my habit to see my students off on Tuesday morning."

Jessie ponders this in silence. Her eyes are squinting.

"Y'know, go down to the draft board as a representative of the Church to point out the madness. Show how the Church doesn't have to be complicit in sending its young men off to war."

Jessie gazes into my eyes. Slowly she begins to nod.

"Maybe someone will see the contradiction."

Suddenly she whirls, grabbing hold of both of my arms like a vise. "Yes, Zach! That's it! But think of it, you could represent more than the Church, couldn't you?"

Puzzled, I watch students wander by us in twos and threes.

"Hey, Padre," one of them yells. I wave.

"What if you represented Death?" In the shadows of the lamplight, Jessie's eyes glow like a witch's.

"Death?"

"Yes. In your habit you'll be Death, don't you see? And you'll be there to see your boys off." With her mouth squeezed, she lets out a low whistling sound and spreads her fingers. A car horn blares somewhere. "And you'll simply be Death."

Suddenly I picture how our Sebastian Community celebrates funerals. The dead friars are displayed in their coffins with their hooded cape draped up over their heads. It's the only time we ever wear them this way, except maybe on Halloween once in a while. I suppose it's to symbolize death, but it's a little creepy to see a friar you know who hardly ever wore a habit lying in a coffin this way. "The death mask," I say as

136

the image grows inside. "Death watching," I add. Jessie is smiling, but she draws back a step.

"You may get in trouble for this, Zach. Are you ready for that?"

Gradually my breathing slows, as though my soul is really present in my body for once. "I don't care, Jessie." The words come out feisty and clear. "Besides, what can they do? I'll just be out for a morning stroll in my habit."

Together we laugh, her small pearly teeth reflecting in the lamplight. Both of us glance at the leaves suddenly rustling in the wind. We turn back toward St. Bridget Centre, and I feel her grasp my hand, hers tiny yet so strong.

We stroll in silence for a few moments before she asks, "Have you told anyone about this?"

"No. Most of the other priests would think I'm crazy." I look at her with raised eyebrows, my heart thumping at the thought.

"Ziggie and I will back you up. Hey, there's one more thing."

"What's that?"

"Makeup. Death is a big role to play, honey, so you're gonna need some. I'll get cold cream and powder and mix up a neat concoction for you. When I get done with you Father Zach, you'll be the best looking Death anyone ever saw." Her voice, so commanding and articulate, overcomes the last of my doubts. I kick some leaves out of our way.

We laugh again. "Terrific. It's a deal then," I say. It'll be just like when my sister Penny and I put on skits for the neighborhood kids in my family's basement.

"I'll leave the makeup kit in a brown bag at the front desk in your dormitory, Zach. Just smear it on lightly and it'll come off with a washcloth." She locks onto my gaze for a moment. Without a thought about the students passing by, she leans up and smooches me lightly on the cheek.

"Jessie, thanks." My face grows warm.

Flip-flopping back up the steps, she spins around at the top. The slender shoulders go back as her hands clasp her waist. Her Belle Masque voice flies across the night breeze as though she is Caesar, "Remember, Zach: I ... am ... Death ... Watching!" She trails it off and smiles before turning back into the dormitory.

With my heart flipping with excitement, I kick the autumn leaves aside again and hurry back down the driveway to prepare my classes for the next day.

The morning of the send-off, I am scheduled to celebrate the seventhirty a.m. Mass for the Holy Redeemer Sisters. Even so, I figure that I have enough time to do my Death Watch at the draft office in town. The makeup Jessie has given me, along with a washcloth in a plastic bag, rests on the car seat beside me. The keys to the Oldsmobile, one of the monastery cars the priests use when we go out for Masses, are moist in my sweaty hand. I close my eyes with a prayer and turn the key.

The weather had changed overnight. A slight fog hangs over the Unitarian Church's slate roof as I drive down Argyle Street toward Auburn. Underneath my black habit, my heart skips like a rabbit's. As I wait for the light to change at the corner of Prosper Street, I glance at my watch and calculate the time again. Ted told me the Selective Service bus was due to leave for Syracuse at six-thirty. It's a little after six a.m. I can see them off and still have plenty of time to drive to the convent for the Mass.

Slowly I cruise over the small concrete bridge, straining to see the Selective Service office below. It's out of sight behind a tree. A parking spot appears on the street a block further on and I duck into it. Shutting off the ignition, I remain still as it coughs to a stop. Strangely, I feel alive, as though for once I am not just playing it safe but taking a stand. Again I glance at my watch: six-thirteen. No more time to waste. Grinning at the Revlon bag Jessie left for me, I quickly zip it open. The jar of make-up gunk feels cold in my hand. Butterflies flutter in my gut.

Six-fifteen. Any curious pedestrians around? I flip down the rearview mirror. No one but a guy a half-block behind me on the opposite sidewalk, walking his mutt. He's already passed the bridge. He stops and looks around while the light from his cigarette flares. Now he starts moving away. Good.

I crack open the jar. Sticking my fingers into the cold, pasty, cream-colored mess, I glance at my reflection in the mirror before swiping my forehead and cheeks in quick movements, smearing it around until it evenly covers my face, even my eyelids. I find a paper towel in the back seat and wipe off the excess. The car fills with the pungent aroma.

This is nuts. I can't believe I'm doing this. What if someone recognizes me? It's even weirder now with the makeup. Lord, help me follow through and not chicken out.

Six-eighteen. I glance up and down the street. A garbage truck and a few cars whizz by. Up the hill on my side a paperboy pedals his bike. I turn so he can't see me as he passes by.

My eyes go up to the mirror again. "Oooh!" With the tip of my little finger I brush some white onto my lips. Perfect. Like Dracula. Even a little scary. I take a big breath. Okay. All set. One last thing. I pull up my hood.

Six-twenty. A deep breath. Oh, I hope I'm not being a fool. This is for you, Lord ... and for life.

Quietly, as though I am a figure rising up out of the nether world, I crack open the car door, slide one leg out, then the other, pausing for a second to lick my lips before emerging like a specter from a nightmare. My adrenalin is surging like a flood tide. I gather it in, and with my habit swaying with the motion of my steps, I begin to float slowly and mysteriously toward my appointed watching place on the bridge.

A faint fog rises through the railing. It's creepy, like a Hitchcock murder scene. Crows perch like sentinels on the tops of the trees, ready to dive and feast on some road kill. A rotting garbage odor rises from the street.

Below the bridge, about fifty yards down and to the left, a yellow school bus is parked in front of the draft office. Its engine is running. Around the bus swarm young men, none of whom I recognize. Secure now in my habit with my hood up and my hands hidden, with the whiteface on and nothing else to do, I watch for some minutes.

Off to one side, partly obscured by a tree, I notice a group of students. Among them I see a couple of veterans, one of whom has an American flag on his shoulder. On the other side of the bus, another group of young people are waving placards: "Make Peace, Not War! … Burn Your Draft Cards! … Nixon's a Nazi!"

Soon the two groups begin taunting each other: "Ho-ho-ho Chi Minh, the NLF is gonna win!" "God bless America, land that I love …" The battle that's been raging in the country for the past five years swirls around the bus. As the minutes tick on, more students and others arrive to join each side. Screams, shouts soon punctuate the dawn air. My stomach starts to churn as two larger than life figures with scary parrot-like beaks emerge thru the mist from the trees. Jessie? Ziggie?

"Yo!"

"Hey, you!"

From behind me, some rough male voices call out from the window of a car that has pulled up by the sidewalk. I keep facing forward.

"Yo buddy!"

"Hey! We're the Auburn police."

I hadn't planned on this. Now what? One thing for sure, I can't afford to miss the Mass for the Holy Redeemer Sisters. Ever so slowly, I turn my head robotically and glance back at the men in the car.

The cop nearest me drops his jaw, a look of disbelief on his face. "Who-are-you?" he asks.

Who am I? Simple. Jessie's words come to me. It is as though I've prepared for this moment my whole life. With her precise diction, I pronounce, "I. Am. Death." I wait for a few moments to let it sink in.

Slowly I turn back to survey the mob scene below, sure now that I am watching a school bus prepare to take my students off to some Vietnamese jungle to kill other young men or to be killed. Hell, no!

"Death? What the ...?"

"What d'ya think you're doing?"

Below us, what look like Army officers begin to shove their way through the crowd, attempting to force the students onto the bus.

Is that Ted in the Yankee's jacket? Liam yelling back at the demonstrators? I told them I'd be here to see them off. I just hadn't told them the details.

The puppet-like figures stand with wings outstretched to block the bus as the protesters link arms with them. Maneuvering to stop this, the vets raise their flag and press forward. Chants break out: "Stop the War! Hell no, we won't go!" Squawking and screaming at the intrusion on their turf, startled crows scramble out of the trees.

"What d'ya think you're doing?" The cop's question hangs in the air.

Ever so slowly, as though I have to tear my eyes away from the fog-shrouded frenzy below, I turn back to the car and look directly at the cops. Then, as though it is obvious to anyone but a moron, I utter a single phrase and let it hang in the fog—"I'm watching." Then I gaze back at the bus.

The bus is revving up its engine now and begins to move. To stop it, the giant puppets lie down in its path. A fight breaks out. A guy in a Yankees jacket grabs the flag from a veteran. It rips. Other vets push him back and he falls into the bushes. More screams. Curses. Someone blows a bugle. Now I recognize Ted's face, his and other faces pressed up against the bus windows looking out. They are yelling something I cannot hear.

"We've got a riot developing down here at the recruiting center," a voice barks from the car behind me. "Better send a squad car down here."

I can't just watch this. Suddenly, as though my whole life of struggle for identity is at stake, my arms shoot up in a "V" sign. A defiant shout roars out of me toward the crowd below the bridge: "I. AM. DEATH. WATCHING!"

"What the hell?" The cops swear as they jump out of their car. For a magic moment it feels like it is all worth it as the rabble around the bus gape up at the bridge, the flag ripped between them, blessed or cursed in some crazy way by a madman on the bridge claiming to be Death.

"You're Death, huh? Who do you think you're kidding, asshole?" A tall Irish cop's ice-blue eyes are like bullets. "Get in the car," he orders. Cupping my head, he shoves me into the back seat. Another shorter, swarthy-looking cop smirks back at me from the front seat. One last glance backward at the bus scene before I remember the Mass at the convent. My watch reads six forty-eight.

All over now. No more figuring out what to do next. Out of my control. Everything is happening however it wants. Yet I'm not panicked, I'm strangely calm as though whatever I need to do next will come to me. If only I can make that Mass.

The police headquarters are just a few blocks away in the shopping district. I am taken through a large receiving area into an inner room. The Irish-looking cop gestures to a seat. He goes out and returns with an older Black man sporting aviator glasses.

Dressed like the others except for a crisp white shirt, he speaks as though he is bored, "You know you're disrupting the peace, don't you? We could charge you." Like wolves around a campfire, the other two cops pace around me.

Aware of how odd I must look in my habit and white-face, a scripture scene comes to mind. When Jesus was arrested, he remained silent.

The captain comes up in front of me. His shoulders and biceps stretch his shirt tight. "If you don't tell us who you are and what you are up to, we can charge you with resisting arrest." His voice threatens, but it's unconvincing. It would sound silly in court. I stare at his boots.

Soon the taller cop pulls the captain to the side and whispers something to him. They pause a moment before the captain nods. As they leave the room, handcuffs hooked on the back of the captain's belt jangle.

The remaining cop, the short guy who has a belly, leans disinterestedly against the stone wall. On either side of his heavy belt, hang a gun in its holster and a shiny brown billy club. He lights up a smoke and blows smoke out of the side of his mouth toward the ceiling. My mind is in a whirl and I need to piss. I want to check the time but don't want them to see that I care. My stomach growls for some breakfast.

Voices approach the door and the other two return. The captain is talking out loud, "He hasn't broken the law. We really have nothing to hold him on." Potbelly against the wall frowns.

All of a sudden I am being rushed out. "That's it. You can go. We've got more important things to do than babysit," cracks Irish.

"Yeah, he—or she?—looks like some religious fanatic. People could get scared."

They all laugh.

I've hardly moved a muscle since I've been seated. Now I adjust my sleeve and steal a look at my watch. A few minutes before seven. I can still make the Mass if I hurry. No one will know. The scared, trapped feeling in my stomach begins to melt. Inwardly I sigh deeply.

"Let's go! Let's go! We don't have all day." They motion with their hands for me to get up and go. I can hardly believe my good fortune.

Slowly I get up and move toward the door. As I do, my shoe catches on the hem of my habit and I trip. Crap! In a swift motion the captain catches me. Swifter yet, he lets go of me when I've regained my balance. In an instant, the contrast between us strikes me—they with their guns, handcuffs and billy clubs, me in my black dress and makeup. Embarrassed, I follow The Irish cop out into the main office. As he holds the glass door for me, I wonder if they might surmise that I am a priest.

Momentarily, the bright morning sun blinds me. I pull the hood down on my shoulders to look more normal. Keeping my head down, I stride the few blocks to my car.

Not many people out at this hour. No one notices. Even if they do, who cares? I did it, and I'm almost home free. When I'm safely in my car, I bow my head and say a prayer of thanks.

Seven-fourteen a.m. I wipe my face clean with the damp washcloth, checking myself in the rear-view mirror. My eyes look wild. I comb my hair, take a long swig of water, and start the car.

It is just a slight movement, hardly noticeable as I glance in the rearview mirror to pull away from the curb. A cop car pulls out from the station house. By the time I approach the red light at Onondoga Plaza, the fat cop is right behind me, a cigarette hanging from his lip. It feels like the devil is sneering at me through the smoke.

Shit! Now what? Will he pull me over? I try to figure out what's going on as he follows me for a few blocks. When he makes a fast U turn at the schoolyard a couple of blocks later, I speed toward the convent. That bastard. Just trying to scare me.

As I enter the old convent, Mother Regina is peering over her glasses at me from the hallway. I wave to her to show that I'm okay, then rush to the bathroom for a pit stop. Unbelievable! Only ten minutes late to celebrate Mass in the statue-crowded chapel. I splash cold water in my face.

Excited, almost exhilarated, I'm also scared. Maybe I can't be honest about my sexual orientation, but at least I've been able to express my anti-war feelings in more than words. Wait 'til I tell Jessie and Ziggie. Moments later, innocent as a lamb and clothed in the brocaded white priestly vestments, I kiss the altar and greet them, "The Lord be with you."

The fat little German nuns respond in perfect unison as the candles flicker, "And also with you."

As a priest, to the nuns I am Jesus' representative and as such I am holy. They treat priests as though we could never do anything wrong, and their faces mirror back our presumed mutual innocence. With my palms pressed together and pointed heavenward, I smile and pray silently, Oh God, I hope I got all the makeup off.

The rest of the service goes quickly. While I receive the Body of Christ and give it to the nuns, I pray silently for my students on the bus. When I send them forth at the conclusion, one younger nun searches my face more inquisitively. I wonder what she sees.

Fifteen minutes later I am back at the college parking the Oldsmobile in its regular spot. As I get off the monastery elevator on the second floor to replace the car keys in the drawer, the Prior, Father Morgan rounds the corner of the common room.

He spots me, and wiggles his index finger. "I want to talk to you." His face has red splotches. His jaw clenches like an alligator's.

Suddenly it comes to me in a flash. The big-bellied cop grinning in my rearview mirror. The sudden U-turn. Of course. He had no need to follow me—he got my license plate number. Under the sweaty, sacred habit my body goes limp as a rag doll, and traces of the makeup cream rise in my nostrils. While I was saying, "Lamb of God, who takes away the sins of the world," the cop was phoning Father Morgan. "Which one of your priests was out in the Oldsmobile this morning? ... out in drag?"

Dummy!

At the end of the 1972 school year I was forced to leave Sebastian College. I had lasted three tumultuous years, the best years of my life up to then because they were the most real. To leave the students, whom I loved and felt loved by, felt like a death. But even if it had enabled me to stay until I was an old man, I wouldn't change a thing. I drove onto Interstate 81 with all my belongings in a U-Haul, remembering Ted's last words to me the day before he left for Vietnam: "You're gonna get fucked Father Zach, but keep it up."

The POW/MIA flag clangs on the flagpole as I blink back to reality. My tea is cold, but I take a sip anyway. As I rise to pay the cashier, my body still tingles from the memory. A familiar voice inside me murmurs: *You can sacrifice your whole life for prisoners like Migo you know, but that still doesn't prove you can truly love someone. You'll never know that until you are free.*

CHAPTER NINETEEN

The earliest I can get to see Migo is the next morning, after the Sunday Mass for the general population. All during the service I am distracted, wondering what Migo's urgent message is about. Norma doesn't know. "Maybe Migo's panicking about his upcoming court appearance," she says.

"I would if I were him," I tell her." She wishes me good luck.

I stand in front of the ancient barred gates at 3 Upper, waiting for the C.O to mosey down the long corridor with his clanging keys to let me in. One of the food service women in a pale blue plastic cap calls out to me as she strolls by, "Hey Father, you being good? You praying for me?"

I wave back, "Hi Julie. Always. And you for me?"

A saucy smile. "Every night, Father."

"I need it, Julie." Catching sight of the inmates through the gate, milling around aimlessly in their jumpsuits, a Scripture passage we just read at the mass comes to me.

To the fatherless be like a father,
and help their mother as a husband would.
Thus you will be as a son to the Most High,
and he will be more tender to you than a mother.

This brings to mind a question Migo recently asked me. Our growing closeness has opened doors between us and he's begun to say anything on his mind. He wanted to know if the Church will ever let priests get married.

I gave him a pop history lesson on the topic, basically explaining that it only became a Church law in the twelfth century to stop priests

THE BLACK WALL OF SILENCE

from passing on the rectory and the parish's financial holdings to their families when they died. That's when he hit me with the question I didn't really answer. "Zach, don't you need someone you can love?"

Laughing at the young man's chutzpah, I told him it's a topic that we need a whole day to talk about. He stared at the floor. His time was getting short and he wanted to initiate a topic I wasn't ready to discuss yet. And given our different roles it didn't seem wise to go any further. Not yet anyway. Could I trust him to keep confidence? What would Sophie say?

Suddenly I hear the click of the heavy black door. The C.O. steps in with a key the size of a monkey wrench, motioning to me. I signal to the officer in the central control cubicle further inside, and he buzzes open another gate. Not recognizing him as one of the regulars, I ask in my mildest manner, "May I see Migo Robinson?"

He eyes me and then my badge warily for a moment. "Your name?"

"Chaplain Braxton." Quickly I show him my picture on the badge. He types it into the computer while he pronounces, "B-R A-C-K . . . " I interrupt, "X . . . It's B-R-A-X-T-O-N."

He stops typing and gives me a disturbed look. Was it my tone? Not deferential enough? One of the thousand threats to power I've learned can occur in jail. Back to the computer. "BRAXTON," he spells it out again. Have a seat in the waiting area." I take my seat, pissed at myself and the game but not wanting to give him the satisfaction of showing it.

When Migo finally appears, his hair is wet and he's rubbing it dry with a towel. A big smile. "Sorry to make you wait. I was getting a shower."

My heart skips. Something about his placid composure combined with his young strength is magnetic to me. A smile jumps onto my face as well. Without children of my own, I've discovered that the inmates, especially a few like Migo, become like my own blood. I almost feel like I'd be willing to die for them, like parents would for their kids I suppose. With all the jail constraints as well as the tragedy of their crimes and plight, I often feel like I do die a little each day when I encounter them. Especially when they get sent upstate for a long time.

"So, you wanted to talk. What's going on? I was worried when I heard it was urgent." We grasp hands and he takes a seat beside me.

Matter-of-factly he begins, "Last week a C.O., the Anglo guy—he nods toward the control booth—threw my Bible and palm cross and the pictures of my family onto the floor. He wrecked my cell during a lockdown search because someone in the cellblock had stabbed another inmate that night."

"What?" I picture the chaos.

"I initiated four grievances against him, but the captain tossed them aside. I was brought back to my cell by this same C.O. The guy grabbed my copies of the grievances and read them. After that he turned to me and said, 'You're dead!'" Migo presses his lips together fatalistically.

"God almighty!" I often hear these stories from the inmates. Usually I just listen, reluctant to get involved in these prison power battles. It's like a chess game with human pawns. I try to listen to it through the C.O.'s eyes too, knowing they are also being tested. "Has he bothered you since?" I glance over at the officers. It looks like they are dozing but they could be watching us.

"No. He just glares at me with an evil eye when I pass him. You can't back down or they think you're a fag, Father. But I don't look for trouble either." He musses his hair and shakes his head like a young lion.

No, don't dare be thought a fag in here! I think of how the victims and offenders are blurred together in jail, especially anything to do with sexuality. The guy who was accused of raping a teenager comes to mind. "What happened to that guy the guards beat up?"

Migo turns to me bewildered, as though I wouldn't really want to know. Staring at the floor, he mumbles, "They dragged him out of his cell unconscious a few days ago . . . somehow his cell was left unlocked." He glances up and whispers, "They banged his head down the steps as they took him out."

Horrified at the image, I cringe.

"He's in a coma now at the hospital." He shrugs at me as though to show me what their life is really like when I leave.

Overwhelmed, I shake my head, "Jeez." What can you do against such violence? I heard that child abusers are considered the worst by the inmates themselves, but I still can't handle the image of a guy being deliberately dragged down concrete steps to crack his head open like an eggshell. Yet I protect myself emotionally from these stories or I'd burn out in a month.

146

"The Muslims, and there are a lot of them in here, Zach, constantly yell at the Catholics over the fact that, as they see it, Catholic priests abuse young boys."

I feel more than ever the sense of a scarlet letter on the back of my clerical shirt as he speaks, and look at myself in shame through the eyes of the prisoners: both the Muslims who so simplistically scapegoat all Catholic priests, and through the eyes of the Catholic inmates who are left on their own to rebut this.

Though I realize Migo was abused by a priest, I tell him, "Most priests are not abusers. Those who do are removed from ministry. At least they're supposed to be. It's a tragedy on all sides."

He shakes his head. I'm not sure what he's thinking. The C.O. and the other inmates are not noticeable through the gate, unless they specifically turn to look. Lunch is about to be served and a commotion soon erupts. Large trays are being rolled up to the front gate on a dolly. The C.O. opens the gate and the trays are pushed through. A couple of inmates barge into the passageway and begin to count these plastic containers out for distribution to the cells, joking and making wisecracks about what the food will taste like. "Ya like rubber hamburgers? Hey, maybe it's horsemeat!"

A Black guy with a beard notices my raised eyebrows. "Want one Chap?"

"No thanks."

"I don't blame you," he chuckles. Migo and I wait until they grab some of these trays and vanish.

"But what I really need to talk to you about is my case," he says. He locks his gaze on mine. "I've decided to take the plea deal. My lawyer tells me it's the best we can do. If I plead guilty to second degree homicide, I can get twenty-to-forty years.

"What?" My heart sinks at the thought of him in prison for all those years. "And if it went to a jury?"

"It could be life without parole." His voice drops to a whisper and his lips twist. "I was wondering, is there any way you can be present at the sentencing, maybe say something favorable about me?"

"My god. I've been wrestling with this question too, Migo. It's like a crucible."

"What do you mean?"

My hands go up and I stretch an imaginary cord, trying to make it as simple as I can for him. "A crucible is like a set of forces that pull you in two different directions. Or maybe it is that they want to crush you together, I'm not sure. All I know is that the choices I have are tearing me apart and I don't know what to do."

His brows furrow. "What choices, Zach?"

"On the one hand, I'd do anything in my power to help lighten your sentence, even help you go free."

His lower lip, usually protruding in a kind of pout, does so even more.

"On the other hand, I'll need to leave the prison chaplaincy in order to do so."

He cocks his head to the side.

"Chaplains aren't permitted to get involved legally in an inmate's case." I wait for him to grasp this.

"Awwww, I didn't know. I don't want you to mess up your work as a chaplain here to help me." His hand momentarily reaches toward me. "Forget it. We'll find another way."

"I saw your sister, Dina, yesterday."

"You did? My little sis?"

"Yeah, she wanted to talk about your court appearance too, what I might do to help."

"What do you make of her? She likes to wear metal stuff, even pierce her body." He looks skeptical.

"On both counts, priest and chaplain, I'm limited by my role. Dina sees me as trapped by this, says I should quit both of these systems so I can speak the truth."

He squints, not quite grasping that someone on the outside could be trapped in a prison too.

"Migo," I put my hand on his shoulder, "being a priest I wear a uniform." I gesture toward my black clerical shirt and trousers. "You and I both wear clothes that set us apart." I point at his orange jumpsuit. "Both of us have sets of rules enforced by authorities."

He listens intently.

"Those in charge often make choices that protect the institution over us."

Migo glances toward the bubble with the C.O.s.

"Each of us have to bite our tongues when something bad is going on around us, right?"

He gets a faraway look. Maybe I've lost him. He's got a murder charge against him, twenty-to-forty years. There's no comparison.

I decide to hit him squarely with my present reality. "Right now, people look at priests with lots of stigma and shame in their gaze. We're all mixed up in their minds with sexual abuse. You can see how this could feel like a prison too, right?" I begin to feel like Peter asking me to understand.

A frown appears on his face. "I didn't realize."

"It's not like it's horrible for me. I can walk in and out of these barred gates in a way that you can't. And it feels great to be able to do God's work with people that the priesthood opens up to me, people like you. But still, sometimes the priesthood feels like a prison."

He nods his head, "Maybe Dina's right."

Out of the corner of my eye, I notice the C.O. watching us through the bars. He's got a quizzical look on his face. Maybe it's time to leave.

"With your court appearance, this feeling of being trapped in my roles comes to a head. As long as I'm a chaplain here, I'm not allowed to support you by my testimony when you stand before the judge. And if I quit as a chaplain to testify for you, I could be forced out of the priesthood."

"What? Why?"

"Because I'll be exposing its secrets."

"Secrets? What secrets?" He blinks. Ignoring the commotion behind him—the lunch guys have returned and are throwing trays around—we sit in silence until they are finished.

I face him squarely, "One secret is that the priest who abused you was a sexual abuser, a serial sexual abuser. That means he was knowingly reassigned to a Church ministry where he could harm other young people even when they knew he had harmed you."

His dark eyes bore into mine.

"It's a pattern in the Church to protect itself. No matter what the cost, this coverup should be exposed. It's bigger than you and Father Alan."

His lower lip juts out, in despair or vengeance, I can't tell. Shaking his head from side to side, a shadow drifts across his face. "So, what can we do, Zach?"

I lean down next to him, my hands folded, my elbows on my thighs. He follows suit. Peter's threat comes to mind: "I'm going to out you as a gay priest to the Church and to the media, including your sexual involvement with your inmate friend." The worst part about such a scenario would be Migo's possible rejection of me as a "faggot," and that he'd see ulterior motives in all my care for him.

"I'll find a way to help you," I say. "Want to pray about this?"

Migo leans his leg into mine. I reach my hand out and he takes it. The C.O. watches through the bars as we bow our heads. I don't care what anyone thinks. I know beyond doubt that I am tending to Christ in prison, and that Christ is tending to me.

CHAPTER TWENTY

Peter ushers me into his office at the chancery. It has been barely a month since our blowup at the Regent but it feels like a year. I need to find out if Peter has done anything drastic in regard to his earlier threats to me, and to plead for Migo's case one last time. When I phoned him earlier and asked if we could speak, he insisted that we meet at his office. "We don't do well in bars," he quipped. Central Park might have been an alternative but I agreed, even though it would put him in charge as usual.

He is decked out in his clerical suit. I'm wearing a gray sweater over my black shirt and trousers. Chuckling inwardly, I recall the time as a young priest in the early seventies when I wore bell-bottoms to a meeting with my provincial. What a rebel I was back then. I've been working my way back into the trust of my fellow priests all these years since.

"Come in, come in." We enter his elegant office adjacent to the main corridor with its oriental rugs and burnished mahogany benches.

It's been four years since Peter's patron, Cardinal John O'Connor, passed away. In his heyday, O'Connor was the singular bulwark against any gay rights initiatives in the city. It was a tough time to be a gay priest. If you came out, you'd be grilled on where you stand on the sinfulness of homosexual acts. The Church hierarchy wouldn't openly punish you for being gay. "Love the sinner, hate the sin" was the new slogan. But you'd be on a collision course in having to uphold the Church's teachings on a whole range of sexual issues. So, theoretically you could come out, but it wouldn't accomplish anything other than a momentary chance to speak the truth. It'd be like a butterfly soaring into the fire.

Besides, it would be presumed that you wouldn't be crazy enough to use the word *gay* in regard to yourself unless you were sexually active.

This, of course, was forbidden by the commitment of celibacy. So gay priests, of whom there were many in New York City despite the cardinal's assurance there were none, were largely trapped in silence as our gay sisters and brothers fought for their civil rights during the catastrophe of the AIDS crisis.

The great organ in the cathedral next door sounds grandly in the background as Peter gently pulls his heavy office door closed behind us. "Holy God We Praise Your Name" brings back images of Benediction services from my boyhood. A calmness comes over me. I've heard that people feel this way when they've finally decided to commit suicide.

Peter moves immediately behind his desk, a huge cherry antique with a massive glass top. On it are a telephone, a Tiffany lamp, a few pens, and a single sheet of paper. "Relax. Take a load off. Would you like some coffee?" He gestures to a couple of emerald Queen Anne chairs in front of his desk. You'd think we were going to do a crossword puzzle together.

"Thanks. I had one earlier at Grand Central."

"Well, where were we?" The old friendly smile I remember.

"We had our encounter at the Regent."

A little snort. "Ah, yes."

"Is it possible we can redo that?" I shrug.

His hand on his pectoral cross suggests that a redo is unlikely, while a sudden crescendo from the organ encourages me to place it all in the Lord's hands. " . . . Infinite Thy vast domain, everlasting is Thy reign."

Just spill it out. "Migo's sentencing date is next month I'm going to make his abuse known in some way to make the case for a lesser sentence." There. Done. I take a deep breath and exhale.

Silently, Peter swings his chair to glance over at the windows. Tall ancient ones with plush maroon drapes, and an ornately framed portrait of O'Connor in his cardinal's robes between them. Afternoon sunlight reflects from tiny dust particles as though to mesmerize us. Sort of casually Peter responds, "Zach, how did you gain knowledge of Migo's assertion that he was molested?" With his downturned palm facing toward me, he eyes his ring.

Strangely, in all the uproar it never occurred to me. Migo shared this key bit of information in the sacrament of confession. Is this what Peter is gambling on? That this is the only way I've discovered this? If so, like all priests I'm bound by a strict requirement never to reveal such information received in confidence under the Seal of Confession, even if it would prevent murder. "He shared this with me a few weeks ago, during one of my visits."

"Under what auspices? As his chaplain? As his confessor?" His fingers cover his pursed lips as they point up in prayer. He continues swiveling his chair.

Gulp. Has Norma told him something? What did I tell her? "Does it matter?"

Ever so slightly, he smiles. He believes he's caught me and my face can't hide it.

Thrown off balance, I lean forward with my eyes wide and plead, "Peter, this young man is being sentenced for murder. He'll be imprisoned for most of his life if he's not helped. Don't you have any . . . ?"

"Zach, don't you care about the sacred Seal of Confession?" O'Connor's falcon eyes beam down at me from the portrait.

"If I've got to break it to save Migo's life, wouldn't you?"

"If you do, your faculties will be removed. You'll no longer be able to function as a priest in the Archdiocese." The velvet drapes rustle slightly as he gazes over his desk at me in silence. "You could be excommunicated."

Aghast at the stakes, I blurt out, "You'd actually do that?" My insides shiver in fear.

"You'd give me no choice." He leans back in his chair with a winning smile, his hands behind his head. So far away, his desk an ocean between us.

"Why must you stonewall this?" I beg, ignoring for a moment the incriminating piece. If Migo's abuse becomes public it will link Peter to a coverup. He could be prosecuted.

"Yes, a man's life must be protected. And a brother priest's life is one I would think you'd do everything to safeguard as well. You told me that I saved your life once. Why can't you do the same for me now?" For an instant, I sense a tone of vulnerability in his voice.

The Brotherhood of Priests. Prostrate on the cathedral floor at ordination. Surrendering our lives—our bodies and souls—to God. What could be more profound? And Peter saving me that New Years' Eve when I was dying inside. How could I abandon him now? I steal a look at his cufflinks, gold with small black crosses. And his ring, the stone square and purple, the sign of a bishop's authority. My inmate-son's black eyes peer out from those crosses.

"Migo's a mixed-race kid with no one to defend him. One of the Church's abuse victims for whom we say we're so repentant." My voice is rising. "You have all the power of the Catholic Church. You've got attorneys up the wazoo." I shift my gaze to O'Connor's portrait, then back to Peter. "You'll never go to jail for what you do. But Migo's expendable, isn't he?" I snap my fingers, "Like that!"

Slowly Peter opens the desk drawer, his glance cast down toward its contents. For a crazy instant I imagine he might have a gun. "And if you testify as you plan to," his voice is low and menacing, "it won't just be your faculties removed. We'll expose you in the media as a gay priest, intimately involved with an inmate he's supposed to be serving as a priest. Instead of me, you may go to jail." He glares at me and snaps his fingers, "Like that!"

"But you'd be lying." My fingernails dig into the doilies. That's not my relationship with Migo."

"Zach, even if you dodge the implication that you're romantically involved with this guy, there are other infidelities to your vows that can be leaked. The media loves that stuff."

My heart flops with the memory of my desperate search for love as a young priest, and Peter's threat to blackmail me over this thirty years later. "You wouldn't dare!" I pound the armrests. "That's confidential information you know from our support group."

"If you don't respect the Seal of Confession, why should I respect your confidentiality?"

In my mind I race back over my struggles with my vow of chastity that I shared with the group while Peter was a member, even while he shared so little. The pain and growth because of this. All the while pray-ing St. Augustine's prayer, "Give me Chastity, Lord." Yet rather than Augustine's ending, "but not yet," I changed it to express where I'm at: "Give me Chastity, Lord . . . *even* yet."

"Peter, my relationships with a couple of guys years ago, one I even considered leaving the priesthood for, were with adults apart from my ministry. They were consenting adults. They didn't endanger anyone and they weren't a crime."

He stands erect with his hands on the desk. He fingers a sheet of paper which probably already spells out the charges he is planning against me. "They were a crime against God and they endanger the Church." It's like he's speaking to a stranger.

All of a sudden in that hallowed place, with the organ strains still hovering over us, I feel reduced to nothing more than a common sinner. Just a faggot, and what do we know about love? I look across the no man's land to a friend who once convinced me otherwise by his arm around my shoulder. How did it come to this?

Gone is our Brotherhood of Priests. I'm just a homosexual, and his threat, demanding that I hide who I am or else, is the weapon that will silence me in this moment of crisis in the Church.

Suddenly my mouth is dry as a desert. With a gnawing emptiness in my gut, I lift myself slowly from the chair. I stare into his blue eyes, steely and unforgiving as cobalt now. But mine are equally hard. Without another word I turn toward the door.

"Zach . . . Zach!"

As I turn the knob, a soft click sounds behind me. When I reach the curb I consider shaking the dust from my feet as the Gospel says. A teenager strolls by, bobbing her head to the music on her headphones. That's when the bomb hits me: Peter taped us.

CHAPTER TWENTY-ONE

2004—

Immediately after the morning mass at the Women's Prison, I escape to Jones Beach. The ocean is where I always go when I want to experience God's presence. This is it. The point of no return. The Gospel that we just heard rammed this point home:

> The Spirit drove Jesus out into the desert, and he remained in the desert for forty days, tempted by Satan. He was among wild beasts, and the angels ministered to him. After John had been arrested, Jesus came to Galilee proclaiming the gospel of God: "This is the time of fulfillment. The kingdom of God is at hand. Repent, and believe in the gospel."

The sky is overcast. It is chilly and smells like rain. I bundle up with a muffler and gloves, along with a jacket and a poncho in case I want to sit down. Only one other car is in the lot. I park near a welcoming booth and find the crooked path through the trees. When it breaks onto the beach at the end, a teeming surf greets me. Low tide. Only broken shells on the wide expanse to the water. A couple of gulls hang in the wind. I walk directly toward the water. It is mesmerizing. Foggy mist hides the horizon where the sky and water meet. Up and down the beach not a soul in sight, just ocean, mist and me.

I don't mind the aloneness. It feels like the cover I need to be in touch with my feelings. Slowly I begin to walk along the water's edge into the mist. It looks impervious about twenty feet ahead, but as I walk the fog keeps opening up around me. As far as I can see in either direction the sea pounds the shore, roaring and seething against some rocks before receding and sweeping back again for another try. It's as though a child is having a tantrum. Or like God Himself is crying out. Or maybe Satan. Mist streaks my glasses and face.

"Father . . . Father?"

My son.

"So glad to sense your presence. I need you badly."

You're doing fine.

"Hah! The vise is tightening. I feel like I'm committing suicide."

I want you to live.

"Me too! But there are no more conversations. It's time to act."

This is what we've been preparing for.

"We? I feel so alone."

You are not alone. I have many servants helping you.

"I believe that, but Father?"

What, my son?

"I only want to do your will."

You are. Keep on doing so.

"Your Church is in great trouble."

Yes, but it will survive.

"The priesthood? The sacraments?"

People will learn to trust again.

"How?"

When the lying stops. When they see no more deceit. When the priests and bishops learn to work together and trust each other.

"When will the pain stop?"

When the people endure it instead of passing it on.

"Father."

What?

"I've sinned that way, passed pain along."

I know. It is good to confess.

"Forgive me."

You are forgiven. Just continue to love others, especially the weak, the poor.

"I only want to do your will."

Keep doing as you are.

"How will I know?"

Pray, and notice my presence.

"In the Church?"

In the prison too.

"I love you, Father."

When you stand before them, I will be with you.

"Father."

My dear son.

I continue toward the receding mist. Like a giant parachute, the sea unfurls its frothy power at my feet. Foam swamps my shoes. A gull whirls and banks into a wave, searching for food. Salty tears mix with the mist on my face. Tears of joy? Feeling held in God's embrace, I continue walking until the mist begins to rise.

The next morning, I shower and do some yoga and meditation, then dress in my black clerics and join the other priests for prayer. After a quick breakfast of granola, strawberries, and yogurt, I plan to visit Migo one more time. On the way downstairs, I check my phone. I had it set on vibrate and didn't check it the night before. Four messages and two voice mails are waiting.

Norma—"Thinking of you, praying for you, give me a call."

Dina—"Padre, I'm saving you a seat between me and Gloria."

My Provincial Superior—"Zach, call me."

Penny—"We love you."

A voice message from the chancery number—"Zach, even if you dodge the implication that you're romantically involved with this guy, there are other infidelities to your vows that can be leaked. The media loves that stuff."

Peter! Ohmygod, the recording! And my own voice—"You wouldn't dare. That's confidential information you know from our support group."

And at last, a message from Steve that makes me smile. "Remember, if you need someone at your back, I've got my knife."

CHAPTER TWENTY-TWO

It's almost 3 p.m. when I get to 3 Upper Block of Otis Bateman. It's just before shift change. I need to see Migo today. His day in court is finally upon us and I want to know if he is ready. The line of blue-uniformed correctional officers is backed up, waiting. All of them, mostly Black men and women and a few Hispanics and Anglos, are joking with each other as they head into another day's work.

Two officers, a male and a female, are frisking the others, making comments about their bodies, the stuff in their pockets, "What's that bulge?" Admiring their hair styles and colors. Laughing loudly. The women bat their fake eyelashes while sniffing contempt. The men grunt and guffaw in a kind of game. All of them have this lingo of their own, with occasional suggestive remarks, including facial grimaces and bodily gestures that usually keep me and the other employees at arm's length.

"Shee-it, you think I give a f*** what he thinks? . . . Oh, sorry, Chaplain . . . You ain't gonna work another late shift for that bitch, are ya?"

Mostly I've come to see this as a way the African Americans deal with the pain and degradation of working in a city prison, locking people up and screaming at them, especially at their own race. Brothers and sisters who for the most part the C.O.s want to distance themselves from but really can't. Seventy percent of the inmates are Black, at least in part because the crack cocaine laws are much more severe than the cocaine laws that white folks break.

"Chaplain, he needs help . . . Some are beyond help . . . What? . . . Hey, Baby Girl . . . Forgive me Father, they led me on."

Perhaps because of these disparities in the law, deep down the C.O.s must feel pity for the inmates that they can rarely show or it'll be used against them. Maybe even make them vulnerable to be attacked or fired or seen as just an empty uniform by their fellow C.O.s. As I watch, I'm envious of their camaraderie, remembering the old days when I felt this with my brother priests.

There's no way I am going to sneak through that lineup and get thru four electronic doors to get to 3 Upper on time for this shift, so I wait. After all the C.O.s get through, the door clangs shut. A middle-aged female C.O. starts to pat me down as I step forward.

"Hi Father."

"Hi," I glance at her name badge. Martinez, probably Catholic, I think. When the pale green metal door bangs open again, I slide through it. While I wait for the inner door, I wonder what it will be like when Migo is sent upstate for a long stretch. As it will be for his family, it will be almost impossible for me to visit him four to six hours away.

When I finally get through the gauntlet into the protective custody area, the officer whom I have a hunch is antireligious shoots me a bored look. I poke my head further into the cramped cage of his office. He's been playing solitaire on the battered computer on his desk though he has a full view through the bulletproof glass of the eighty or so cells on two levels.

"Chaplain Braxton," I announce with a verve they respect, even though he sees me often. "I'm here to see Migo." I read aloud his inmate number. Automatically I offer my badge for him to check. He squints to read it, and sizes me up with a stare.

"We're about to feed them now."

An inmate is mopping the space with a horrendously gagging disinfectant to keep it clean for the trays of food, trash bins, hampers, and other items coming or going, stacked in the passageway. The officer surveys this scene and hesitates before halfheartedly pointing a finger toward the upper tier. "He's in cell 187 if you want to go up."

The C.O.'s invitation goads me to move. Except in an emergency, or when I was very new and didn't know any better, rarely did I visit an inmate at his cell. This is both for their privacy and for safety sake. Maybe on this shift it is different. Besides, it's crucial that I speak with Migo today.

Up the stairs I go, two at a time, passing a few inmates as I make a beeline directly to Migo's cell. The thick metal door is locked. For a second I stand there, glancing through the 4"x 6" barred window. I don't want to intrude, yet I'm intrigued to get a glimpse of Migo's small world again. Only on my first visit did I encounter him this way. I peek into the semidarkness. He's seated on his bed in a pair of long johns.

Spotting me in the window, his face lights up. Was he meditating? Jumping up, he moves quickly to the window. "Zach! What a surprise."

My grin mirrors his. I thrust my hand through the window bars to shake his. I notice the small desk with a few books, his journals and poetry. The toilet with no lid. A dank smell too. No air or plants. Nothing to give life.

"What's up?" he asks. His eager brown face presses against the bars. His lips, eyes, the bright teeth bared in a grin—or is it a sneer—I take it all in, so happy to see my son, my brother-friend as he refers to me.

"Sorry to be busting in on you like this, I wanted to see you." Stealing a look at his lithe torso, his thighs, solid against the restraint of the long johns, I turn aside shyly.

"It's all right, but I can put my coveralls on if you want."

"No, don't bother. I'm only going to stay a minute. Tell me, are you all set for Wednesday?" The sudden mention of his day in court crashes through our joy.

"As ready as I'll ever be. I'm actually glad to get it over with. You coming, Zach?" His eyes widen with hope.

"Yes. I'll be there. Nine o'clock, right?"

"Yes. Great. They wake us up at three-thirty though."

"Oh man." I remember what I heard about how inmates due in court are awakened in the middle of the night, taken in chains by prison bus to the criminal court downtown, left together in a holding room with no chairs, and given a peanut butter sandwich.

Finally called if their case is ready, they are returned to the jail in late afternoon. All of this regimen can stretch out for months if they have a jury trial. But Migo has made his plea deal so his sentencing will be just before a judge.

"I'm glad to get it over with, no matter what happens."

"Did you tell your lawyer that Father Alan abused you fourteen years ago?" I whisper, not wanting to be overheard by the inmates coming and going.

"No. It'll make things worse, prove that I intended it." Then a confession from this mostly upbeat guy, "Father Zach, I'm scared."

"I bet."

"I know I did something horrible. I killed a man, even if he harmed me." I notice the scar above his eyebrow.

"What are you afraid of?"

"The future. All those years locked away, and maybe that I'll never be forgiven."

I wait, not wanting to take him off the pain yet, his need for God in a place I cannot touch.

"Zach, I was at my lowest then. I was living with my father and couldn't hold a job. My father kept telling me I was no good. I was on drugs, crack, trying to numb the pain, the loneliness. The loneliness, I never felt it so bad, and no one cared. There was no one I could talk to about it, no one to share my feelings with. I was never so lonely in my life."

I nod my head like I understand.

"I was filled with pain and confusion. It could've been anybody. I even wanted to take my own life and looked up ways to do it on the Internet, but I wasn't brave enough. I had been arrested for a robbery and was on house arrest. I didn't know what my future was." He waits as I listen to what the judge should hear.

"When I discovered that Father Alan was abusing some kids in his parish, I couldn't stop remembering how he did that to me. When me and Chooch went to confront him that day, in no way did we plan to kill him, but all my anger came rushing out. I wound up giving him all the pain I felt in myself."

I imagine this strong young man standing in front of someone who abused him. Something snaps and all the anger of a beaten-up childhood comes pouring out. "I bet ninety percent of the guys in here have stories about their hidden rage pouring out of them like this," I say. I'm searching, trying desperately to make sense out of this for him and for me. Also, the images of his rage make me a little scared for myself.

"You know what gets me the most," he says, "Father Alan's sister, Bea. She was like a mother to me. When we went over to their house the day after the murder, she was crying so bad. She came up to me and asked, 'Do you know anything about who killed my brother? Did you have anything to do with it?'"

He pauses, takes a deep breath. "I hugged her and told her no. I was like Judas, giving a hiss-kiss. I feel most regretful about that."

"A hiss-kiss," I repeat, picturing Judas' betrayal of Jesus. I watch Migo's lips curl into a mournful twist. He'll have to live with this. Hopefully he won't give up hope like Judas did.

Backing up a few paces further into the cell, he falls silent.

I peer into the gloom toward him, then peek back over my shoulder. I catch sight of a prisoner in a cell across the balcony. His light bulb is on, his silhouette framed in the barred window. Has he been watching us? Over the railing down on the ground floor, I hear the food trays being distributed. The TV blares out some prison show. Guys yak on the public phones. Others play cards. Over all of this, a vague body odor mixed with disinfectant hangs on the walls. Shifting my head sideways to the control booth, I notice that it is dimly lit. The C.O. is engrossed in solitaire.

Turning back to Migo, I glimpse his shadow a few paces back in his cell. Our breathing is in synch. My left hand rests at the window. Like a vine unfurling in the spring, it begins to reach through the bars. I want so much to assure my son of the Father's love for him. Slowly I reach out to him, my palm upturned chest high. Only silence. The commotion below dies down.

A crazy thought comes. The memory of a religious order in history where the monks take the place of captured slaves. I break the silence. "I'm an old goat, Migo. You've got so much of your life to live yet compared to me. If I could, I'd switch places with you. I wish I could say something so you could get a lighter sentence."

Is that sniffling? Inside the six-by-ten-foot cell, he hovers back in the shadows. I try to imagine what he's feeling. Will we ever be this close again? Like God's hand toward Adam, my hand curls open for him. No response.

Maybe I won't be able to see him after he is sentenced. I can offer him a ritual to remember. He knows it's the way we often say goodbye at the end of our visits. "Want to pray?"

Silence except for my breathing. A slight movement. Soon the feel of his hand on mine. Warm. Pulsing. Blood to blood. Suddenly both of his hands grip mine in the darkness. I'm almost ready to cry out in fright, but instead it hits me with wonder: Migo's caressing my hand.

As much to spiritualize the sensation as to prolong it, I start to pray. "Father-God, look down on this dear son of yours. He's about to be sentenced like your Son, Jesus, was long ago. Standing before a judge with his whole young life hanging in the balance, please hear his sorrow and forgive him any sins he's committed."

"Please, Father-God." His hands squeeze mine.

"Let the judge see in his eyes the eyes of your Son. And give him the humility and courage that Jesus had to accept what comes. But if possible, please give him another chance. In Jesus' name I pray." Somewhere a door clangs.

In response to my prayer comes a gift I could never have imagined. From this murderer whom I've come to love, from this young man whose lips I enjoy seeing curled in a smile comes a kiss. A kiss, tender and innocent as though from a baby, presses against the knuckle of my hand. Like the touch of God's lips, like a . . . that's when I hear footsteps behind me.

"Back up, chaplain!" The correctional officer grips my arm roughly and pulls it through the bars. "What's going on here? And you . . . " his evil eye shoots through the bars at Migo, "I warned you before. You're dead!"

CHAPTER TWENTY-THREE

From the front seat of my car, I watch the C.O.s stream through the parking lot for the next shift as they chat on their phones. I'm still shaking from the encounter at Migo's cell. Though the C.O. acted so triumphant, and with a wicked grin wrote my badge number down for his report, I want to take it as the action of an overzealous C.O. In case he presses forward to make an issue out of it for either of us, I even have damaging info on him from the earlier time he threatened Migo.

I retrieve my phone from the glove compartment where I had stashed it earlier. Something about the sheer numbers of C.O.s makes me decide to contact Norma. I text her and leave a brief sketch of what happened. She responds before I'm out of the parking lot. "Zach import u write detail descrip of what happ. Send 2 me. Keep low-key if poss. Love, n."

When I get home, I email a more in-depth report to her, leaving out the fact that Migo kissed my hand. Why blow the thing out of proportion? Good Lord, it never stops. I add a P.S. "I need to talk. Can we take a walk tomorrow?" Ten minutes later, her message comes back: "Yes. Meet in Tuckahoe parking lot at 2. Love, N."

As soon as I pull into the parking lot, Norma's bumper sticker catches my eye. A few years ago she introduced me to this lovely paved trail that meanders like a snake through the woods on the banks of the Bronx River in Westchester County.

In the springtime, swans glide like royalty on small ponds linked by the river, a stream really, that gurgles over pretty waterfalls and then calms down enough for an egret to stalk for its lunch under the rustic footbridges. Bicyclers and joggers pump themselves up beneath lofty elms and maples, oblivious to the sound of the occasional Amtrak train speeding by this Eden in the City. Sometimes they're oblivious to walkers like Norma and me.

With her hair pulled to the side in a new style, Norma sneaks a smoke as she sits with the car windows rolled down. We wave as I drive past her in search of a parking place. As I approach her moments later, she's leaning against her car in her black slacks and top. She dresses in black for these outings because she's always fighting "my weight," as she calls it, except when she occasionally feels daring in the summer and wears her white tennis skirt. She notices me and drops the cigarillo on the pavement, squashing it with her sandal.

"Hi darling." She's been calling me this for the past year.

"Hi." Quickly we reach to smooch, her chin tilting up so I won't smudge her lipstick.

A smile lights up her face. Norma's love is her main gift to the world, not just for me but for everyone. The Mother of All Captives.

"Don't you look sharp," she says. "Shall we walk toward Tuckahoe or Bronxville?" She tucks her car keys into her cleavage.

"It doesn't matter." I shrug.

"It's Tuckahoe then." As we watch the traffic zoom by, I grasp her hand. We hurry across and then I let go.

Something seems different about her. The hairdo? A tone in her voice?

"Did you get my email?" I ask as we dodge a bicyclist careening toward us.

"Yes, and I think I get the picture. But tell me why the officer was so upset." Her gaze focuses on the trail.

"Migo and I were actually praying about court tomorrow. Our hands touched through the cell window."

"Is that all?" She searches my face for a reaction.

"To be honest, that wasn't all." I stop in my tracks. "He kissed me."

"What?" Her eyebrows shoot up.

"My hand! He kissed my hand, Norma." Shaking my head at how provocative it sounds, I pull her off the trail so a guy walking a bulldog with its tongue hanging out can pass us.

"You didn't include that in the report." She frowns.

"Norma," I thrust my face down close to hers, "do you really think anyone reading that report will think that a kiss is innocent?"

"Well no, but . . . " She starts to walk again.

"It'll create a controversy that's ridiculous, and this right before his trial. What mystifies me is what was on the C.O.'s mind, barging up on us like that. I'm not sure what he saw, but I'm certainly not going to put in the report that Migo kissed my hand. They'll never understand."

"Understand what?"

"That Migo and I are just friends. I love him like a son."

"Oh Zach, we're in the middle of a national uproar over sexual abuse. You're a priest. All of you are suspect, so a kiss on the hand won't be seen as innocent because you're his chaplain."

"Norma, I'd never use my chaplain's position to harm people, and I'm celibate."

"It doesn't matter. You've got a power position over him, even if he is behind bars."

"Hmmmmm." I picture how I often hold hands with the male and female inmates when we pray, how I place my hands on their heads when they ask for a blessing, and the occasional shoulder bumps at the Kiss of Peace, all of this overseen by the C.O.s and the other inmates.

"The prison environment, with all the rules and locks and bars, permits a closeness between us that isn't so easy with people on the outside," I say. An Amtrak train roars by and we turn to watch until it passes.

"Right, and these rules protect both of you . . . unless you reach through the bars," she says with a smirk.

"Unlike the inmates, I have inner restraints too," I say. "Most of them are in jail because they don't have such discipline. They never learned to internalize the rules, and it isn't just about sexuality. It's about many of their impulses."

"I agree. So don't put the kiss part in your report." We walk separately for a while, occasionally bumping against each other lightly as we gaze at the trees and the stream until Norma says, "Is that what celibacy is for you, an inner restraint?"

"I suppose." I smile at her curiosity, a curiosity others might have about priests' sexuality too, but rarely mention.

"Priests are strange with their celibacy rule. It doesn't matter whether you are straight or gay. It's like you have protective bars around you that keep women at a distance. Keep men at a distance too."

I feel the pain of this distance. "Well that doesn't stop my imagination. If a fantasy does come up about someone, I brush it away, especially if it is someone I am involved with in a pastoral way.

"So what do you do with it on lonely nights?" We're walking side by side and she turns to look directly at me.

"Acknowledge it to myself for one thing. People don't understand. They think because we take a vow of chastity once in our lives that our sexual drives evaporate. I try to channel these feelings into ministry and friendships, and especially into my relationship with God." We watch a squirrel chase another up a tree.

"Doesn't it ever get to be too much? In the springtime, don't you want to have someone?" She waves her hands toward the trees.

"Sure." I glance behind me, not wanting to be overheard. "Sometimes I feel like screaming on a moonlit night, Norma, and it's not just in springtime." I place my index finger over her mouth. "Shhhh! Let's just enjoy the scenery, okay?"

"Okay." We stroll until we spot a small footbridge ahead that we've stood on before, and we head toward it. Leaning over a rail covered with scribbled initials, we watch the swirling pools below. Norma leans down and picks up a pebble and tosses it into the stream below us. As it sinks, the ripples spread out towards the shore.

"I suppose sexuality is involved in all of our relationships," she says.
"Yeah."
"Maybe I'm jealous of your feelings for Migo."

"Norma, I have fond feelings for you too. Can't you trust that I love you and him? C'mere." Slowly I pull her hand up and kiss it. Her eyes fill as I watch her briefly. Then, wanting to avoid getting mushy, I look back down at the stream.

Both of us watch the stream in silence as the traffic rushes by on the parkway. The sun starts to fade behind the trees. Norma begins to say something, but stops, then starts back on the trail. I don't follow immediately.

When I see her pause in front of a tall sycamore, I hurry to catch up. At our feet a bed of early-blooming hyacinths pokes out of the roots.

"Ooooh Zach, look. They're intoxicating." She stoops to smell them. I bend down beside her. Together we breathe in the fragrance.

"It's getting late," I say as a train's horn sounds, "and there's something I almost forgot to tell you."

When she stands, I say as nonchalantly as I can, "I believe Peter has a tape recording of our last conversation at the chancery. When I testify tomorrow, he could use that to blackmail me with the Cardinal, especially if my testimony implicates him."

Her mouth drops open as she covers her heart with her hand. "God help us. When will this stop?"

"When we're not afraid to be real."

We listen to the traffic and birds and trains all woven together in their suburban concert. In a while Norma says, "Let me worry about the tape."

A duck quacks below us and I turn to watch it. When I turn back, I notice that Norma's usual smile has vanished. "Zach. . ." There's an odd sound in her voice. "I need to tell you something too."

"Tell me something?"

"You'll hate me. I'm such a damn fool. I don't know what possessed me." Her hands go to her face.

A tremor goes through me.

"I didn't want you to get hurt tomorrow, Zach . . . " Her voice is low and strangled. Her eyes plead as her hands squeeze mine. "so I spoke to the C.O. beforehand."

My jaw drops in horror. My breathing stops. Pulling away, I back up a step. *Oh God, my friend, my darling, a scorpion!*

Suddenly spooked, the ducks take off.

"I wanted . . . I only wanted to protect you," she stutters. A shadow of fear darts across her face. A chasm opens up between us.

"Protect me!" I spit out the words like venom. "Protect me from what?" The wind suddenly swirls the leaves around us like ghosts.

"From harming yourself." It's her little girl's voice. "I'm afraid for you, Zach, that your priesthood will be destroyed tomorrow. I wanted to stop you somehow . . . please, please understand."

"From harming myself or from being myself!" I begin waving my hands.

"I wasn't thinking, don't you see? I was blinded by my need to help you."

"Do me a favor, will you? Stop trying to run my life! I can take care of myself." My voice is a dagger, severing the cord between us.

Norma's face flushes beet red. I watch tears roll down her cheeks. She sobs softly as I glare at her with disgust. I'll never be able to trust her again.

People pass by on the footpath. Some glance our way. Most keep chatting or listening to their iPods. I stare at the ground.

When I can't bear the agony anymore, I take a step toward her. She makes little gestures as though to push me away. She continues to cry, the tears dripping onto her black sweater. In a while I reach for her shoulder.

Traffic whizzes by and a bird tweets from the trees. I remember a bench we passed a little earlier. "Let's go over there," I point. Grasping her hand, moist from the tears, we lurch like two beggars toward a home base.

We sit side by side in silence, mostly just watching rivulets in the stream or an occasional bird or squirrel hop nearby. The backs of our hands touch up against each other. It feels like the hand of a stranger.

At one point, she turns slightly toward me. The sun is behind her. In the shadows, her face looks wrecked but somehow even endearing.

"Forgive me, please Zach?"

Forgive! That word, that cry so necessary in this world of conflict. That challenge, which I so easily foster in others. It's my turn now.

But I can't. She screwed me. She set me up to be seen as an abuser. Migo is screwed now too. Even if I forgive somehow, I'll never forget this. Half numb, I try to speak but words won't come.

Just a tiny peek from her before she murmurs, "I'm afraid I'll lose your friendship . . . and I'd die without it."

My wall is up and she sees it. Except for the sounds of the traffic, we sit in stony silence. I watch the shadowy patterns on the path. "We better get back to our cars before dusk," I finally say while standing. Norma looks up warily. We begin to walk briskly back toward the parking lot, each alone with our bitter thoughts.

Before retiring, I strip down to my underwear. Lighting the oil lamp in front of my Jesus icon, I sit on a cushion and twist my legs into the lotus position. Jesus's stern face looks out at me.

Closing my eyes, I try to let my mind go blank. Honking cars from the street pull for my attention, as do my feelings about Norma's betrayal. Soon my legs hurt. I shift, releasing one leg a little.

I long for a sense of deep stillness, of security and peace in the silent presence of God. I need this, especially for court tomorrow. As I often do, I simply wait for this presence. It can't be forced. Breathe in, breathe out . . .

Twenty minutes later, my body and mind still haven't fallen silent. The warm, peaceful feeling that usually comes over me is missing. I hear a toilet flush. The oil lamp flickers and a whiff of scent tickles my nose. The knot inside my chest is still there. Glancing up, I see the crucifix on my wall, the one I stained with black shoe polish to show Christ's love for prisoners, the one with Migo's eagle feather taped to Jesus' hand. I whisper, "Here's to Three Feathers, ready or not."

It's the same crucifix that I took from Peter's room when he left the seminary over thirty years ago. How is it possible that we were friends back then? His voice comes back to me.

I'm going to out you as a gay priest to the Church and to the media . . . including your involvement with your inmate friend.

Any accusation against me now, and I'll be presumed guilty until proven innocent. Who will believe me? I better shut up. But if I really want to help abuse victims, I've got to break out of this prison of silence.

We have to close ranks or they'll destroy us.

I am part of the Church hierarchy, part of the system that should have been keeping watch out for the wolves among us. We let the lambs be stolen. I feel responsible somehow.

And you're getting involved in this now? Let it play out.

All this silence in the Church—about AIDS, about speaking out about women's ordination, about the presence of gay and lesbian people in our midst, about sexual abuse and its coverup—a thousand voices crying out to be heard.

Don't betray the brotherhood.

I'm furious that I'm trapped in this position, caught between the bishops and the people. I don't want to betray the Church, Jesus, or my brother Sebastians.

Don't betray yourself!

Therefore do not be afraid of them. For there is nothing concealed that will not be disclosed, and nothing hidden that will not be made known. What I tell you in darkness, speak it in the light; and what you hear whispered, preach it on the housetops.

—Matthew 10:26-7

CHAPTER TWENTY-FOUR

1987—

I t's the Sunday when Dignity/New York celebrates its last liturgy at St. Francis Xavier Church in Greenwich Village, a time I am angry in a way I've never experienced before. The whole congregation is angry, yet it is one of the best liturgies I've ever participated in. There is all this rage that we are never supposed to feel as Christians, let alone show, and we are doing so together at a "Mass of Expulsion."

In October, 1986, the Halloween Letter, as it is called by the gay community, is issued by the Vatican Congregation for the Doctrine of the Faith, headed up by Cardinal Ratzinger. This document, officially named "Pastoral Care of Homosexual Persons," describes homosexual inclinations as "objectively disordered." It also concludes that Church premises cannot be used to foster any pastoral activities that do not support this teaching.

A few months later, Cardinal O'Connor of New York issued a directive to the pastor of St. Francis, ordering him to stop permitting Dignity to use Church facilities for their ministry. The new Vatican document shows clearly that Dignity contradicts Church teaching on homosexuality, he is told.

It doesn't seem to matter to the cardinal that this group of hundreds of gay and lesbian Catholics and their friends have worshipped at the parish every Sunday night for over ten years, or that they are being devastated by AIDS. The Church must keep its image publicly pure, so gay and lesbian Catholics who disagree with its teachings are expendable.

I can still hear the chanting. A festive, almost pregnant, spirit causes an electric current to pass between us as we greet each other on arrival. St. Francis Xavier Parish is filled to overflowing with a thousand men, women, and children; married couples, parents, siblings, friends of gay and lesbian people, black and Hispanic people, clergy, and laity.

Most of us sense that this is one of those historic moments that happens only a couple of times in your life: when your beliefs go on record; when you experience the cost of discipleship, even though you won't know until eternity whether you were right or not. There is a palpable sense of community that can only be felt when you are under siege.

I begin to vest along with the dozen or so other priests who are concelebrating, including some from our support group. Up to this point, I've kept a low profile in the Archdiocese, preferring to offer private support for gay Catholics and be available for counseling. I haven't joined the other priests, mostly members of religious orders, who regularly celebrate the weekly liturgy for Dignity at the church.

Even though some photographer might snap a picture and send it to the cardinal, I tell myself that it is worth the risk to be part of such a historical witness of faith. As an officially ordained representative of our Church for twenty years, I can't bear to hide in the shadows while the gay community is booted into the streets in the name of Jesus Christ.

Two parts of the service engrave themselves on my heart. The first is John McNeill's speech, which he delivers during the Rite of Expulsion that follows the Mass. John, who is the godfather of the Roman Catholic gay and lesbian movement, is a Jesuit priest who was forced out of his religious society a few months earlier because of his refusal to remain silent any longer about his positive teaching on homosexuality.

During his speech, a rhythmic chant from the congregation begins. Low and erratic at first, it gradually flowers into a full-throated communal shout that fills the enormous church up to its rafters as though intent on reaching God's ears. "We are the Church! We are the Church!" The refrain booms off the Gothic columns and stained glass windows.

It is as though we can't help but remind ourselves and the absent cardinal that the Church, no matter how grand and beautiful, is not just a building, nor is it the private possession of a few righteous people.

We shout to let everyone know that the Church isn't only the Vatican or the bishops, but includes all of us who are baptized. Finally we are getting to the core of the Gospel: Christ died for all of us and lives in all of us, especially those who are considered sinners.

For me to raise my voice in Church is frightening, especially because I hear my anger in the group's passion. I hear my own anger, swirling all around me and inside me. Some people in the crowd raise their fists. The roar grows louder until it seems that we all might burst.

Our rage comes out, a rage that is usually buried deep inside. This rage, at God or the bishops—it doesn't matter—severs the umbilical cord that links our sense of self-worth to someone else's approval. Excited at the release of anger, I feel free.

Standing around the altar with the other priests, I realize what an important moment in our history this is, especially because we are doing this not just as individuals, but as a community of faith who has just received the Eucharist. It seems unbelievable to me and I smile across at McNeill.

At the conclusion of the ceremony, the second unforgettable memory engraves itself on my heart. The congregation takes this new understanding of ourselves out of the Church building where we've been nourished for so long and carries it into the city streets. It is one of the saddest and yet most inspiring moments of my history as a Catholic priest.

The pastor, a young Jesuit priest, is at the podium describing the sequence of events that led up to this expulsion. He and his Jesuit superiors begged the cardinal to understand how his action would deeply wound the Catholic community at St. Francis Xavier, but he wouldn't budge.

"I told the cardinal that the gay and lesbian Catholics are fully incorporated members of our parish," he says. "They serve as lectors and Eucharistic ministers, work in the soup kitchen, and as home visitors for the elderly." He fights back tears as he explains this to the congregation.

"As pastor, I am under the cardinal's authority," he tells us. "I have no choice. I have to let Dignity go."

"No! No!" the congregation cries out.

At this moment, a female member of the parish council approaches the lectern. Leaning in to the mike, she says in a halting voice, "I can no longer be part of such proceedings. Cardinal O'Connor is dividing Christ's Body. I'm resigning from the council."

The congregation applauds her.

At this point, John McNeill invites the entire congregation to stand. The paschal candle, which represents Christ's triumph over death at Easter, stands like a pillar of strength in the sanctuary before a fifty-foot sheet of purple cloth that cascades from the ceiling to the floor. To symbolize that we are united in one baptism, he invites us all to light our candles from the paschal candle.

Meanwhile, the lights in the Church are gradually extinguished until only a single spotlight shines on the purple cloth. The Easter candle and the thousand little candles lit from it spread the Light of Christ into the darkest corners of the Church.

Drumming begins behind us, a rolling cadence that synchronizes with the pounding of our hearts. Solemnly we turn and follow the drummers out of the Church into the streets, while above us the organ pumps out "We Shall Overcome." Tentatively at first, hardly knowing what to do next, the procession begins to sing the civil rights hymn.

In the streets of Greenwich Village, hundreds of gay and lesbian Catholics march abreast toward Sixth Avenue, headed to the Gay Community Center, which will be our future home for liturgies.

I look back with others to see the Church door darkened. St. Francis Xavier, the gay community's place of worship in New York, is now a sorry-looking shell. Its life-blood is pouring out because the bishops can't see past dogmas to the people they are meant to serve.

My anger turns to sorrow, even then despair as I watch my candle flicker and almost die out in the night breeze. As I guard it alongside McNeill and the other priests, our eyes are drawn upward. Many people in the apartment windows are gazing down at us. Even though many of them have no time for the Church and its homophobia and hypocrisy, they sympathize with our position.

On a balcony, I watch a young man in a black tank top flash a thumbs-up sign. It gives me hope. A small voice echoes within me, *We are the Church! We are the Church!* Meanwhile the drums roll, *But you're out! You're out! You're out!*

CHAPTER TWENTY-FIVE

Bronx Supreme Court 2004—

Finally, it's here. Migo's day in court. The sun is streaking the apartment houses pink when I awake, while my belly tumbles over and over as it did half the night. My son, my brother, my friend, only twenty-nine years old and his life, his youth, will be gone.

I approach the court building and weave in and out through a throng of people streaming toward the revolving doors. For the most part they are Black or Latino, representing the poorer, rougher edge of the city. The ones whose neighborhoods are rampant with competing gangs, few jobs, broken families, violence, trauma, drugs, and the crime that flows from this.

Cops and lawyers, mostly white, are mixed together in this crowd. We're told to remove our belts, all electronic devices, metal objects, keys, wallets, coins, and assorted paraphernalia and place them in baskets where they are sent through the metal detectors. We're reminded of the dangerous world we live in as we're sandwiched up against each other in the elevator. It zips us to the third floor with the victim and offender families, indistinguishable unless you happen to know them.

I'm early, but already a few policemen and court employees are milling about. Some of the family members, a few of them holding babies, begin to hover near the doorway to the courtrooms. No one I recognize, though in my black priest garb I get a few nods. Tingling with fear and even some excitement to have finally gotten to this day, I take a seat on a long stone bench outside the courtroom.

Peter's phone message is still on my mind. *There are other infidelities to your vows that can be leaked. The media loves that stuff . . .* and my retort,

You wouldn't dare. Closing my eyes, I take slow deep breaths. I need to calm down, link with the Holy Spirit, *Do not be afraid, I am with you.* I also try to link with Migo who's in a cell down below somewhere.

"David Colfax. Migo Robinson's lawyer." A chubby guy with a mustache and what looks like dyed hair breaks into my prayer. He offers his hand, palm down.

The whole saga flashes before me: the arguments with Peter, Dina's pleading, Sophie's encouragement, Norma's betrayal, and Migo's last look. I grip the attorney's hand, "Father Zachary Braxton."

"Pleased to meet you, Father. Are you prepared to speak?"

I swallow hard. "Yes."

"Fine." He gives me a riveting stare. "Just don't say anything that offends the other side."

I try to figure out what this means as he moves away. Something about him makes me uneasy.

A little later, Dina arrives with her partner. There are a few other family members I don't know, ones I've seen in family pictures.

"This is Gloria. I told you about her."

An attractive woman with short blonde hair, a little older than Dina, shakes my hand with the tips of her fingers.

"And Eddie, my cousin," she motions to a gawky pimply-faced teenager behind her, "This is Father Zach."

The kid's sullen brown eyes scan me up and down. My outstretched hand hangs in the air.

"You ready, Padre?" Dina mumbles into my ear as we hug.

"Yes."

"Me too. The family's counting on us."

We sit on the bench and wait, silent, perhaps praying. My legs are trembling. Soon we are ushered in. As the heavy doors are swung open, you'd think we were entering a church: pews in the back where the families sit, a lectern for witnesses, a jury box, a court reporter's station, two long tables, one for the prosecution, and one for the defense, and above all of this, a raised polished-wood dais up front where the judge presides. Like a priest, I think.

Both sides of the crime sit in the same row only ten feet apart. I'm between Dina and Gloria. Cousin Eddie is slouched on the other side of Dina. I take a peek at two distraught women down at the other end of the bench. One is the murdered priest's mother, Dina tells me, the other his sister. The double tragedy strikes me. Suddenly it occurs to me that I'm not really neutral in the way I'm sitting. The two families may not be looking at each other, but I can. I do. Butterflies swirl in my stomach.

Soon Migo appears. Led in by a court officer, he's dressed in a long underwear shirt with beltless khaki pants. Corn rows crown his head. The officer hovers beside him. With only a split second to search for his family, he quickly scans the room. I don't catch his gaze. From now on we will only see his back.

Double doors up front suddenly spring open. "All rise," the court clerk's voice booms.

The judge sweeps into his perch above us with his black gown flowing behind him like a penguin. He looks determined, yet something about his manner appears kind. "Please be seated," he says. He welcomes the prosecutor, Alexandra Banores, and the defense attorney, David Colfax, by name.

"We are here today for the sentencing of Mr. Migo Robinson, following a hearing on March 11, 2004, in which the defendant pled guilty to second degree murder in the death of Alan Ferber." That he is a Catholic priest goes unsaid yet hangs in everyone's mind because of the public controversy.

I stare at the back of Migo's neck. No emotion visible from this son I've learned to love. *Oh God, help him.*

Dina grips my knee as the prosecutor describes how it happened, "In the course of a robbery, battered to death with a baseball bat, multiple blows that left the victim's face unrecognizable, left for dead." For the first time since he confessed to me, I consciously look at Migo as a murderer. My heart freezes.

The priest was Migo's pastor, I recall. Father Al to everyone. Known to Migo's family for over fifteen years. Both families weep as the stark facts are read. This is the first time I've heard the horrifying details. "The arc of the bat goes up . . . comes crashing down." I feel like throwing up.

The judge continues, "I've relied on the sentencing guidelines of New York State, the Presentence Report prepared by the Department of Prisons, the defendant's prior record, and any additional information submitted by the prosecution and the defense." He peers down at them, the prosecutor a slim and surprisingly young woman in a navy blue power suit with straight auburn hair cascading to her shoulders, the defense attorney middle-aged and stocky in his tweed jacket with a mustache that hides his lips.

"The sentencing guidelines for second degree murder are a maximum of twenty-five years to life in New York State. This is my direction in light of the defendant taking responsibility for his actions that led to the death of Alan Ferber. In addition to the Presentence Report, I have received numerous requests from both sides, asking for more severe or lenient sentencing. These include letters from the victim's family and his parishioners as well as fellow priests; also letters from the defendant's family and friends, including one from his grade-school teacher."

My mind begins to blur as these legal intricacies wash over the courtroom. It is as though we are speaking about someone I don't know.

"What are your recommendations?" the judge asks the prosecutor.

Ms. Banores slides around her table. A slight smile appears on her lips before she looks over her rimless glasses. First she acknowledges the judge, "Your honor," then a nod to the rest of us, lingering momentarily on the victims' side. Moving methodically to take her place at the lectern, she folds her arms, as much to contain herself as to be combative. A last minute side-glance toward Migo, who stares straight ahead, completes her ritual. *Oh God, this is really happening.*

"Your honor, there have been accusations in the media against the deceased victim, Fr. Alan Ferber, allegations that he sexually abused certain individuals. These unfounded allegations occurred over six years ago, exceeding the statute of limitations. The victim was never charged, and on the contrary, Fr. Ferber was a blameless and holy man. Therefore, I ask the court to ignore these allegations of abuse history in the presentence report."

What a crock! They expect abuse victims to get over their trauma in five years?

"Duly noted." The judge jots on his pad.

Stroking her hair back, she recaps the crime and its effect on Father Alan's family and loved ones: "Horrible crime, heinous nature, unprovoked. The defendant is a danger to society."

I watch Migo's shoulders slump ever so slightly. "Unprovoked, my ass!" Dina stage whispers into my ear. We trade glances as the judge stares down toward us.

The prosecutor finishes her address. "The state recommends the maximum sentence, twenty-five years to life."

The judge makes notes again. "Anything else?"

"No, your honor." At Migo's age, that sentence may as well be the death penalty.

"Mr. Colfax, what does the defense recommend?"

He rises, twirling the edge of his mustache. Nodding to the judge, he strolls back and forth between the judge and the gallery. With his hands clasped behind him, he begins in a raspy and sincere voice: "Your honor, as you can see, accusations against the victim have surfaced since his death that throw into question his moral character. These involve serial sexual abuse of young people who trusted him." He pauses for this horror to sink in, glancing back at the gallery. "And whose parents trusted him too."

"No!" a voice from the priest's family erupts.

The judge glares. "There will be no interruptions. If this continues, you will be asked to leave the courtroom." Some low weeping sounds trail off. "Continue Mr. Colfax."

"We know that the statute of limitations were exceeded, but these young people have been traumatized by this abuse. They are just now coming forward. Due to the present law, they cannot have their voices heard in this courtroom, but you can listen to them your honor, and take this history into consideration regardless. Rather than my client being a threat to society then, the unfortunate victim was a threat." Gasps from the victim's family. The judge glares down at them again.

"I wish to respectfully recommend leniency in your sentencing of my client based on this new information and the following additional factors: that Mr. Robinson has been exemplary during his time waiting for his sentencing, that his prior criminal record has been nonviolent, and that the extent of his young life ahead of him offers the court an opportunity for mercy."

"Why should these new allegations make your client any less guilty?" the judge asks.

Momentarily, the attorney seems stymied by this retort. I can't read Migo's posture. Dina leans into my ear and whispers, "I could tell him why."

"Your honor, I'm not suggesting that my client is any less guilty of murder. To this charge he has already confessed. But only that you take this information and other parts of the memorandum into consideration." He looks at the judge with a pleading look.

"Will that be all?"

His attorney throws a quick glance toward Migo, "Yes, your honor."

The judge scans the courtroom, probably weighing these various calls for justice and mercy and how they might be balanced.

What a helluva job. Like God's, I think, except that the judge has to face both sides. Who does he dare disappoint?

"Mr. Robinson," the judge motions for Migo to stand. "Have you and your lawyer read and discussed the presentence report?"

"Yes, your honor."

"Do you wish to say anything to the court in regard to your case?"

Shoulders slumped, trousers hanging off his butt, Migo seems to be searching for words. "I'm sorry Father Alan was killed," he says softly as he looks up. He turns slightly toward the gallery. "I'm very sorry for your loss. I know you don't believe me . . . that you must hate me . . . but I ask your forgiveness." Blinking, his glance darts toward Dina and me. "And another chance, to show you that I'm not a monster." His voice fades and he drops his head.

"Anything else?"

Migo shakes his head.

The judge gathers his papers and sits up. "Do you understand the terms of the plea agreement and do you knowingly and voluntarily agree to plead guilty to the crime described by the assistant district attorney?" he asks.

At first, silence. "Instead of the real possibility of life without parole if it goes to trial, so this is a big break," his lawyer had told him. I remember thinking when I first heard of this plan; it's like he has to stab himself in the heart.

Out of Migo's mouth tumbles a barely audible "Yes." He sits back down.

So that's it? It's all over. Whatever else happens is just for show? I glance back and forth between the two families, nervous, memorizing my testimony as best I can, still unsure.

The judge takes a swig of water. He then invites the prosecution and defense to present any witnesses.

The prosecutor's voice rings out, "I call upon Mrs. Virginia Faber, the mother of the victim."

All eyes follow a slight woman with gray hair pulled up in a bun. A hush fills the room as we follow her deliberate steps to the witness stand. There is something quite dignified about her though you can see that she's broken. Everyone looks at her except Migo.

Virginia is the mother of a priest, a prized role in her working-class neighborhood. This religious claim to fame has helped her through a rough marriage and many difficult times. Now her darling, one of God's beloveds, is not only brutally murdered but accused of being one of those despised pedophile priests: a Man of God who preyed on children; the scum of the earth; better that a millstone be hung around his neck. Gone, murdered, defamed in the media with no chance to defend himself . . . so his mother will.

"Raise your right hand. State and spell your name." She does so. "Do you solemnly swear or affirm that the testimony you are about to give will be the truth and nothing but the truth, so help you God?"

"I do, so help me God." Gazing blank-faced out at the crowd, she folds her hands on the lectern as though in prayer. "I am Virginia Faber," she begins softly, "Alan Faber's mother. Father Alan Faber." Her beaten voice gains strength as she continues. "During the past few months, my family has watched with horror the charges against my son. Sexual abuse incidents from years ago were smeared in the newspapers and on TV. How could a priest ever do such terrible things?" She pauses and stares us down with disgust, her look saying, How could you believe such things? Her voice begins to crack and she clears her throat.

"We couldn't formally challenge these charges against my son until a trial. The lawyers for the Archdiocese told us not to, you see? Think how it would feel to hear your child destroyed . . . " her voice trails off at first, then lurches back as she glares out at us, "Day after day your parishioners looking at you as a traitor, your family despised. You've got no idea. People I've known for years looking upon me as someone who raised an evil child, even someone they'd be glad to kill."

Like Migo felt? Dina grabs my hand. I search beyond her to see Eddie. With his hands jammed into his pockets, he looks like he is somewhere else. *Could he be one of them?*

At this point, Virginia turns to face her son's killer and a mother's steel heart cracks, "Migo, you came to our house. Father Alan took you on trips." The voice is plaintive, almost coaxing, like she is back at one of those family scenes. Suddenly a wild animal cry bursts from her throat, "Migo, how could you kill your priest? How could you murder your friend?" Her hands are raised in the eternal question. If Migo can't answer, maybe God will.

Stunned, no one moves. Nailed to our seats by her question, we wonder too. It could be that she screamed this only once, but it echoes in waves over us in the courtroom. In this case it is the cry of a victim's family as well as a perpetrator's. We all hold our breath.

"Thank you, Mrs. Faber. I am very sorry for your loss," says the judge. Virginia shuffles back to her seat as the journalists scribble.

"Is there anyone else?" the judge asks.

"Yes, your honor." The prosecutor turns to the assembly.

The younger woman with Virginia raises her hand and stands. She is fortyish, dressed in a gray pants suit with stylish streaked blonde hair. She waits for the judge to acknowledge her before she strides quickly to the stand, her high heels clicking like a clock of doom.

Looking directly at Migo, who is now slumped with his head down, she begins in a kind of nasal whine. "My name is Beatrice Schiavone. I am Father Alan's sister."

I recall Migo's regret, *I told her I didn't do it. It was a hiss-kiss, Father Zach.*

"Alan was my older brother and my hero. He has been a wonderful priest to so many people. Even if, and I say if because we are still innocent until proven guilty in our country, aren't we?" She turns from the lectern to eye the judge and then back to the rest of us. "Even if Father Alan committed the crimes he's accused of, why does that possibility wipe out his entire life before us and before God?" Her question stings us as she wipes tears from her eyes. "What makes sexual abusers the most hated people on earth? Tell me, worse than murderers? Many have been abused themselves, yet we gladly send them to prison where they can be abused more, or shrug it off as justice if they are killed. Even if they get out of jail, their pictures are all over the Internet and they have to live like lepers outside the city, hide under bridges like fugitives."

Focused on the bench in front of me, I picture Migo getting caught up in the stinking swirl of sexual abuse charges in prison. Abusers and the abused get morphed into one, perhaps being prey to gangs of thugs who apply their own kind of justice behind bars.

Beatrice surprises us though. Her voice becomes tender. While whining, she reveals her own desperate inability to understand and forgive this crime that cries to heaven. "Migo, every weekend, when I babysit for my granddaughter, she asks me, 'Gwammy, where Uncle Alan?'" Beatrice dabs her eyes with a tissue. "At first I made up stories to protect her . . . and you Migo. But you know what I say now? I tell her, 'Uncle Alan isn't coming back anymore, baby girl. He's never coming back.'" She pauses for what seems like a lifetime. Even Migo cocks his head briefly to look her way. At that moment she drops her curtain of pain between us, "I will never forgive you Migo. I hope you spend the rest of your life in jail." Her curse ricochets off the walls and stabs us.

Even the judge's mask of neutrality cracks for a second as Beatrice, sobbing now, strides back to her seat. So it'll be life without parole no matter what sentence you get, Migo.

The judge moves some folders. He's ready to wrap up this part. But no, the prosecutor stands. "There is one more witness, your honor. I call on Bishop Peter Mueller."

CHAPTER TWENTY-SIX

*P*eter! *What the . . . ?* I never noticed him enter the courtroom. The crowd murmurs. Slowly and confidently he strides toward the podium. I spot Norma. She must have come in with him. We haven't spoken since the argument. My eyes search hers, but they are expressionless.

I notice she's holding something up, though it's partly concealed. Her mouth is pronouncing something silently. Only when she drops her hand back down does it dawn on me. Somehow she got the tape from Peter!

"Raise your right hand. State and spell your name." He does. "Do you solemnly swear or affirm that the testimony you are about to give will be the truth and nothing but the truth, so help you God?"

"I do." A tremor in his voice.

Remember, you're swearing to God, Peter.

He folds his hands over the edge of the lectern, his purple ring evident for all to see. Clearing his throat, he smiles down at us. "My name is Peter Mueller, an auxiliary bishop of the Archdiocese of New York. I am here to speak in behalf of Father Alan Faber who is no longer able to defend himself." He pauses, letting it sink in, "despite the recent character assassinations in the media."

"Bishop Mueller," the judge interrupts, "stay focused on your own testimony on behalf of the victim, please."

Peter faces forward and continues. His voice becomes measured, like honey from the rock. "For over twenty-five years, Father Alan was a faithful priest in the Archdiocese. His parents, sister, and friends are faithful parishioners at St. Joachim's Parish. During a robbery, he was brutally murdered by this man, Mister Robinson." Peter glances quickly toward Migo and then at his ring.

Tell the truth, Peter. A bishop is supposed to represent the Church and Christ.

Peter's voice intones Jesus' cry for the poor, "My dear friends, your loss is incalculable. The Church's loss of Fr. Alan is irreplaceable as well. Yet I ask you, is it still possible for us to remember the example of Jesus at such a time?" He gives a quick look toward Beatrice and her mother. "Our Lord forgave the thief crucified next to him."

My god, he's trying to show us he's got a heart.

He raises his hands as though to implore us with this image. He nods to the judge. "However, we also know this is a court of law. We can't expect the state to simply forgive people. We have to be held accountable for our crimes." Peter hesitates as we hang between Jesus and the judge. "This court can punish, yet it can do so with mercy."

The judge's mouth twitches.

Peter goes on. "Surely the defendant knows the gravity of his action, that he has destroyed the life of a human being. And a priest of God," he adds for a punch. "With the Faber family's cries ringing in his heart today, he can weep and pay a price." Peter stands back from the lectern. He takes a deep breath. As though surprised at where his compassion is taking him, he adds, "but he can still be rehabilitated back into society at some point, can't he?" Like Pilate's wife, he's trying to keep Jesus's blood from their hands.

Gazing at the gallery he asks, "We don't have to further the violence in this city any more than is just." His magnanimity floats out over the courtroom like fog. Peter wants to soften our human instinct to retaliate. "Therefore, I respectfully ask the court to consider leniency in the sentence of Migo Robinson today."

Done. Marvelous, Peter. Mission accomplished. But were you a prosecution or defense witness? What's left for me to say now?

"Will that be all, bishop?"

"Yes, your honor."

Ever so slightly Peter bows to the judge, one authority to another, and heads back to his seat.

"The prosecution rests," says Ms. Banores.

The judge pauses, to take it all in I presume. Turning to Dina, I whisper, "Are you ready?"

She simply stares at me and nods. "Are you?" Her jaw twitches.

The judge calls out, "Does the defense wish to present witnesses?"

"Yes, your honor." Mr. Colfax rises and motions to Dina.

With her nose ring and some tattoos visible, Dina slowly ambles to the lectern. Her shoulders swing ever so slightly from side to side in the Bronx street style. As she takes her oath, she looks a little uncomfortable in the blouse and denim skirt she's wearing, and her hair isn't quite as punked up as I remember.

Facing steadily out at the assembly with a mix of defiance and vulnerability, she starts, "When Migo was five years old, our mother would make him watch as she beat me and my sister. Our mom was paranoid schizophrenic." Her voice falters. "My brother became different after that." She glances over at Migo and puts her hand up to her heart. "Even as a child, he always tried to protect me.

"Yeah, he's been arrested a few times, possession of some pills and attempting to steal a car once. But he was with a gang then, and he wasn't even the instigator, so it was dismissed. He even studied for his G.E.D when he was in jail the last time." She tapers off, not sure whether she's helping or hurting her big brother.

Give her the words, Lord.

Not sure where to go next, Dina brushes the hair from her forehead. You can see that she's thinking. All of a sudden she makes a gesture with one hand. "But why?" she calls out to us as incomprehension flashes in her dark eyes.

At last, the spell is broken.

She answers her own question. "Up to this point, my brother was never violent. Why all of a sudden would he . . . ?"

"Miss Robinson," the judge warns, "if you continue on this line of thought, your testimony will be stricken. This is not a trial. It is the sentencing sequence of a guilty plea."

I steal a peek at the Faber family. Beatrice is stoic, but glued to the testimony. Virginia clutches a handkerchief to her mouth.

Yes, tell us why, Dina.

She stops, her fists clenched at her waist. It doesn't matter if she can't say more. Her question jams into our consciousness anyway. Why? Why the ferocity of smashing him with a baseball bat? Except for Migo, only Dina, Norma and I know why. And Peter.

"Will that be all?"

She nods grimly and shuffles past the Faber's without a look as she returns to her seat. Her cousin Eddie shifts to make room for her, muttering to himself. The stenographer clicks away at her keys.

The defense attorney motions to me. He's twirling his mustache again, making little curls at the end. As I rise to speak, my mind suddenly floods with all the questions, threats, points of advice from others and myself over the past months. Sophie's insistent voice pierces through all the others, "Don't betray yourself."

I walk past the priest's family and glance at them briefly. I don't look at Migo, rather at the judge. Taking my place at the lectern, I swear the oath as my heart tumbles crazily in my chest. Opening my folder, I hear my voice begin to recite in a slow almost mechanical rhythm from my notes.

"Before he is sentenced, I would like to say something about this man, Migo Robinson. *He's a murderer.* As his chaplain at the prison, I have come to know this young man as a good person. *Don't say anything that will offend the families.* This is not to say he is incapable of doing harm, even killing someone. He has already admitted this." I steal a glance at the families. They stare back. *Twenty-five years to life!* For Migo's sake, I have to bring out my feelings here. I've got to touch these people if I can.

"Nothing can bring back the life of Father Alan." My voice trembles. I smell fear. *Where is your courage?* I push on.

"There are no winners here. Nothing can undo the harm done to his family, especially to his mother and sister who grieve before us at this very moment, numbed and suffering for what Migo did in a moment of passion . . . "

"Father Braxton, please refrain from interpreting the specific motives of the case."

"Most of all, nothing can undo the harm done to the heart and soul of this young man himself. He has told me more than once, 'I beg God to forgive me. I only ask for a chance to make it up.' So with deep feelings for both of these families, I wish to join Bishop Mueller in a plea for leniency in Migo's sentence so that he can indeed be given that second chance."

Across at their table, Migo's lawyer whispers something to him and he nods back. "One last thing." I go for it. Taking a crumpled piece of paper out of my jacket pocket, I wave it toward the judge. I can see he's impatient, but he motions for me to go on anyway. "In closing, I wish to recite a poem. Migo calls this 'A Prayer for Unity.' He wrote it himself while in jail."

As I dwell in the Divine Mind,
I pray that Your life, O God,
be lived through me,
that every thought and action
be a reflection
of the loving expression within.

He's a murderer.

I pray the Lord
for all people,
of all creeds and cultures,
whichever path they choose,
that it may lead
to the One God.

I will never forgive you Migo. I hope you spend the rest of your life in jail.

Stealing a look at the murdered priest's family, I continue.

I pray for my enemies as well,
for anyone I have harmed,
and for those who have harmed me,
that all may learn to forgive,
and to love with God's infinite compassion,
and be given a chance to start over again.

When I look up, I see Migo blinking.

I conclude, "In Christ I pray. Amen," and stuff the paper back into my pocket.

"Is that all, Father Braxton?"

Though not fully satisfied, I'm about to say yes. What else can I do for my friend. As I turn to step from the witness stand, I spot Dina's face. Only a sarcastic sneer perhaps, like the one she gave me in my office. Her voice from that day drills back into me: *Easy for you to say, Padre. Why isn't the Church willing to defend my brother? At least try to make up for the harm it's done when it didn't bust that priest's ass long ago? Let me clue you in, Father Zach. People see all priests now as potential perps. It's over for you guys unless you do something drastic.* My hands start to tremble.

There's no way I can sit down. Not before doing something to stop the inevitable, whatever the cost. Someone coughs. My breath comes spastically. A simple question pops out of my mouth. Frozen in place, I ask, "It wasn't just a robbery, was it Migo?" I look over at him.

Migo is caught off guard at first, but slowly his head turns, the cornrows slightly askew. The stenographer stops typing. There's a sense of the room holding its breath. Migo's bottom lip juts out and he grimaces. "No!"

"Why did you murder Father Alan, Migo?" I call out to him with my hands waving. "Even the presentence report doesn't mention it."

"What's going on, Father Braxton?" The judge calls out.

I stare across at Migo, remembering his reticence, *They'll think I'm a faggot, Zach.* And my challenge back to him, *Don't be a victim. Take responsibility for yourself.* His eyes are glued to the table. I decide to break the silence at last, "I'll tell you why."

"Zach, wait!" Migo is up on his feet. The court officer immediately tries to restrain him.

The defense attorney's head is rotating between Migo and me.

Migo blurts out, "Fr. Alan sexually abused me when I was fifteen years old."

"Objection, your honor." Ms. Banores leaps to her feet, her dark hair swirling. "Where is this new evidence coming from? And why now?" she calls out.

"It's from his pain," I shout, "and it's his last chance to get the truth out."

"Order!" demands the judge, his finger pointing at me.

"He was abusing those kids I knew," Migo's voice rises, "I went to the parish to confront him. We got into a fight."

"I believe him," I say, my hands raised to the gallery for reinforcement.

192

"Order, order!"

Peter is standing, shouting from his place. "Fr. Zachary's testimony is suspect. He's a gay priest, romantically involved with the defendant."

"Whaaaat?" Migo and the families gasp.

Colfax, the defense counsel is up, his hand pounding his desk. "Strike that from the record, your honor!"

"It's a lie," I shout back at Peter. "I'm Migo's chaplain. He's locked up in prison. How could we be sexually involved?"

The judge glares furiously at us and bangs his gavel. In a barely controlled voice he says, "One more time, I'm warning you, Father Braxton."

Shaken by Peter's wild accusation, I'm desperate to hide somewhere from the madness. Dina's voice prods me once more, *Padre, I still think your best solution is to leave the priesthood and to say why, that you want to protest the Church's coverup of sexual abuse by these pedophile priests.*

"Father Braxton?" The judge is clearly frustrated, his face blotchy red. "Return to your seat now."

Peter's challenge comes back to me, *Zach, Zach, we have to close ranks or they'll destroy us.* "No, I'm not finished," I blurt out to the judge. Fiercely, with months of pent-up anxiety ready to fling to the wind, I jab my finger at Peter and shout, "Bishop Mueller, you knew that Father Alan sexually abused Migo, didn't you?"

Peter gapes in shock and fury, his eyes ablaze.

"And that's why you're so intent to cover this up, isn't it."

"This is insane. What are you talking about?" Gritting his teeth, he looks ready to leap over the bench.

"Order! Order!" The judge sees his courtroom imploding. "One more outburst and you'll all be held in contempt. "Court officers, take charge!"

Cousin Eddie's voice erupts from the gallery, "You knew about Migo?" he yells to Peter. Transfixed, we all stare at him. Dina restrains him while his face contorts with rage. "You knew that priest was an abuser and you sent him to mess with us? I hope you rot in hell, you bastard."

Peter's face becomes chalk white. My heart pounds with fear and something else . . . exhilaration?

"Clear the courtroom!" shouts the judge, banging his gavel over and over.

Pandemonium breaks loose. Both families erupt in shouts and threats. Quickly everyone scrambles for the exits as the court officers move toward us. While an officer rushes him out a side doorway, Migo shoots me a long questioning glance.

I may be arrested, I may be tried and thrown into jail but I never will be silent.

—Emma Goldman

CHAPTER TWENTY-SEVEN

I slowly raise my eyes and gaze out at the stream winding its way through the trees. On the other side, traffic whizzes by like another universe. An occasional jogger or biker blurs past the bench where I'm sitting on the Bronx River Trail. It's the same one that Norma and I often sit on to watch the egrets. Just a few weeks ago we sat here like bitter strangers.

So much has happened since the trial ended. Everyone has been affected. It's like we all went over a waterfall, Migo most of all. I picture the look he gave me when Peter outed me in the courtroom: *Father Zach is a gay priest! Romantically involved with the defendant.*

Cringing again at the memory, at the feeling of my clothes being ripped off in public, I reach in my coat pocket for Migo's letter which I received this afternoon. My eyes glisten as I re-read it for the fourth time.

Hi Zach!

Sorry not to have written 'til now, but I've been adjusting. I finally got sent to my home jail. It's a place called Fishkill. I'm working out, and writing in my journal. Could you send me that book on writing you spoke about? I would really appreciate that. I want to write a book about my life so far. You'll be in it.

How are you doing? I miss you and our talks. It is hard to get to know people here. You've got to keep your guard up.

I have to be honest with you. I wish you weren't a priest anymore. I wish you could go out and find your soul mate and relax on the beach, and write all day and just live the rest of your life happy and not alone. You've devoted your whole life to helping people. I don't think it would be wrong if you focused on yourself a little. I just really want you to be happy because you deserve it.

Would you do me a big favor? You've got to live 'til your eighties so you and I can go out and watch the mountains together when I get out. Okay? (LOL).

Zach, it doesn't matter to me whether you are gay or not. And this isn't a hiss-kiss! You will always be my father, brother, friend.

I love you.

Migo.

My eyes close and I picture him locked away in an upstate prison for at least the next eighteen years. Thank God the judge reduced his sentence to eighteen to forty because of the abuse evidence that came out, so it was worth it. Even so, his whole young adulthood will be spent behind bars.

Dear Lord, bless my son, my friend. Hold him close and keep him safe in there. One day we'll walk together outside and . . . Tears brim.

Oh God, is it myself behind bars that drives me to want Migo free, the prison of my hidden orientation that gives me compassion for others' struggles?

A jogger races by, a thirty-something guy in a Fordham sweatshirt. Nice looking, well built, he catches me looking for a second and smiles. I realize I'm smiling too.

Most of all, Lord, I praise you and thank you that Migo isn't put off because he discovered who I am.

Why do you need to call yourself gay, Zach? Norma's question comes to mind.

Need to? It's who I am, Norma. Can't you accept that? She hates labels. We're all bigger than labels, she says. She's right. But I tell her that as long as our Church keeps making this part of our sexuality bad and something to be ashamed of, it's worth claiming it openly to show them they're wrong. It's like her reasons for resigning her position with the diocese. She couldn't stand the hypocrisy any longer.

Because she loves me, it's hard to trust Norma has my best interests in mind when it comes to this struggle in the Church, We're slowly building back our trust again, but I'm gun-shy now about how friends can sometimes betray you.

Peter comes to mind with his challenge. *You need to choose whether you are gay or you are a priest.*

Why, Peter? You know that at least half of the priests are gay. The Church couldn't survive without us. He holds onto the idea that gay priests can't be celibate. How does he know? Even if some are sexually active—like some straight priests—the Vatican fosters this idea to blackmail us into hiding.

An egret moves stealthily from behind a bush and catches my eye. Slowly, slowly it lifts its spindly legs so as not to alarm an unassuming fish soon to be its supper. It spies me and freezes, its searching eyes barely visible alongside its thin beak. Holding my breath, I sit motionless. Gradually it turns back to its prey. One leg up and held, then placed down ever so carefully, carefully . . . *strike!* Like lightning, it's got one, wriggling its last . . . *gulp!* If you're not on the alert, the Church hierarchy can devour you the same way.

Hmmmm, I'm still kinda paranoid. I better talk to Sophie about this. I pull my phone out, then leave a message asking her for an appointment. I imagine that she knows by now what's been in the headlines: "Gay priest defends murderer! . . . Bishop accuses chaplain of tryst! . . . Murderer links victim with abuse! . . . Priest involves Church in coverup! . . . City of New York to Launch a Grand Jury Investigation." *Mother of God, show me the way.*

"Hi Zach, Come in, come in." Sophie's eyes sparkle as though I've risen from the dead.

"Hi." We embrace briefly. "I'm still reeling from the tidal wave that's swept over me. It's like I'm just coming up for air."

A wizened smile. "Tell me. You didn't betray yourself, did you?" The soft voice.

"No. And it feels so damned good." I sink into the chair.

"I was so proud of you when I heard." She takes her seat across from me while Snooky scratches his ear.

Leaning back in the chair, I stretch my legs out. "It was unbelievable."

"You must be so relieved."

"It's been so long since I've felt this way." A shiver goes through me as I let out all the pent-up emotions of the past year.

We rest without speaking until I notice the clock ticking. I gaze around the small room: the clock, the candle, the crucifix, the window with the tree branch.

"What a journey you've been on," she says.

"It's like a new self is being born, and I want to hold onto a thread so I have a trail to return home if I ever get lost."

"What thread? Lost from what?"

"From my relationship with God for one thing. That's the thread and that's home for me."

"Intimacy with God."

I quickly add, "And intimacy with others too. I've discovered that it has to include intimacy with others or it's dangerous."

"Intimacy can always be dangerous. It has to do with letting someone else into your heart and soul. We actually have to consider someone else as well as ourselves."

I think of my yearning for intimacy, my taste of it at times in the past as well as my fears of it. "Yeah, I'm still trying to get it right."

"What about your situation at the prison, the threats to you in the chaplaincy now. What's happening with that?"

"Sophie, the charges of my abusing Migo have been dropped, thank God. Norma wrote up a report that downplayed the C.O.'s assertions. I've been warned not to testify in court for an inmate again."

"Whew."

"What this has taught me though is that I hope to develop a relationship with a man like the one I have with Norma."

"How might you do so?"

"It's difficult, and not just because I'm a priest. Something about men inclines us to make things sexual rather than see friendship as a goal in itself."

"A lot of sexual abuse is not just sexual. In fact it's even more about power," Sophie says.

"Power?"

"Did you ever hear this phrase? 'Men play at love to get sex, while women play at sex to get love.'" She brushes a lock of hair back.

I tilt my head to ponder this, wondering how this plays out in same-sex relationships.

"I believe we're hard wired this way. Men want power and women want relationships." A faint smile creeps onto her face, her lips and eyebrows crunched with a question.

I think about Peter and me, our back and forth between relationship needs and power struggles. A more immediate struggle comes to mind. "Peter threatened that I can be excommunicated from the Church for breaking the Seal of Confession about Migo's abuse."

Sophie's eyes widen.

"But a canon lawyer informed me that a confessor can reveal these things in an emergency . . . if the penitent gives him permission, as Migo gave me. I grin and spread my hands as though handcuffs have been unlocked.

A smile breaks onto Sophie's face.

"But the biggest challenge still waits out there for me."

Squinting, she asks, "What's that?"

"The Black Wall of Silence. It's not magically going away. The Vatican wrote a directive to my provincial, stating that I'm forbidden to speak in public on anything to do with homosexuality or sexual abuse."

She presses her lips into a line. "What can you do?"

I sit up in my chair, gripping the armrests. "I'm outside that prison wall now, Sophie, and I'm never going back inside again." A kind of snort escapes me.

"Even if it means you might be forced out of the priesthood over this?"

Swallowing, I glance up at the crucifix above the door, then through the window over her shoulder. "My Sebastian Community is standing behind me for now, and that's important. But even if they cave in, I'm not going to be silenced."

I watch her nodding.

"That's been the whole struggle this past year and my whole life. The wall is broken down now, and it shows it's got no power. Our whole Church needs to look at these issues honestly."

"But why stay and fight such a long battle?"

Rising, I begin to pace back and forth. "It's because I love the Church—its rituals, the sacraments, and the Gospel."

Sophie gazes impassively at me.

My hands are gesturing to make my point. "The Church, broken down beggar that it is now, is God's *anawim* or little flock where I receive these sacraments and sense God's presence in the Eucharist and the people's faith." I search for an image that will make my commitment clear.

Turning, I continue as Sophie sits with her hands on her lap. "I guess I could even say that I am willing to lay down my life for this little flock of Christ's as he did for me. A good shepherd doesn't flee when the wolf comes. That's why I don't leave." From her look it dawns on me that my voice is quite loud.

"But the Church leadership will never accept you as a gay priest," she says.

Feeling my blood rising, I stand still. "Don't you see, Sophie? It's not about the hierarchy accepting me. That's not the Church I live in any more. If I waited for them to accept me, I would wait forever. It's the people in the pews who are the real Church, the men and women in prison, my family and true friends, the Sebastian Community."

"So you stay in a system that will never accept you, that says you're disordered."

She's goading me on but I can't stop myself. Sitting back down, I look directly at her. "It's not about anyone else accepting me, Sophie." It's as though it's taken me my whole life to blurt out the obvious, "It's about me accepting myself."

"But what about intimacy?" she insists. Jumping off his chair, Snooky runs over and looks up at me and whines.

Words from a man I loved once bubble up from my heart, a relationship where I learned about intimacy:

You could have had everything.

I love you but I won't leave the priesthood.

And I can't stay.

He walked away then. Later I heard he found someone else. Sometimes on a moonlit night his voice rises up inside me. Tears come. My hands reach out for him to hold me . . .

"A lover isn't even enough for me now, Sophie. I've tried that and I can't be at peace hiding a relationship with someone I love. For me it's got to be all or nothing. I call this being Single for the Lord."

"You mean celibacy?"

"No. That word is so negative. Single for the Lord is positive, relational. And I don't care what the Church leaders or anyone else says or does. This love of Jesus for me, a gay priest, and for all of us without a bunch of preconditions, is what I want to speak about. No one, not even the Pope, is going to silence me about this."

Sophie's jaw clenches. For an instant, it seems like the jawbone of some ancient Gaelic Warrior Queen.

Soon a bird tweets. I glance out the window then back to her. "Sophie, sometimes when I'm celebrating Mass or preaching, I feel my spirit flow out across the altar to reach into people's hearts: women and men, gay and straight, the beautiful and the less beautiful. 'This is my Body, given up for you,' I say at these moments. This is what the Eucharist is all about, and what priests are meant to be."

I've heard her speak of this mystical communion during retreats. She sips her water slowly, places it back on the table. Her misty gray eyes gaze across at me.

I think of the long struggle in life, the competing forces that want to win, and the road that lies ahead. "You and Norma tell me life is all about intimacy, Sophie; Peter tells me it's loyalty above all; and my driving force is honesty. But it's really all of them mixed together isn't it? There's no magic compass to tell you when to choose one or the other."

It may be the afternoon sunlight streaming through the window. Or that I've tried to open up my heart completely to her over the years. Or that she sees I'm just being myself. Whatever the reasons, Sophie's face glows.

"Zach, I understand now why you can't leave the priesthood, no matter what they decide about you. Anymore than Jesus could leave you, me, any of us—forever."

Back in his chair, Snooky's head rests on his paws. The tree branch waves at the window. Birds chirp. No more words are needed. The old nun's shining eyes and smile merge with mine, while below us at the base of the Englewood Cliffs the mighty Hudson River flows down to the sea.

Later that night after dinner with the other friars, I head up to my room. It's been a long day and I'm tired. Instead of flopping down on the rug as I usually do for some goodnight moments with the Lord, I put on an Enya CD. Her haunting Irish voice will lilt my stress away. Pulling the blinds closed, I slip into my pajamas. I light a candle and switch off the lamp.

I take the eagle feather from its place behind the crucifix. Migo once told me it would guide me. When I asked him what that meant, he said, "Native people believe their journey in life is like the eagle's journey. The eagle soars between heaven and earth, never nests on the ground." I wanted to ask him more about this, but we were interrupted.

Slowly raising the feather above my head, I begin to sway with Enya: "Who can say if your love grows, as your heart chose, only time?" In the oval mirror with its antique golden rim I grin at myself: the skinny but strong shoulders, the lined face, the eyes that hold so many stories. It's like Jesus' eyes looking at me: big, silent, smiling.

Reflected in those eyes I see a young boy hiding in a closet from his father, a teenager getting out of a stranger's car, a guy saying goodbye to his girlfriend. Looking deeper, I see a young seminarian with a friend's arm around his shoulder, a man embracing another man's body in the glow of a streetlamp, a priest and a prison inmate holding hands while they pray, a gay priest sitting on a bench with a friend.

A few old dream-stoppers try to interrupt: *What will people think? What will I do if the Vatican challenges me? What will become of me?*

Stepping away from the mirror, I continue to sway with the feather. Laughter bubbles up. Breathing rhythmically, my spirit fills the room. "It's been a great life, Jeshua. Thank you. I wouldn't change a minute of it no matter what." Dancing more sensuously with the feather and the shadows, I lift up the memories as a gift to God.

CHAPTER TWENTY-EIGHT

Confessional, Our Lady of Angels Parish, six months later—

"Please bless me Father for I have sinned, it's been over a year since my last confession."

That voice . . . Peter?

"I've got some difficult things on my mind, things that torment me at night and give me no peace."

"If you can speak about these things, it will help." *God, help me!*

"Is that you, Zach? I was hoping you might be here."

"It's me, Peter."

"I need to confess.

"Mmmmm."

"I . . . hurt some people."

"Yes. Go on. What happened?"

"Will you keep this secret?"

I am silent.

"Zach, I need to know before I go on."

"How did you hurt these people? I won't break the seal."

"I hid the truth."

"Mmmmmm. Go on."

"I let a man go to prison when I could have defended him."

Migo. "Yes."

"And there were others I harmed as well."

"Who?"

"The young man who was abused when I reassigned Fr. Alan. Others like him."

"Yes."

"But we needed them to remain silent . . . for the good of the Church."

At last. "Can you talk about this? Get it out so it doesn't chew at your insides forever?"

"I was trapped between two sides who could be hurt."

"Two sides?"

"If I helped the priests, the abuse victims were left to suffer on their own. If I helped the abuse victims, it would implicate someone else I'm sworn to protect."

"And who is that?"

I hear only Peter's breathing.

"Peter?"

"The Cardinal. He's ultimately responsible for everything that goes on in the Archdiocese."

"Hmmmm." *Help me, Lord.*

"It could even go further up." I hear strained breathing on the other side of the screen.

"So Peter, what is it you're really telling me?" *And why are you telling me?*

"I feel a deep regret, Zach. I have trouble sleeping. And I want you to know what my motives were, so you don't think that I'm just a bastard."

"You actually care what I think?"

"I know you won't believe me, but I do care. I always have. And I need to tell you in a way that you will not be able to destroy the Church."

"Destroy the Church? You think that's my goal?"

"From my position it feels like that."

"So . . . and you're using this sacrament to continue your game?"

"Game? It's not a game, Zach. I guess you'll never understand. But I honestly desire forgiveness so I'm seeking absolution from you"

"Aren't you forgetting something?"

"Forgetting? . . . What?"

"Me."

Erratic breathing ruffles through the screen.

"If you really want to clear your conscience, then you might confess that you hurt me as well as Migo."

"Perhaps. But I realize now that your hurting me was part of it."

"Hurting you. How?"

"You turned Norma against me, said some horrible things about me in that bar. Most of all, you betrayed our bond."

"Our bond."

"Our brotherhood of priests with Christ, to protect each other at all costs."

"Peter, I'm sorry you were hurt by my actions, but I needed to help Migo. He was a defenseless inmate, so I had to confront you."

"Maybe. But you seemed to take delight in it, as though you were getting back at me, as though some hurt from the past was at stake."

"You're right. It hurt when you left me."

"Left you?"

"Yes, our friendship in the seminary. Your acceptance of me back then gave me such hope. After you left and rose higher in the Church, I felt pushed away by you."

I wait for a minute. The kneeler creaks on Peter's side.

"Peter, are you there?"

"I'm sorry I hurt you then. I wish I could undo a lot over the years, but it's not that simple. Maybe we can forgive each other."

"Peter, you outed me as a gay priest at the sentencing, made me look like a sexual predator in the media, cost me my good standing at the prison. We can't go back."

"Probably not."

It's bigger than you and him. Don't get sidetracked.

"This is your confession, Peter. I have to give you a penance before I can give you absolution."

"So what's my penance?"

"That from your new position in Rome, you'll actively work to make up for the damage done by sexually abusive priests in the Church."

His breathing stops. We stare at each other through the screen.

"And promise to pick bishops who will respect people's different sexual experience in the Church. Above all, promise to stop the sexual violence."

"You know I can't make these promises."

"Why not?"

"It would compromise my loyalty to the Holy Father."

So it goes all the way to the top. "Then I cannot give you absolution."

"Please Zach, you must absolve me."

"When you finally grasp what's really at stake, come back and promise these actions, Peter. Only then will I forgive you in the name of God and the victims."

I wait a few moments for Peter to respond. Except for a creaking window, our muffled breathing back and forth through the confessional screen is the only sound in the dusky church.

Bong! Above us the Angelus bells begin to toll in the tower.

The angel of the Lord declared unto Mary, and she conceived of the Holy Spirit. Bong!

The confessional space feels suffocating. I sense Peter's hypnotic gaze through the screen.

Behold the handmaid of the Lord, be it done unto me according to your word. Bong!

Thy will be done. It's what the authorities always want from us. Surrender your body and your mind as well, and believe that doing so is blessed.

Peter coughs. The scent of his musky cologne drifts through the screen.

The Word became Flesh, and dwelt among us. Bong! Bong! Bong!

Gritting my teeth, I grope for the knob of the confessional screen. All I have to do is slide the wooden panel closed. The whole weight of Church history claws at my brain to stop me. No, no, this is the moment. As I slide the panel shut, Peter's fist pounds on the other side.

An exultant shout rises up in me as I stand to exit the confessional. Stepping out, I search the darkness. A dozen pews away a woman has her head bowed in prayer. Quickly I move down the side aisle with my black tunic brushing against my legs.

A pungent smell of candles and incense hovers in the still air. My heart pounds as my fingers creep up to my Roman collar. It's as though this symbol of the priesthood has a stifling grip around my throat. I imagine flinging it into the darkness in one grand gesture of liberation.

Behind me I hear a door click.

"Zach, Zach . . ." It's Peter's voice, mellifluous and coaxing, "Don't leave us."

Leave you? Leave the Church? "It's my Church too, and nothing in heaven or hell can take it from me," I shout. The woman in prayer looks up.

In a flash, as though the wings of a thousand doves are set loose, the old black wall of silence crashes inside me. Lifting my right hand over my head, I grip my Roman collar like a victory baton. The collar that has fed and stifled me, liberated and tortured me, revealed and hidden God from me for so long.

Exhilarated as when I first experienced love, I soar like an eagle toward the doorway and freedom.

EPILOGUE

2015—

Everything has changed since the Latin American Jesuit, Pope Francis, was elected last year. He wants the Catholic Church to be a poor Church, reaching out to the poor and disenfranchised.

The Pope tells young Catholics to "make a mess" by their questions, and to take the Church into the streets.

He says that we will not find the Lord unless we truly accept the marginalized.

He visits prisons and washes the inmates' feet, including a woman and a Muslim.

He has set up a commission of international experts to advise him on safeguarding children from sexual abuse.

He wants to get rid of careerist Vatican officials whom he describes as a leprosy on the Church.

He challenges bishops who obsessively preach about abortion, gay marriage and contraception. He says if a person is gay and seeks the Lord and has good will, "Who am I to judge them?"

He tells the bishops that they should speak openly, without fear of upsetting him, and listen humbly.

He wants the church to be the voice of the voiceless.

"I am a sinner," he says of himself. "It is the most accurate definition. It is not a figure of speech, a literary genre. I am a sinner."

And most strikingly, "Jesus Christ has redeemed everyone by his blood, not just Catholics."

"Even atheists?" he is asked.

"Everyone."

So, does the Black Wall of Silence still exist?

Does the Roman collar still muffle priests' voices?

Can we really trust that the Church will change its approach to covering up sexual abuse?

Can anyone's voice, particularly nuns, be respected when they have a different viewpoint from the Church hierarchy?

Is the ordination of women still taboo to speak about in the Church?

Can we speak honestly about sexuality issues, including homosexuality, and whether celibacy is required for the priesthood?

Can we really speak what we believe in our conscience without fear of being excommunicated?

Is the Catholic Church truly a home for the marginalized and the voice of the voiceless?

Pope Francis' words and pastoral actions are stunning. They give the Church and the world hope. People who aren't even Roman Catholic are moved by his courage and sensitivity. But the Church is not one person, even if he is the Pope. Francis is going to need every one of us to work along with him to accomplish his dreams. And we must pray that he survives long enough to accomplish this resurrection in the Church.

The End

ACKNOWLEDGMENTS

Got no check books, got no banks.
Still I'd like to express my thanks—
I got the sun in the mornin'
And the moon at night.

I want to thank Irving Berlin for this refrain. It grounds me in gratitude for life itself, and for the simple gifts of morning and evening. It undergirds my desire to give thanks for all of those who helped me in the writing of this book. Many times during the process I thought of how a woman may feel giving birth to a baby. Breathe, breathe...trust the process. Oh sure! The following people helped me to keep breathing and writing until the baby was born: First of all, Judy Scher, my editor and friend of over twenty-five years; my writing would be stillborn without this wonderful and creative woman and accomplished author; my gifted and diverse readers, who offered me their precious time and wisdom: Rev. Bob Frueh, Rev. Donald Reilly, OSA, Richard K. Taylor, Dr. Patricia Kelly, April Gagne, Mrs. Teresa Egan, and Sr. Andrea Nenzel, CSJP. I give thanks for the groundwork and encouragement of my writing class colleagues, Debbie Wong, Ken Paprocki and Patricia Jackson; my teachers, Michael Kaye, Stacia Friedman, and Rob Rebele; my copyeditor, Barbara Crawford, my first and only agent, Barbara Bowen, my first publisher, Michael Leech, the Dogear Publishers team, Tarren and Julian at Hopeworks, NJ, Dave Stys, my website designer, and Brother Bud Knight and the Christian Brothers Community at Lincroft, New Jersey, for their hospitality. And to the many others in the writing/publishing/marketing business who have guided, challenged, and cheered me on when I might have given up, I thank you from the bottom of my heart.

I am deeply grateful for my religious brothers, spiritual guides, consultants and ministry colleagues who have shared their spirit and kindled the embers when my writing fire was going out: my Augustinian brothers, especially for Frs. Tom Casey, Tom Hennigan, and Marty Keller who've guided me in this whole process from the other side; my mentors, counselors and spiritual directors throughout these years: Bro. Aelred Shanley, OSB, Fr. John McNeill, SJ, Sr. Gail Demaria, CSJP, Sr. Bernadette Kinniry, SM, Michelle Hyman, Ph.D., and Rev. Carl Sword, OHC; my professional consultants, Ann Butchart, Rev. William Wallace, O.S.A., J.D., and Dr. Paul Schaefer; for my faithful colleagues in our Adeodatus Prison Ministry Program, including all of those men and women in jail who told me that they were praying for me and my writing and still do.

I give thanks for all of my friends who have asked me how my writing was progressing, or put up with my absences or moods or preoccupation, or who said a prayer for me and encouraged me in my goal, especially for Anne Gentile, my soul friend and 'the wind beneath my wings,' who shows me by her own life how to trust my deepest voice and to let it ring. Last but not least, for each and every one of my family members, including those who have gone before us into the Kingdom--the in-laws and out-laws, their children and their children. They have given me their love, hope, forgiveness and joy in the great gift of our family life, which is the inspiration and source of all of my story-making. And so. . .

> Whether we have checkbooks or banks,
> May we all express our thanks,
> To the One who graciously shines upon us,
> the sun in the morning and the moon at night.

ABOUT THE AUTHOR

Paul F. Morrissey, OSA, an Augustinian priest, currently serves as a prison chaplain and spiritual director in Philadelphia. He is the author of a memoir, Let Someone Hold You: The Journey of a Hospice Priest (Crossroad, 1994), which won the Christopher Award and the Catholic Press Award, and a pocket pamphlet, Together To God: Praying the Augustinian Way, (Liguori, 2013). Fr. Morrissey's writing has appeared in a variety of newspapers, magazines and books, including, The Philadelphia Inquirer, America, Journeys, and Let the Clock Run Wild. He has a special fondness for interactive writing, including an international newsletter for gay priests and religious, which he edited from 1977-90, and Voices From Prison and the Edge, a quarterly newsletter of Adeodatus Prison Ministry, which he has edited from 2007 to the present. Each of these highlight the first person stories of those for whom the newsletter is written, the goal being to empower people to speak with their own true voice as a way to foster Gospel freedom. Before studying for the priesthood, Fr. Morrissey graduated as a Civil Engineer from Villanova University and went on to work for Sikorsky Aircraft in Connecticut. After entering the Augustinians, he began his studies at Catholic University and graduated with a Licentiate in Sacred Theology. Later, he received his doctorate in spiritual direction from Weston College in Cambridge, Massachusetts, and eventually became a Fellow in the American Association of Pastoral Counselors. His ministries have included teaching Theology at various Catholic universities, establishing a draft counseling center, ministering to the gay and lesbian community in Philadelphia, serving as spiritual care coordinator for the home hospice program of the Visiting Nurse Service in New York City, founding a pastoral counseling center in New York, and establishing the Adeodatus Prison Ministry Program in Philadelphia. It is Fr. Morrissey's deepest hope that his novel, The Black Wall of Silence, will promote a much needed conversation on sexuality, gender and power in the Catholic Church and beyond. The website, www.Blackwallofsilence.com hosts a blog to foster this conversation, which Pope Francis has encouraged among all of the faithful, to speak our truth without fear.

A Conversation with Fr. Paul Morrissey, O.S.A.

Q. You've been a Catholic priest for over forty-five years. What inspired you to write your first novel at this point in your life, and how much is it based on actual events?

A. I figure that I better write some of my feelings about life down now before someone else does it for me when I am gone. Like most novelists, I have pulled from my life to weave experiences and relationships into a story that will intrigue readers.

Q. Why haven't you simply written a memoir?

A. About ten years ago I did. But when my family read the manuscript, many of them were aghast. They pleaded with me not to publish it because it might get me in trouble with the Church. On the other hand, some of them felt that it should be written, that these issues need to be discussed in the Church if we are going to be real. I put it in a drawer for five years until I got the idea to write a novel instead.

Q. When you rewrote it as a novel, did you leave the troubling pieces out?

A. Not really. I believe a novel allows an author some deniability. What I have written is not about any specific person, not even myself, but all the characters are in me in one way or other. In other words, it is different from an autobiography. Like a film or play, this enables a reader to enter into the characters with some distance. It allows the author and readers to discuss the interactions and behaviors in a novel without the distracting dynamic that it is referring to the author or anyone else in particular. In some way it is like the parables that Jesus used to teach with.

Q. Won't this still create some problems for you and your Church superiors? Don't you—or some of your characters—make statements in the book that contradict Church teaching—on sexuality for instance?

A. When asked about this, I will keep reminding people that it is a story. It is fiction. I made up the plot and the characters. I am quite happy to discuss what these characters stand for with anyone who has read the book. I know I will also have to be prepared to address what I believe about Church teaching at some point. One quote that gives me courage to do this is Pope Francis' response when asked how he feels about homosexuals: *"Who am I to judge?"*

Q. What is your goal in writing such a book, a book that exposes secrecy in the Church, a book that raises the issue of gay priests, among other provocative topics? Especially the explosive implication that the silence of gay priests is an atmosphere that contributes to the cover-up of sexual abuse? Do you actually believe that this will be helpful to the Church, or that people want to know such matters?

A. Pope Francis has also called on the entire Church to prepare for a synod in September 2015 that will address sexuality, marriage and family issues, and related issues that the Catholic Church needs to converse about. The Church is losing many people, especially middle-aged people and our youth, who no longer take us seriously because we don't speak—or listen— in believable ways to them about these topics. My goal in writing this book is to foster this conversation that the Pope has told bishops around the world to host so it is not just the bishops talking to themselves.

Q. In the novel, you have shown the struggle between loyalty to the Church versus honesty to one's conscience through the Bishop Peter and Father Zach characters. How is it possible for a group like the Church to survive if it allows everyone to practice openly what their conscience speaks to them?

A. Maybe it can't. If so, we should be more open about this. In other words, tell people that the Church leaders have to speak for the main body in their teachings. If you in your conscience break with this, you must be prepared to be marginalized, even excommunicated—for the good of the whole. That is what Jesus' life shows us. Just don't be surprised. However, the Catholic Catechism, edited by Pope Benedict XVI, says the following about conscience: "Deep within his conscience, man discovers a law which he has not laid upon himself but which he must obey. Its voice, ever calling him to love and to do what is good and to avoid evil, sounds in his heart at the right moment…For man has in his heart a law inscribed by God…His conscience is man's most secret core and his sanctuary. There he is alone with God whose voice echoes in his depths." (#1776). If the Church teachings do not reflect the conscience decisions of its people, then the Church is living a lie.

Q. In the novel you show the role of women in the Church through the characters of Norma and Sister Sophie. What can you say to women that will give them hope in the Church, a hope that is worth remaining for?

A. Sister Sophie would say, "Oh please!" Seriously, women have been the core of our faith from the beginning, and they have always been pushed aside. Mary Magdalen was the first one Jesus appeared to on his Resurrection Day. She ran to tell the disciples, as Jesus instructed her. They didn't believe her, as Scripture says. This treatment of women's experience by men, especially in the Church, has been going on ever since. It is a heresy that women are not allowed to proclaim the Gospel in our liturgies. No matter, I would not encourage women to leave our Church unless they cannot live hopefully in it. The Church needs women. I need them. Especially when this dialogue is opening up, we need women's voices above all.

BOOK CLUB DISCUSSION QUESTIONS

1) Which character in *The Black Wall of Silence* most intrigues you? Why? What would you add to this character to spice her/him up?

2) What about the sexual abuse crisis in the Church most fires you up?

3) If you are/were a Catholic, what would you advise Pope Francis to do first to address the issues raised in this book? Any advice to him from people of another faith? Atheists?

4) In reading this book, what did you learn about the Catholic Church that surprises you? Gives you hope? Causes you despair?

5) Are you more inclined to loyalty or honesty in your relationships? Your support of organizations you belong to, including your own family?

6) Is a 'gay priest' a contradiction to you? What would you advise a gay priest about coming out today? Is celibacy—being 'Single for the Lord'—a viable option for a person today? For priests?

7) What is the best thing the Catholic Church could do to show it believes in women's gifts and role in the Church? Short of ordination, what can Pope Francis do to send a signal about this?

8) In what areas of life is your voice likely to be muffled? Is any of this self-inflicted? What price do you pay for this? What do you gain from it?

9) Are there any other questions that this book raises for you?

10) Any advice you would offer to the author? A theme for a sequel?